I0822266

DAKOTA MONROE

SHADOWS OF THE CROWN

Shadows of the Crown

Book One

Dakota Monroe

Copy editing and proofreading: K. Morton Editing Services, L.L.C.

Cover: Drakana at GraphicSoulArt

Internal illustrations: Dakota Monroe

First Edition 2024

THE EPHEMERAL REALM

AURORIA

MENEAU OCEAN

FROSTWELL

GRENPORT

ELYSARAN

EBONWOOD

VEXAIL

VERDANTIA FOREST

CINDARA DESERT

THE AETHER REALM

WHISTERRA

SKYDENCE

LUMARNA

MERIDIAN

OUNTAINS

VALORIA

EBELAN OCEAN

INVALLE

THALASIRE

GEL'S PASSAGE

Content Warning

This book is a dark fantasy romance, with topics that some may find disturbing or triggering.

For the full list of warnings, please visit dakotamonroe.com/contentwarnings

To those who grew up reading fantasy and have been searching for something a little darker and sexier.

Chapter One

Ariella

Maybe I should fuck him before I kill him.

Not with my own flesh, of course, but the hilt of my blade would certainly do the trick. He deserves it after what he did to that woman. My lips curve at the thought. I could do it. My only instructions were that his death had to be caused by a blade to his heart, and nothing was mentioned about what pain I could inflict beforehand.

Fuck, I might just do it because of how long he's taking.

A chill sweeps through my bones as the coldness from the brick starts inching its way into my cloak. I spin my blade through my fingers with practiced precision—one of my better habits. Sighing deeply, there's a heaviness in my posture. Anyone who was unfortunate enough to see me would quickly turn the other way. Lucky for them, though, I'm never seen in the shadows.

"If looks could kill."

If I had a copper for every time I heard that one, I could probably afford a night in the Eldorian castle.

Just one night is all I'd need to kill the king.

A quick stepping pattern pulls my focus, and I tilt my head to listen closer. These steps are hurried and moving with purpose. The thumping gets louder than the muffled conversations humming through Valoria, and I know this is my target. He always walks this alley home, though never with such haste. I roll my eyes, because *of course* someone had to tip him off that the guild was looking for him. It was probably Isolde, that bitch. She loves to push me to my limits, but I'm in no mood for these games today.

I close my eyes to the sight of the alley. There's barely any light in this part of the city; but no matter, I can feel my target's essence like the glove on my hand. My essence yearns to be released, and I nearly growl in frustration at its insistence. I've neglected it for too long, not releasing the building power, and now it's trying to fuck with my assignment. A masculine scent hits my nose, replacing the heavy, wet mustiness that's been circling me these last hours. The target reaches me, and using the hand not gripping my blade, I tug on my umbral strand, weaving opaque shadows into existence, casting my target into complete darkness.

The hitch of his breath hits me like the most pleasant song. My shadows caress his sweat-licked skin, allowing me to see that this is indeed the one I've been waiting for. I once sliced the throat of a man who I thought I was to kill, but he turned out to just have the same hair color and build as my actual target. Unfortunate for him, but annoying for me, as I had to explain why there were two bodies instead of just one.

His pulse quickens, and I smirk at the adrenaline he has swirling through his veins, helping him focus on trying to find a way out of his fate. There is no way out, but I let him plan for a moment. Their expressions are so much more rewarding when you give them a chance to hope first. My leathers rub together, causing a light squeaking to echo through the silence. My boots come down hard enough to let him hear me, and his pulse quickens even more. His breaths strain—I scrunch my nose at the smell of whiskey floating from his direction. Of course he drinks whiskey. Seems to be the poison of choice for those who also enjoy raping others.

The reminder of his crime sends hot rage through me, tasting like burnt honey on my tongue. I want to get this over with; I'm tired and need to release some of my unused essence. But this man deserves a painful, horrible death. If it were up to me, I wouldn't kill him. That is a kindness after what he's done. I'd drag him back to the guild and do to him what he did to the girl. And unlike him, I wouldn't be foolish enough to get caught. He would stay under my care for a long, long time, suffering a repeat of his crime every single day until I was satisfied with his punishment. That would likely be never, but that theory is negligible.

The target whimpers as I step closer, my lip curling at the sound. He feels powerful enough to use an unwilling woman for his pleasure, but I come into the picture and he immediately pisses himself to death? Pathetic.

"Please," he sputters in the direction he thinks I'm located. "Please, I have a family. I have money I can pay. Just please let me go!" I chuckle lightly, and he spins around to face me, eyes widening when he sees my form directly behind him. I allow the shadows to dissipate some, giving him enough light to take in the face of his killer as I remove my hood.

He spits out some incoherent words at the sight of me, his body now trembling hard. A foul smell drifts toward me, and my eyes flit downward to see that he did indeed piss himself.

"By the Angel!" His legs give out and he drops to his knees, bones cracking from the impact. He can barely form his next words through his sweet fear, making me smile for the first time in days. "Silver Wraith, please, I beg of you. I beg for your mercy." He lowers his head to the wet stone, bowing before me like I'm some Aether here to grant him pardon. I'm not known for mercy—no, the people of Eldoria know me for my darkness. My ability to be silent and unseen until my blade is in their throat. The last thing their eyes witness is my silver hair hovering above their nauseating faces.

He moves to kiss my boot. "For fuck's sake." I swing my foot into his face hard enough to send him careening into the brick wall. He curls in on himself, tears and snot covering half of his face.

Why did I have to volunteer for this assignment? Clearly a blind, elderly woman could have taken him down without any trouble. I just wished for a job that wasn't one of the king's requests, though I likely will not be volunteering anymore because this is so much worse than being bored at the guild.

"You're fucking pitiful." I tilt my chin to the sky; maybe I should use my psionic strand to have him jump off the building in front of me. There's no one around to see me weaving, and I really do not want to be associated with his death. It's embarrassing, honestly. I groan—that won't work because the guild was hired to kill Samuel, and it would be quite suspicious if he just happened to jump from the same building I'm tasked with waiting next to.

No, I can't. There would be too many questions.

"Let's get this over with, then," I sigh and crouch next to his whimpering body. "You know why you're being targeted, yes?" He shakes his head and I grab his throat, lifting him from the ground and slamming the back of his head into the wet stone.

"Don't fucking lie to me, Samuel. You know exactly why I'm here. Now tell me." A spark of hope lights his eyes momentarily, as if he thinks admitting his crime is my requisite for letting him go free. Imbecile.

"I—I hurt someone."

"You hurt someone." It's not a question. He did, but I want him to elaborate. All of my targets confess to their crimes before I take their life. And if they refuse? Well, the guild would have a temporary prisoner, I suppose. But my reputation always proves useful, because these bastards are too frightened of *Eldoria's deadliest assassin* to keep their truth hidden for long.

"I hurt someo—" I squeeze his throat, and he looks to my eyes for any hint of safety or hope. He won't find it. Even if I wasn't here to kill him, he wouldn't see either. My face is always the mask I wish others to see...nothing else. And right now? Samuel sees death in my gaze, and a promise that it will be much worse for him if he chooses to lie to me again. "I killed a woman." Every bit of fight, what little he had, abandons his limbs and he goes slack in my hold.

"Now you get it," I praise sweetly. "You won't be leaving here, Samuel. I will not show you mercy, and I doubt the Angel will, either. Not after you raped and murdered Olivia." I laugh to myself as my anger demands more than his life.

"You're lucky the method of your death is not my choice," I whisper sharply, and watch his brows furrow as his body registers the blade in his chest. I only nicked his heart, which will prolong his suffering for a while; it's not enough to sate the hunger in me that wants to make him pay in full value for his crime, but it will have to do. This was not my revenge to have. I'm only the executor.

I pull the blade out, smirking when he drops to the ground with a heavy groan. I wipe the blood off the sleek steel using his shirt and continue to twirl it through my fingers as I lean back against the wall. Suddenly, I'm no longer annoyed with having to stay in this frigid, damp alley. The pained whimpering coming from my target is entertainment enough.

I close my eyes and imagine it's the king's life sputtering away in front of me, instead of Samuel. As soon as the light left his eyes, I would weave my forbidden temporal strand, taking time back a few moments so that I could watch the second he dies over, and over, again. Weaving that type of essence would ensure my death, if murdering the king didn't first. That's fine with me; preferable, actually. There's nothing left for me here once I get my revenge on him. Maybe Isaiah, but he would easily live without me. He doesn't need my protection anymore.

The muffled voices from a nearby tavern get louder—it must be later than I thought. Looking toward the rapist, I frown when I see he's already dead, and I missed the best part. I bend to feel for a pulse, or spot any slight breathing, though there is neither. I sigh, frustrated with my wandering thoughts. I wouldn't chance weaving my temporal strand on him, though, so I will just have to endure the disappointment.

The clamoring outside the alley increases and I stand to take my leave, almost feeling sorry for whoever finds this grotesque mess. But I'm not being paid to clean things up...I snort under my breath. I wouldn't despite being paid—Samuel's body deserves to rot in this cold, empty place for a while.

I slip out of the alley, pulling my hood up to hide my easily identifiable hair. I'm fond of the color...it's the same color my mother's was, and it feels like I hold a piece of her with me. Unfortunately, no matter how much I love the silver strands, they're very recognizable. Being the only person in the Eldorian Kingdom, in the physical realm even, with this color makes it difficult to go unnoticed anywhere I am. So I hide it most of the time, allowing myself to travel without the constant stares and whispers.

I wish I could weave my shadows everywhere, but no one alive knows that I possess the ethereal affinity. I cannot use any of those strands when others are around, because if I'm found out, I will be executed. Not only is the ethereal affinity illegal, my father told me to never report my third affinity. It's bad enough that the kingdom knows I possess the other two, making me a useful object to the royals. But to be a universal weaver? There's only one weaver in history who was known to possess all three affinities, and she was sacrificed to the realms for her essence.

According to the official documents, I have the living and elemental affinities, and can only weave the flora, aero, and kinetic strands from them. They've no knowledge regarding my ability to weave all the strands from each affinity, as that would also make me a big target in the eyes of the Eldorian royals.

So I keep my secret from everyone, including Isaiah, and allow the king to use me as his personal killer. He's never met me, as that would look bad for his reputation; but whenever he sends an assignment to the guild, he always requests the Silver Wraith to complete the job. And I do. Gladly. One day, I will use his preference for me to my advantage; it may allow me to get close enough to sink my blade into his heart.

Killing him just like he did my father.

I push the consuming thoughts away and focus on the damp stone under my silent feet. The streets are nearly empty, as expected, which is a relief for me. Being around many others has never been a comfort of mine; I prefer the darkness and solitude. My thoughts keep me company enough, and these assignments allow me to move about the city without the expectation of conversation. I can just breathe in the empty space around me and bask in the city's quiet.

I stretch my neck, attempting to coax cool air into my cloak. It's warmer than usual this season, though it's my fault for deciding to wear my fleece-lined leathers instead of my regular ones. I always get hot in these, and yet just like to torture myself for some reason.

The sound of clanging hooves drifts from the corner of the next street, and I immediately duck into the shadows. I'm very familiar with the sound of the royal carriages. I watch as the large horses come into view, and my brow furrows. Why would one of the members of the royal family be out at this time of night, let alone in this part of the city? The crimson red and deep gold accents contrast the otherwise white carriage, the colors clear as day even under minimal moonlight. There's a royal guard stationed on each side of the transport, wearing their signature black slacks, with a crimson jacket and gold padding at the shoulders. Interesting, though, that their uniforms are not the usual ones you see on the guards at the castle. These are form fitting, almost like the material gives them more freedom to fight. *There's no reason they should need them out here*, I think, but then shrug as I remember that people like me exist. I'm the reason they need those hideous outfits.

It's surely just the king searching the lesser essence district for someone innocent to punish. Seems to be a favorite hobby of his. My fists clench, and I force my legs to move in the opposite direction, toward the guild.

Otherwise I will do something foolish from my pent up rage and ruin all the work I've done these last two decades.

Soon.

Chapter Two
Ariella

Warmth hits my face as I step through the front doors of the guild. It's a large building, one of the nicest in Valoria. It's also the largest guild in the Eldorian kingdom, next to Meridian. The guilds aren't just for training killers; we all have different jobs here, but it's mostly a home for those who don't have one. They help children learn how to weave and control their essence, and teach them how to defend themselves. But the guild in each of Eldoria's cities possesses their own group of assassins...some people call us the Weavers of Justice, as the royal guards are good for nothing more than being practice targets.

I do not think of us that way. Murdering people, even if they deserve it, shouldn't be celebrated. The Angel would say I have no right to take lives in the first place.

But the Angel isn't here. I am. And I'm good at what I do...I just don't toast to completed assignments.

"Back so late, Ariella?" A familiar, nagging voice scrapes the inside of my ears, and I have to fight the nausea that rises. "What, did your target give you a hard time?"

"Shut the fuck up, Isolde." I march in her direction, towering a few inches above her five-foot-four height. She always has a twinge of fear flicker through her upturned eyes when my full attention is on her, though she's gotten better at hiding it. "If you mess with one of my assignments again, we'll have a problem." My voice is low and threatening.

She tries to smirk. "Oh yeah? And what are you going to do, Ari, kill me? Velora will have your head if you do." A slow smile spreads across my face, and hers falters at the sight; her skin pales further, nearly matching the color of her bright hair.

"Last time I checked, Velora doesn't run the guild. Marek does." I tilt my head and narrow my gaze at her. "And he would reward me for being the one to *finally* rid us of the house parasite."

She snarls in my direction, and I have the urge to remind her that this is why she isn't the best. Why she doesn't get chosen for things: because of her inability to control her emotions. But I internally scold myself, because that would probably be taking it too far and cause her to snap. I mean, I wasn't lying. Marek wouldn't be particularly upset if my blade slipped, but he would scold me for causing any more drama amongst the students. So instead of provoking her further, I turn and leave the common room.

The hallway to my dorm is dark and full of serene shadows. Thankfully, everyone besides Isolde seems to be sleeping, so I do not run into anyone as I step into my room and tug on my umbral strand to ward the door. No one in the guild would be brainless enough to enter my room without expressed permission—which I've never given to a single soul—but the wards still afford me a sense of ease. Locks can be picked easily, but to recognize and undo a ward? That person would need access to the ethereal affinity, and I'm the only person I know who has it. It's not impossible for others to possess that affinity, just very rare.

My shoulders drop, muscles relaxing as I sit on my single bed. The room itself is simple; I have a wooden dresser with large shirts for sleeping, several pairs of leathers, and a few other undergarments and active wear items. The bed is small, covered in white sheets and a gray quilt. Each dorm has a standard wooden desk and chair that matches the other furniture, in which I have a few papers on top. There is a small pile of boots and running shoes next to my door, along with a thick leather jacket for when the weather cools.

But that's it.

I've never wished for anything more. My focus in life has been on essence control, physical training, and ever-changing plans that all have the same goal: kill the king. I have no need for material items, and no time to care about them. Some might say the lack of personality in my own room is depressing, but I say it's smart. If I ever need to leave, or if I get killed, there's nothing here that I would care to come back for. Nothing to miss.

I lie back and decide to weave excess essence, knowing I will not be able to sleep if I don't—my body feels too jittery to even remain still for a moment. I usually choose strands that wouldn't have any lasting effects on my surroundings, as I do not desire the questions that would be inevitable if someone spotted the damage. I tug on my kinetic strand, lifting papers from my desk and a pair of boots from the floor before spinning them around the room in opposing patterns.

Whenever I release essence, I always work on control. Most are strands I cannot practice outside of this room, so it's important that I force years worth of training into these brief sessions.

I think of each strand as its own muscle—if I fail to work a muscle for any length of time, I lose some of its strength and my control over it. But, the spectral and temporal strands are two that I never practice with, though I'd argue those are unfortunately the most important to have control over. I shudder. Communicating with spirits of the Aether feels...wrong. Or so I tell myself as an excuse to not do it. Also, fucking with time has consequences—ones I'm not yet willing to pay. So I leave those strands alone and work on the others.

When I'm satisfied with my ability to manipulate objects, I snatch one of my blades and cut deeply down the length of my wrist. This would be a fatal cut to most, though it forces me to really focus on my vital strand. While it's good to practice with essence, I find it helpful to learn how to use it in different situations. Teaching myself to not panic from bad wounds is important, especially for when I make it into the castle. Chances are, the royal guards will strike me before I see the king, and I cannot let those wounds slow me down. I will need to heal them as I move and not allow their severity to cloud my thoughts.

I pull on the strand, this one located deep in my chest, and coax it to my left arm. A dim light passes through my fair skin, traveling swiftly to the injury I created, and I watch in awe as I instruct it to seal the wound shut. A small amount of the light peeks through as it works the top layer of my skin, and I smile. Some of my strands almost feel sentient, as if they're another entity living in my body—I chuckle. They likely spend their time cursing me for how foolish I am with my safety.

I practice a few more strands in the elemental and ethereal affinities before I feel sated enough to sleep. There are some strands—like the fauna from the living affinity and psionic from the ethereal—that I cannot practice alone. Those must be subtly used around other beings, and I do not necessarily enjoy invading the minds of others...it's strange existing in two bodies at the same time.

Sighing, I stand to strip my leathers and slide on a shirt, ready to lose myself to the darkness for a while.

Green, unfeeling eyes stare back at me as I ready myself for the day. I throw on a tank and shorts, needing to run after I meet with my mentor. I grimace at the bright sun shining through the window—it's likely already too fucking hot outside, and my lack of attire will be less than helpful. I pull a band over my thigh and sheathe my blade, because Angel damn me if I'd go anywhere without one.

That's the caveat of having the reputation I do...there is always a target on my back.

I step from one of the two private bathrooms available on this floor and walk down the stairs to Marek's study. I knock twice on the dark wooden door and wait for permission to enter. Marek is hunched over a stack of papers that I'm pleased are not my responsibility. The room is dimly lit, as always—he prefers to only have two lamps, instead of an overhead light, as the brightness bothers him just as much as it does me. The sleek floor doesn't creak as I step to his desk, remaining silent until he's ready to address me. We may have an easy, casual relationship, but he's still my mentor and I always show him the respect he deserves.

There have been times I've regarded him as my second father, though those flitting thoughts never last long, as I quickly begin feeling guilty for pushing my own father to the side. He certainly wouldn't think of it that way, and I know he would prefer me to have a nice relationship with *someone* in my life, but I cannot just change the way I feel.

I sit in the large armchair across from him, folding my hands across my lap. Marek's getting older, and it's obvious in his features. Patches of gray streak through his hair, lines crease next to his eyes when he smiles, and he sometimes has that look about him that says he wants to leave Eldoria and find a peaceful, quiet home in a neighboring city. Those looks are more frequent lately, to my dismay.

He breathes a lightly groaning sigh, sliding his glasses off his face and setting them onto the table. He sits back in his chair and crosses his arms, pinning me with a glare. I learned the differences between his stares very quickly after I arrived at the guild, never knowing how useful that skill would be with other people. This one says, *"really, Ariella?"* and I roll my eyes, knowing exactly what he's referring to.

"She was being a bitch, Marek. You know how she gets," I exclaim, feeling like a child being scolded even though I'm twenty-seven. The man is lucky he's the only person in the realm I'd allow to speak to me in such a way.

He raises an eyebrow, tilting his head to the side slightly, which means *"and you think it was acceptable to threaten her just because she was rude?"*

"Yes, I do—in fact, you yourself taught me to threaten anyone that has shit to say about me. It's not like I was actually going to do anything..." I sink back in my chair, shifting my eyes to the painting behind my disappointed mentor. And because I refuse to ever keep my mouth shut, I mutter under my breath, "She didn't need to know that, though."

"Ari, you insulted her and now she's making it my problem," he groans. My gaze snaps back to his, and I can see the laugh he's trying to hold in.

"Kick her out if you do not wish to deal with her dramatics." His jaw clenches, and whether he's considering strangling me or not, I cannot be sure. "At least I'm honest. Would you have me lie to her instead?" I press, knowing I've swayed him to my side.

Of course I did. He can never say no to his favorite student.

I smirk at his narrowed eyes, making it clear he's lost. Again. Marek has always been fond of me, which is likely why I'm the only student he's ever mentored himself. Every other student is under the direction of Velora. I'm not sure why he chose me when I was brought to the guild twenty-years ago, though it's not difficult to guess that he saw what happened to my father.

Everyone saw.

"You will be the death of me, girl," he mutters the same eight words he's said to me since day one. Grabbing his glasses and sliding them back on, I know he's done with his obligatory scolding and ready to move on to other topics.

I lean forward, resting my elbows on his large desk as I set my chin on combined fists. "You should be thankful I'm here to entertain you in your old age; otherwise your grumpy ass would meet the Angel without ever having laughed a day in your life." He chuckles, shaking his head and pulling out a folder with the name Samuel written at the top.

We have a tradition of discussing my assignments once they're completed; he likes to be informed of what happened, but it's much more than that. As my mentor, he has always asked me to describe what I did during the job. What essence I used, what fighting or weapons—if any—and where my thoughts were during. Why did I make the decisions I did? Once I explain the details, we work through anything I could have done differently.

I may be the best killer in the realm—according to Marek—but there is always room for improvement. I used to be so annoyed whenever he would say that to me, but now I appreciate the expression. He's right, I can always be better; and I work very hard to surpass my own frustrating limits and high expectations.

He scans the basic notes in the file, re-familiarizing himself with the specifics of why we were hired for this job. Once he's finished, his tired eyes find mine expectantly, waiting for me to start. I explain how I waited in the alley, sneaking up behind Samuel when he entered. He listens as I describe how I killed him, and what I was thinking during those hours. It was a relatively easy assignment, as the target put up no fight and died quickly, so I'm done speaking within a couple of minutes.

I leave out the information about my use of ethereal essence, of course. Though I think he's known for a while that there are things I haven't told him about my essence. He'll never ask, as he wouldn't put me in a position to choose between our relationship and my safety, but he sometimes looks at me as if he sees more than I've ever let anyone see—which I ignore. My parents were the only people who knew of my universal essence, and unfortunately, the one sharp memory I have of my father is him desperately begging me to never tell another soul. I trust Marek completely, and think of him and Isaiah as the only family I have, but I'd demand he slit my throat before I confessed my darkest secret.

I wait in silence while he watches me with calculating eyes. He's surely trying to determine how I managed to sneak up behind the target in a narrow alley when he was walking toward me. We stare at each other for a moment, and I raise a brow in challenge. But he nods, resigning to the fact that this is one of those questions he will not ask and I will not answer.

"Well, do you believe there was anything you could have done differently?"

Yes. I need to control my anger better, as it once again put me at risk of getting caught by outsiders.

"No, I don't believe so," I say instead, feeling fidgety, my muscles begging me to move.

"Pride is improvement's rival, Ariella." He pins me with a knowing look, and I keep my face neutral and voice silent. "You're dismissed. I would have you work with Julia and Noah when you get back." Standing, he pockets his hands, looking overly stressed. "They're falling behind, and between you and me, you'll catch them up faster than any of the others."

I nod and turn from the office, walking into the common area. There are a few students huddled around a table, eating breakfast before class this morning. I used to be jealous of those who could make friends easily; especially in a place where we're taught everyone is our enemy. But now I've learned the benefit in solitude, as I am the only person I've ever been able to truly rely on. Sure, I have Marek and Isaiah, but that will never be the same thing.

I step out of the doors and walk slowly down the steps to the cobblestone street below, stretching my neck and shoulders. It's early morning, but the sun has already brightened the tops of Valoria's buildings. The mountains behind the guild shine too brightly at their peaks, where snow forever rests. I spin, not wishing to be blinded today, and focus on the beaming castle in the distance. Fire races through my veins, and I suddenly have the energy for double my normal run today.

Taking the last few steps down, I brace to begin running when a hand grabs my shoulder. I snatch the target's wrist, twisting it under as I turn to face whoever dared to grab me. I see my best friend's pained face and smirk. He knows better—it's his own fault.

"All right, all right, Ari!" I release him and cross my arms, raising my brows at his audacity. "Fuck, you get stronger every day." He glances at me and laughs at my unbothered expression.

"One of these days I won't hesitate to snap your arm, Is." I jerk my head toward the path behind me and we start running.

I can *feel* his eyes burning the side of my face, but keep mine forward. "You are a wonderfully wicked woman, Your Majesty." I throw my head back and laugh; Isiah loves to string words together like that, something he's been fond of since we were children. When we met for the first time he said to me, *"Wow, you have superbly, striking, shimmery silver hair!"* Marek had to hold me back from ripping his balls off at what I had thought was an insult, only for us to become friends the next day.

He also has taken to calling me majesty, though I keep asking him not to. He insists that such a powerful, strong, beautiful woman like me is wasted in the lesser district. That I should be in the castle, wearing silky fabrics and having tea with the royals. The thought makes me gag—there's not a chance he would ever find me associating with any of those deplorable people. Maybe Vespera, the young princess, though I'm sure the rest of them have gotten their venomous claws into her already.

"What's on your mind today? You seem distracted," he asks, ripping me away from my consuming thoughts.

I peek over at him. His tousled, dark hair bounces with his movements, and deep brown eyes bore into mine, worry etched into their creases. My gaze lands on the scar running across his left cheek, and I look away from the bleak reminder of my failure to protect him.

"I'm just tired. I got back late and didn't get much sleep." A partial truth, though Isiah knows there's always something more than that. Thankfully he doesn't press, always understanding when I don't wish to talk about things.

We continue to run, Isaiah following my lead as I turn us directions we rarely go. He doesn't question me, though, trusting my resolve enough to shadow me to whatever destination I have in mind. Eventually, we stop on a street in front of the castle gates, and I rest my hands on my hips as I get my breathing under control.

The royal guards do not even look our way, though I'm sure they're used to many people stopping to gawk at the Eldorian castle. I cannot see much past the wall that surrounds the extremely large building, but through the gate I spot a fountain that takes up a good amount of the courtyard. The fountain is made of deep, gray stone; in the middle is a griffin standing on its back legs—facing the sky—roaring, while water shoots from its beak. I've never seen a griffin up close, which makes me wonder if the fountain accurately represents their size.

Behind the fountain, the castle rises as tall as I imagine the Elysaran mountains to be. That's definitely an exaggeration, but I swear the castle, and the land it's on, is as large as Valoria. Honestly, who needs that much space? There are children brought to us every season, who are hungry and on their last thread of life...all while one singular, unforgiving family lives *here*? It's fucked up. I guarantee they don't utilize more than fifteen percent of it. That space could be used to shelter those who need it, even if just for a short time.

I shake my head; I don't know why I plague myself with these thoughts. The king would never do something so generous as to offer unused space to us *lessers*.

Fuck him. Fuck their whole family.

Isaiah places a gentle hand on my arm, comforting me in the only way he knows how. He's a tender soul—always in touch with others' emotions. Ready to be a helping hand to anyone who is going through a hard time.

He knows what the royals did to my father. He knows about the nightmares that I still have of that day. His room is directly next to mine and the walls are not soundproof, so of course he's aware of the terrors I hide behind them.

He doesn't, however, know of my plans. He doesn't need to. Everyone will find out soon enough.

Chapter Three

Ariella

Noah releases a frustrated sound for the eighth time this session and throws down his blade.

"I can't do it, Ari! It's impossible!" He exclaims. His eyes gloss over, and I can tell he's trying hard not to let the tears fall over the edge.

I kneel in front of him, looking into his sad azure irises. We do not always know the age of the children that are brought into the guild, but I would guess Noah is around eleven. He runs his hand through his hair again, making it look like someone twisted a fork through the blonde strands.

"I know this is difficult—" I start, but he interrupts, shouting at this point.

"No, you don't! You're good at everything you do, no matter what it is...I can't even hold a blade right!" His lip trembles, but his cheeks remain dry.

I bite the inside of my cheek hard—comforting others and offering soothing words is not a quality I possess. I'm not good at this, especially with a child. "Noah, where do you think I started? Hm?" I watch as he processes what I'm trying to say. "I was just as young as you once. When I got here, I couldn't even hold a kitchen knife correctly. That's why they gave me to Marek...I was completely hopeless and needed the extra training. But I worked hard, pushed myself out of my comfort space, and now here I am."

Was that good enough?

His eyes well up a little more. *By the Angel, please don't cry.*

"You mean you used to be worse than me?" He rubs his temple, avoiding his eyes, and I can see some of the heavy emotions dissipating.

Okay, maybe I can do this.

"Yes, I was much worse than you!" I smile at his strained laugh. "I'm not giving you a heavy blade to upset you. It's important that you learn how to wield different weapons, especially ones that aren't made for your stature. Because when you're out there," I point at the window to my right, "you may not have access to your favorite blade. Maybe you'll need to use someone else's. And if that were to ever happen, you'll be thankful you know how to adapt."

I inwardly cringe at my words. I was struggling to talk on his level, so I'm not sure if he'll understand what I'm truly saying. But after a few moments, he grins widely and nods.

"That's a good idea. I want to be able to use any weapon, just like you." He reaches down and picks the blade back up. He's still battling his fingers to hold it properly, but there's a determined look on his features now. I definitely underestimated him.

I stand fully, continuing to show him and Julia the different ways to grasp their weapons. I make minor adjustments in their grips, demonstrating why certain ones could be harmful if used.

Isaiah sits against the wall, watching us. He was *too tired* after our run to help me with them physically, but insisted he could still use his voice, which earned him a big eye roll.

"Doing good work, Ari!" I suck on my teeth and slowly turn my gaze toward him, narrowing my eyes. He bursts out laughing as he shoves another grape into his mouth. "What? I'm just complimenting you!"

"You could help instead."

One side of his mouth crooks up, and I know he's about to say something annoying. "And interrupt your perfect teaching? No thanks. I'm happy to sit here and make sure you keep doing good." His amusement doesn't earn him a pass, so I grab a blade by the sharp end and twist my body to fling it at him. He has no time to register what's happening before it's embedded in the wall next to his head, so close that it presses against the skin of his ear.

He jerks away a second too late, his mouth dropping open as he looks at me. I blink, daring him to take the bait.

"Oh, okay...you want to challenge me? All right, let's go," He chuckles playfully, stalking toward me. If he weren't my best friend, I could see myself being attracted to him. He's muscular and toned, with smooth, honey skin, and sharp facial features. But I could never ruin what we have for a good fuck—because that's all it could be.

The only person I'm willing to commit to is myself.

I laugh at his exaggerated movements and attempt to speak, but the door opening snags my attention toward Marek and Velora walking in. Is and I share a confused look before turning to focus on our mentors. Marek never enters the student training room, so this is strange. Especially with the hard look on his face.

"Julia. Noah. You're dismissed for the day," Marek says to them. Noah jumps in the air before remembering he's holding a sharp weapon, and carefully walks over to the wall to place it back on its mount. Julia waves goodbye to me before skipping her way out of the room.

"What's going on?" Isaiah questions when no one speaks. He has never appreciated the power of silence like I do.

"Could you both follow us down to the briefing room?" Velora remarks sharply. She's not pleased about whatever has happened. We follow, walking down a set of stairs just off the common area to a dimly lit hallway underground. There are several rooms down here used for information that is to not leave the ears of the guild. We enter the briefing room, where a large, round table sits. It holds sixteen chairs, though we no longer use them all. Not since Mikah was killed during an assignment and her sister, Mabel, ran from the guild, convinced it was her fault.

I don't know where she went, though I do wonder if she's still alive. She and Mikah were always kind to me, even though I can be a complete bitch sometimes—well, most of the time. It devastated the entire guild when we learned what happened that day.

Isaiah and I sit next to each other, across from a sneering Isolde, while the others file into the room. There's eleven assassins along with our mentors, and then Jaxon. Jaxon is our strategist; he creates the plans that are given to us for each assignment. While we do our own research at times, Jaxon seems to know everything about everyone. He knows where they frequent, who their close circle is, and where they'll be in a few days time. He uses this information to map out where the kill should take place, and how it should be done. While everyone in the Eldorian Kingdom knows the guilds aren't just for educating orphaned children, we still try to make things as clean as possible. Sometimes they look like accidents, or just petty theft with a side of murder. Jaxon changes our methods frequently, ensuring that a kill couldn't be pinned on the guild in the event someone jumps on a power trip and attempts to take us down.

Once we're all sat, Marek sets a piece of thick paper down on the table. It looks like the type that's used for announcements around the city—the ones that hang inside different businesses to garner attention for something. Marek folds his hands in front of him and meets each of our eyes before speaking.

"King Thalion has sent out a proclamation to all the guilds in the kingdom; even the one in Grenport. It states the castle will hold a...competition, of sorts." My forehead creases as I contemplate what this has to do with us, and wait for the old man to make his damn point. "This competition will be for members of the guilds. And while it's not stated directly on the announcement, it's implied that the king expects each guild to offer three assassins for this competition."

None of us speak. What the fuck? Why would there be a competition for assassins?

"Now," Marek continues, "clearly Thalion is just bored and looking for a good show from those of you trained to fight. But to the public, he will most likely make it benefit his reputation. Either way, this is something we cannot refuse."

"We brought you all down here to first ask if anyone would like to volunteer." Velora's demanding voice takes up every available space in the room. "Before you decide, you should know that you will be required to live at the castle during the competition. Also, the winner will be given some kind of reward. That is as much information as we have—anything else will be told to you upon arrival for the competition." She leans back in her chair, her stern face watching each of ours carefully. She wears her dark hair short, cropped nearly flush with her scalp. She's a tall, severe woman, and has never really liked me. I'm sure it's just because Marek chose me as his, while she mentors the rest of the students. Despite that, she tries to demand things from me, though I consistently remind her that I do not answer to her requests. I take great pleasure in watching her skin flush a deep red each time she becomes angry with me.

But I have no desire to bother her right now, as I am nearly trembling at the opportunity that has presented itself to me. I've been trying to figure out a way to get inside the castle for years...just to get close enough to that smug bastard. I wonder if the Angel does listen to prayers? Certainly someone in the Aether realm heard me, if not the Angel, because there's no way this gets handed to me the day I visit the castle for the first time since I was six.

I know Marek will insist on me going whether or not I volunteer—I have a good chance at winning against the seventeen others, and it will be expected for the capital's guild to take the crown in this competition.

"I will go," I speak up before the others get a chance. They would most likely wait for my comment first, anyway.

Marek looks at me, approval in his gaze, and nods to confirm the decision with the rest of the group. "Who els—" he begins, but Isaiah quickly interrupts.

"I will, too," Marek shoots him a glare, and his eyes widen before adding, "Sir." If I didn't insist on keeping my features blank around everyone in attendance, I would've laughed so hard at his face right now. He looks like he just met a griffin.

My mentor glances at me, and I give him a barely perceptible nod, indicating that I'm okay with Isaiah joining. There's no reason for him not to; and it will be nice to have him there. I likely will not be leaving the castle alive, because I refuse to waste this opportunity, but he will be okay without me. At least I'll have the opportunity to say goodbye before I'm executed or imprisoned for the rest of my life.

"Okay, Isaiah," Marek says before turning to the others. They discuss who else should join Is and me. Isolde, of course, creates a big scene about being the final one to go. But much to my, and everyone else's amusement, Velora shut down that idea quickly. Isolde would certainly embarrass the guild, using the competition as an excuse to try besting me in the war she seems to think is between us.

After a few minutes, it's decided that Raine will join as the final member. Raine is tall and slender, and one of the quickest people we have in the guild. His speed could be very useful in the competition—though if just for him, or all of us, I'm uncertain.

It's disappointing that there were no extra details given in the proclamation. Would the guilds be working in teams? Is this an individual competition? Will we be competing physically against each other, or some other way? How long is it expected to take? All of this information would have been useful in determining who to send, as we could choose those of us with the needed strengths. Though that is certainly why there wasn't any other information...now that I think of it, Marek mentioned that the king didn't ask for us directly, so how is he sure we're the ones needed?

I stand and walk over to my mentor, grabbing the paper to look it over while the others continue talking.

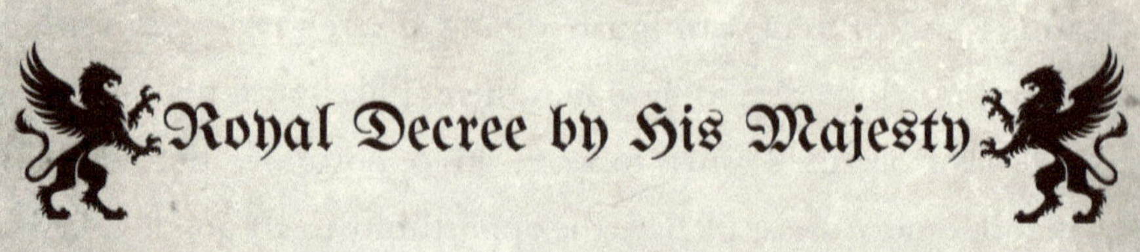

Royal Decree by His Majesty

By the sovereign decree of His Royal Majesty, King Thalion Blackwood, ruler of the Eldorian Kingdom, and protector of the people, it is hereby ordained that each esteemed guild within the boundaries of our glorious Kingdom shall, with utmost haste and loyalty, dispatch a trio of their most skilled and discreet members to the hallowed halls of the Royal Castle. These chosen individuals shall partake in an illustrious series of trials, crafted by the King himself, where the victor shall receive honors and rewards befitting their prowess and cunning.

Let it be known this royal summons extends to the guilds within each of the revered cities of Eldoria — the valiant Valoria, the majestic Meridian, the luminous Lumarna, the stalwart Frostwell, the verdant Grenport, and the formidable Invalle. Failure to present precisely three members from each city shall be deemed an act of defiance against the Crown and shall incur the gravest of consequences.

These participants are expected to arrive at the castle gates upon the advent of the next full moon, prepared to endure the span of the trials. It is essential for each member to embody the virtues of discretion and adaptability, qualities held in high regard for their significance in matters of statecraft and strategy. While the nature of the trials remains a guarded secret, know that they are designed to test the limits of both mind and spirit, seeking those who possess the cunning to navigate the unexpected and the resolve to act with decisive precision.

So decrees King Thalion Blackwood, in his wisdom and foresight, for the prosperity and security of our great Kingdom of Eldoria.

Sighing, I hand the page back to Marek. The king was certainly not subtle about who should be sent for the competition, and it sounds as if the trials will be both physical and mental challenges.

I slip from the briefing room without being dismissed, ready to prepare and spend the next two weeks training from sunrise to sunset. Of course I could use those skills in the competition, but I have one chance to figure out my way to the king.

I will not waste it.

Chapter Four

Caspian

Bright sun beats down on my face, causing heat to caress my body. I despise sweating in my formal attire; it's stiff and soaks in every bit of moisture, causing it to become sticky and uncomfortable. But there's nothing I can do about it until my father is done with his speech. I wouldn't even dare adjust myself, as that would earn a disapproving frown from him, and whatever gossip the crowd in front of us made up. The people love to talk about anything they can get their hands on when it comes to my family. We always need to look calm and put together in front of them, otherwise chaos would reign.

A few years ago, Vespera and I were visiting shops in Valoria to help her pick out a gift for a friend. While in a dress shop, I held up two gowns for my sister to scrutinize—though they looked exactly the same to me—and a group of ladies spotted me through the window. I watched as they pointed in my direction and laughed with each other, assuming they would move along with their day. That was certainly naïve of me—the next day, there were posters drawn, some of me holding the dresses and some of me wearing them. They generously gave me the front page of the morning papers for days, the headline reading "Is Prince Caspian keeping secrets?". Each day, the articles discussed how I was using my sister as an excuse to look at dresses for myself, quoting opinions of those who falsely claimed to know me. They alleged that the only plausible explanation for my appearance in that shop was because I wish to be a woman, and Vespera was helping me in my journey.

I couldn't go anywhere without being stared at more than usual, and everyone laughed at my every move. Eventually, I'd gotten so sick of the inane rumors that I had a gown brought to the castle so that I could wear it during a nice, long walk through Valoria. The next day, there was suddenly other news to make the front page—and since then, I have just minded myself in public, attempting to avoid another *scandal.*

"I will reward the champion in gold," my father's deep voice booms through the city streets. Whenever he speaks to any size of crowd, he requires one of the castle staff to use their aero strand to send his voice skimming across every available surface they can reach. He does not enjoy being ignored. "This is an opportunity for one of the less fortunate in our kingdom to have a chance at the life they've always wanted."

I fight to keep from rolling my eyes; he's not doing this for the *"less fortunate,"* as he so nicely put it. He's requested the kingdom's assassins to be in attendance...I'm sure they could benefit from the large winnings, though I am uncertain why he's insinuating this is a competition for anyone in the guilds. I shake my head—it doesn't matter, I suppose. He will do what he wishes, regardless if it's comprehensible to everyone else.

The competition has afforded me a new opportunity, as I've been tasked with organizing each of the trials. And with their nature, it wouldn't be possible for just anyone to complete them. No—everything the assassins will face has been tailored to their specific skills.

"...rooms prepared for each of our guests, as well as a private indoor training arena, so they may prepare for their trials without the prying eyes of the court." He laughs loudly, and the crowd follows along. "My son, Caspian—" He gestures to me, and I bow my head to acknowledge the crowd, "—will oversee the care of our guests. We, of course, want to ensure a pleasant stay for them." He continues with the rest of his speech, though it brushes right over my wet, sticky, dark hair instead of hitting my ears.

I focus my attention on the crowd; there are always more people than I expect that show up to these things. The king's words will be featured in the paper, and they're not mandated to be in attendance. I understand how much some love their king, but I've heard the hate-filled comments of others when they think I am not listening—it's interesting that more do not feel such things about my family.

The streets extend further than I can see, completely filled with people that prevent any traveling parties from passing through this part of the city. Movement catches my eye not too far ahead of me, and I spot a group of four women huddled together, giggling. Three of them are in lightly fitted dresses, each with a color that represents the season. Deep crimson, crunchy orange, and even the green of the mysterious trees in the Verdantia Forest. The fourth woman has stunning, long hair—somehow darker than mine—that slides over the skin of her smooth arm as she turns to look at me. A red hue appears over her round cheeks, and I allow the corner of my mouth to tilt up as I wink at her. Her eyes widen before the others grab hold of her and try to keep their squealing to a minimum.

Women are simple creatures. A little attention and a smile have them falling to their knees, ready to suck their way into my life.

Or maybe they do it because I'm the prince—the thought grates my nerves.

It's why I do not allow myself to get close to many others. Intentions are easy to conceal, and people will sacrifice anything to be in the good graces of my family. Even fucking me, only to ask afterward if there is an open position in the court I could recommend them for. I cannot blame them, though...we have everything we could ever want, and more, so why wouldn't they try to get a taste of that? I wish my father would give back to the kingdom. To our people. They're the reason we have food, metals, trades, and even the military. Our advances in technology from Lumarna have allowed us to have even more luxury at the castle. We would have none of this if not for our people, and they deserve much more than we give.

That will change when I'm king.

"The competitors are to arrive in three days, at which time we will hold an initiation ceremony in the castle arena." He pauses, smiling at the hundreds of people who are hanging on to every word. I suppose this is exciting, as it is not an event that has ever been held in the kingdom. "Please, join us in their introduction—meet those who will represent the cities of Eldoria in this esteemed competition!" Cheering breaks the silence of the crowd, many of whom are whistling at the conclusion of my father's speech.

Thank the Angel this is over. I badly need to wash my skin and be free of the commotion before the competition starts, and I have no opportunity to remove my mask.

I remain stationed in the same position until my father is fully out of view, only then allowing myself to retreat from the uncanny heat and walk back into the castle. Gavriel falls into step next to me, both of us keeping silent until we're in a private space where our conversation will not be heard.

I peek over at my guard, smirking at how I'm not the only one affected by the heat. His light hair has melted to his skin, nearly covering the dark of his eyes; I chuckle to myself, causing him to knock me in the shoulder. I nearly return the gesture when two ladies of the court turn the corner—my sister's ladies—spotting me and swiftly ending their conversation to bow. Gav and I stop, waiting for them to rise as they insisted on blocking the entire hallway with their exceptionally large gowns.

"Stella, Marion. You both look lovely as ever." I reach for a hand from each, placing a breath of a kiss to the top before letting them drop.

"Thank you, my prince, you are too kind!" Marion spits out; my stomach whirls at the eagerness in her voice, jaw clenching though I keep my smile in place.

"Might I also add how dashing you look yourself!" Stella glances at her pale friend before looking back at me. "My prince, I was wond—" I don't let her finish, knowing that she's going to ask something of me that I'm not able to refuse. According to my father, it is unacceptable to not spend time with the ladies when they request.

But I'm not obligated to say yes if they don't request it in the first place.

"My apologies, ladies, I must be going. Many things to accomplish before the onset of the competition." I nod briefly before stepping around them and hurry to my room.

Gavriel attempts to hide his laugh. "Go vanish in the glades, Gav." I roll my eyes, attempting to feign anger, but the amusement leaks through my voice.

I don't believe I could ever be mad at him. He's been my personal guard for over ten years, though I rarely think of him as such anymore—he's the only person I trust completely within these stone walls.

I was seventeen when we first met, eager and ready to follow in my father's footsteps. He was a couple of years older than me, though the youngest in the royal guard. I spotted him being pushed around by some of the more seasoned sentries, and though their jesting was to be expected, there was something I didn't like about what I saw. I stopped their advances, snatching Gav's arm and pulling him with me to talk where the others wouldn't overhear.

I smile at the memory.

"What's your name?" I question once we were alone.

His wide, nervous eyes meet mine before he whispers, "Ga—" his throat clears, "Gavriel, Your Highness."

"Do they do that to you often, Gavriel?" His brows furrow. "The other guards. Do they harm you often?"

His mouth flops twice before he's able to answer. "Oh, no, Your Highness, they just like to joke around." I raise a brow; it's clear he's lying, most likely not wanting to cause punishment for the others.

I don't think I'm allowed to do this...but, fuck it. "Okay, Gavriel. From this day on, you will be my personal guard. Your room will be next to mine and you will have no interaction with the others unless I, or the king, deem it necessary. You will train with me daily and report to me instead of your current commander."

My father was indeed angry. Not only was I forbidden to choose my own guard, but I'd chosen the youngest one, with the least amount of experience, who seriously needed a lesson in confidence. I pleaded with my father, and he eventually agreed to allow it as long as I had a second guard of his choice until he felt comfortable with Gavriel handling things himself.

We've been good friends since.

Closing the door behind us, I walk further into my room, depositing my sword against the bed. I strip my jacket, grimacing as it peels from my body in sticky increments. I throw that and the rest of my soaked clothing on the ground for staff to take care of. Not bothering to hide my nudity from Gav, I turn from the large bed to walk into my bathroom, sighing when my feet press into the cool tile.

A hiss falls through my lips as I step under the shower—the cold water stings for a moment, but I allow it to take over my body, numbing my senses and cooling my emotions.

"I can't figure out what Thalion's motive is for this competition," Gav's voice breaks my concentration, and my gaze snaps up to find him leaning against the vanity, eyes closed as if he could rest there comfortably. "Sure, he says it's to give back to the people, but that can't be true...otherwise he wouldn't have just assassins attending. What is the purpose of that?"

What is the purpose, indeed. I'm unsure of my father's intentions—I've been mulling over the different possibilities for weeks but have come up with nothing plausible. Does he want to see the murderers of the kingdom? People he allows to exist under the guise that they discreetly deliver justice? My lip curls.

Or could he truly just want to help them? Is it possible he believes the assassins have it the worst out of everyone else, and they deserve the first chance at winning the gold?

Regardless of the reason, I'm also confused about my role with them. I understand organizing the trials and creating tasks that will test all of their abilities, but to oversee their care? What purpose could that serve? Surely they're trained enough to handle the competition, and could use the equipment we'll provide them to train on their own? Maybe they'll feel more comfortable having someone from the royal family with them each day. I'm sure for the ones who are leaving their cities, being here will be a new, daunting experience.

"I don't know my father's reasons," I mutter, scrubbing soap through my hair—one Gavriel truly enjoys teasing me for, as he claims it's too feminine for a prince.

But when is the last time he brought a woman to bed...

He gives me a knowing, pitying look. He understands how difficult this position is for me—being the king's son. I wish to be fully supportive, but some of my father's decisions do not align with our family's supposed values. This competition, for example. Giving back to our people is good and necessary, but to do so in this way? It is not even truly *for the people*? I'm...conflicted. But, I will continue to support the crown, and the kingdom, even if I do not always agree.

I finish rinsing off and step out of the shower, tugging on my kinetic strand to drag over a towel, lest I continue swinging my dick in Gavriel's face.

"Show off," Gav murmurs, and I laugh at his uninterested tone.

"How many times must we argue about this? You weave pyro, which is significantly better than my kinetic or aqua. Plus, it's more impressive in women's eyes." I wag my eyebrows suggestively, and he barks out a laugh.

"Please—if I took even half as many women to bed as you do, I would believe that."

"You," I finish pulling on a loose, comfortable pair of pants and poke him in the chest, "have the better essence. I have the better title." I jump backward as he reaches to shove my shoulder. Laughter builds inside my throat as I dodge his attempts to tackle me.

He catches my left leg and I topple to my side, throwing my hands up before he can begin his attack. "Okay, I surrender!" Sitting up to push him away, a wicked smile curves my lips before I mutter, "Go play with your fire. Find those women you were just bragging about." His eyes narrow, cursing under his breath as he stalks out of the room, leaving me alone.

I lie back on the rug, focusing my eyes on the cream stone that surrounds the residential parts of the castle. I trace the patterns as my eyelids grow heavy, creating a new story for myself with each crease and fold.

Chapter Five

Ariella

A light drizzle catches my skin as Isaiah and I walk through the *illustrious* Eldorian castle gates. I keep my hood up, as most of the others I see outside, not desiring to be soaked by the time we're done with whatever this ceremony is. I also do not wish to alert each person here of who I am just yet. It's absurd, all the competitors gathering in the castle's arena just to show us off to the people. I will not be able to get a good look at the other competitors, considering the offensive weather today.

Though I will not complain—it has been too hot and dry. The crisp, damp air feels particularly nice.

I stop, now face-to-face with the griffin statue in the castle's courtyard. It is much larger this close than I expected—I still wonder if that is the actual size of griffins. How else would they have made such statues if not from studying them first?

I suppress a shudder and continue forward, not peering back to be sure Isaiah is following—he will. It will be nice to have a friend in my last days, though publicly showing a partiality toward him will only put a target on his back. We must maintain the appearance of indifference when around others; as if we are only acquaintances because we come from the same guild.

My eyes struggle to adjust when the sun peeks from the dark clouds, illuminating the arena we're being led to by a few guards, all of whom are draped in nauseating red and gold. The large arena behind the castle is known for hosting bi-annual tournaments, where soldiers from our military stronghold—Frostwell—compete to be assigned as castle guard. I curl my lip. That particular city has always confused me; why would our military only be stationed behind the capitol? Not that we're enemies to the realm's other cities, but the placement lacks logic.

Well, it is the Blackwood family who made such decisions...

The thick, humid air dampens my skin, seducing my hair to stick across my neck like an obsessed lover. We walk a wide path around the annoyingly large castle, which is rather empty. To my right is a small hill that leads down to training grounds, where several weapons lie sprawled around the mats.

Two men circle each other at the center of a mat, my eyes close enough to watch sweat drip down the muscles of the one not wearing a shirt. The sun illuminates every curve to his body, forming shadows along the many lines. He lunges for his counterpart—a guard, I presume, as the standard issued jacket they are all given is thrown off to the side. The two tussle, their laughter reverberating through the grounds as neither can seem to get the upper hand. Pathetic.

The shirtless one twists his hand before one of the swords rushes to rest in his palm. Kinetic strand...interesting.

Our path begins to lead us from view, the hill growing higher the further I walk. At the last moment, the elemental weaver turns, wild eyes meeting mine briefly just as the land covers him entirely.

A finger taps against my thigh. The giddy anticipation I feel to look the king in his eyes is a confession the worst of tortures couldn't pry from my mouth. I want him to see me. Recognize me.

Fear me and what he knows is coming for him.

Whether he is aware of who I am other than the wraith, I've yet to discover. Though I've half a mind to show him exactly who he invited to his castle the moment I step into the arena.

I won't, though. No...I did not imagine the moment of his death for twenty years just to fuck it up on impulse. I will wait and watch. Plan.

I suck in a breath when Isaiah shoves my shoulder. "You good?" My head snaps to his, causing his eyes to roll.

"Why wouldn't I be? This competition is a mere game for the king's amusement—child's play, if I'm to be specific." He chuckles, shaking his head.

Raine snorts from my other side, waving a hand toward the arena. "Yeah, for you. The rest of us weren't born knowing how to perfectly wield a blade," he mutters, sucking his teeth.

"Yes, well, we all have our talents, Raine. You, for example, would likely do well in the theater—I've yet to meet someone else that is just as dramatic." My head tilts, and I hum. "Actually, take Isolde with you. That woman must be good for *something*, and it certainly is not at the guild."

He grimaces, shaking his head. "No thanks," he drags out his words, and I almost smile.

Cheers reverberate through the space just beyond the tall stone structure of the arena. Sentries stand at each entrance door, though the ones guiding our group veer to the right where a tunnel appears. I slow, nodding for Isaiah to walk ahead of me as the tunnel is only wide enough for one person at a time. My hands itch to drag him from the enclosed space, but standing at his back will have to do. Too many people have already seen us here; I cannot walk away now.

Despite the suddenly bright day, light does not reach very far into the tunnel, completely surrounding us in darkness for a minute. I unsheathe my blade, pushing off my hood and angling my head to listen behind me, my relief unfound even after we emerge from the opposite side unscathed. I twirl my blade, scanning the arena twice before focusing on the assessing group we approach. There are a dozen assassins here already, all huddled in their respective guilds, I assume.

From the wide eyes of my competitors to the mutterings of the audience, I tense and settle into the calm awareness that aids my mind in such crowded places. Especially when so much attention is on me.

Our trio halts next to the others, turning to face the gilded throne that awaits my subject himself. I focus on the details of the thrones instead of the whispers—four in total, all gold with red cushioning, though it's easy to discern which is for the king. I doubt he could have made it more obvious if he tried. At least twice the size of the others, intricate carvings through the back that are filled with a glimmering ruby in each.

"My, my..." a lazy voice drawls from my left. This should be interesting. "Never in my wildest fantasies did I imagine meeting the Silver Wraith at such a...lowly competition. The tales of your merciless ways reach even the far corners of Frostwell, though I must admit how disappointed I am that they do not speak of your beauty." The pale man appears in front of me, arrogance exuding from his every movement. His broad shoulders are covered with worn leather, likely cracked from the cold of the mountains just as much as from his frequent training. Red, curly hair rests sluggishly over his thick head as his nearly black, amused eyes drink in my body.

When his gaze finally meets mine, clearly expecting a reaction, I raise a brow and wait. A dark smile tugs at his lips, his eyes flitting to someone in the group before returning to me.

“Not much of a talker, huh?” No answer—his brows furrow. “That’s fine...I never enjoy the screamers, anyway.” The darkness that passes through his features confirms that he certainly prefers to bed women who are crying and struggling, rather than willing.

He steps closer, the heat of his body warring with the sticky air around us. He looms several inches over me, curving his shoulders as if to intimidate me—I nearly roll my eyes. “I’m Jeth, by the way—and now that we’re familiar, what do you say you give me a tour of your room when we’re done here?” A couple of the other assassins snicker behind me.

I lean toward Jeth, looking up at him with wanting eyes. He smirks. “I say that the next time you dare to get this close to me, my blade will gladly find a new home.” His forehead creases just before I drive my knee into his cock and lean back to kick his chest hard enough that he flies backward, spraying sand when his body smacks into the ground. He groans, cupping his groin as two other men rush to his side.

“I’m fucking fine. I don’t need your help.” He shoves them away as he stands, pinning me with a hateful glare. “You’ll regret that, wraith.” I drag my eyes to the audience, where the king occupies the once empty space in front of his throne. His beady eyes stare through me for a moment until he seems to remember where he is, focusing a thoroughly practiced smile at the thousands of people watching.

"Citizens of Eldoria, welcome to trials that mark the first of their kind! Where members of our kingdom's guilds will compete for a single victory, upon which they will be rewarded handsomely." Cheers ring through the arena, movement from my peripheral turning my head to the right, where the final three competitors stand—I must have missed their arrival when Jeth insisted on signing his death papers. The king raises a hand, effectively quieting the noise. "There will be three trials, the likes of which will remain hidden until they begin. Each competitor will be given a room in the guest wing of the castle, where they are required to live while they remain in the competition. However," he mutters icily, training his eyes over all eighteen of us before speaking again. "You are permitted to leave the grounds when you are not attending a trial or training—you are not prisoners!" He chuckles, moving on to announce other rules I do not particularly care to listen to.

No, I'm interested in him.

He makes loud gestures with his arms, as if he must act out each word he spews. Not one strand of his light hair flows with the breeze, remaining perfectly styled on his imperious head.

"Ariella Mistaire," he spits my name thickly, attempting to disguise his disgust, though the curl of his lip gives away his true feelings. I intertwine my hands behind my back and smile at him challengingly. He averts his gaze. "Isaiah Cheral, and Raine Nicolae join us from Valoria's very own guild!" Applause. My jaw clenches as he introduces the rest of the competitors. Jeth and his two companions—Bessan and Jaspar—each wave to the audience when the king utters their names with a sense of pride. "—Obren Sparre, and Ally Dimir traveled from our wonderful Meridian to be with us today!" The group to my right stirs, the raven black haired woman casting her eyes downward when attention shifts to her.

The king dismisses our groups, shifting his announcement to what the audience can expect, though his eyes remain on me as I walk from the arena. Even when I cannot see him any longer, I feel his gaze searing through my back.

I've already grasped his attention—perfect. I breathe deeply, feeling much lighter than I did an hour ago. Staff wait just outside the tunnel, two stepping away from the dozen to step in front of our trio.

"Welcome. We are to escort you to your rooms," the smaller woman says quietly, bowing her head as she turns to lead us down a different path than we arrived on. She peers nervously over her shoulder, quickening her steps when she sees we've followed. Her crimson dress must be extraordinarily uncomfortable, the thick material covering her arms and down through her ankles.

The woman next to her lightly touches her shoulder, motioning us inside a small entrance at the back of the castle. Where more royal guards are stationed...it seems the king is taking no chances among his new *guests.* As if a few sentries could stop me from killing him.

I chuckle, Isaiah's head snapping to me at the sound. I shake my head slightly, thankful he lets the behavior go in favor of being friendly with the staff. His kindness will kill him one of these days.

"What are your names?" The women share a look before the older one answers—the smaller one's mother, I realize. They share the same pale blue eyes, sandy hair, and lithe frames. Amada and her daughter Corine. I study the castle as we walk through endless hallways, Is pestering the women with ridiculous questions. Which garden is the prettiest? What's the best food that's served here? If you walked at a normal pace from one end of the castle to the other, how long would it take?

"Nineteen minutes if you utilize the main halls, though only fourteen through the service passages." The entire group pauses at my answer, though Isaiah just laughs and waves me off.

"Ignore her—she does that," he mutters, pushing us along. I raise a brow at him in a way that says, *"don't ask questions you don't want the answers to."* He flattens his lips, facing forward.

Each hallway we enter has the same uniformity, much to my liking. The colors, however, are not. Cream, stone walls form pillars and grand arches where a gold chandelier hangs from each. In between are gilded lamps jutting from the walls, while the floors create square patterns with cream and red tiles.

It's all very...royal.

We enter the guest wing, where there are fewer arches and more doors. I sigh, rubbing sweat from the back of my neck. The assassins who come from guilds that lie days away should be given rooms during their time in the competition, though Valoria's guild is a mere hour walk from here. There is no logical reason for Isaiah, Raine, and me to stay here.

Images of the king's death flash through my mind, and suddenly the prospect of having access to his home for a few weeks doesn't seem too burdensome.

"Ms. Mistaire, this will be your room..." Corine remarks, pushing open a door and stepping to the side. Isaiah looks over his shoulder and winks, Amada showing him and Raine to the two rooms next to mine. I walk through the doorway, clicking my tongue at the simple setup. A large window on the far side looks over Valoria, a wooden desk positioned next to it. Toward the center of the room is a large bed, which surprisingly isn't dressed in crimson.

I cannot say the same for the rug that covers most of the floor, which displays the royal crest—

"I'll have a bath drawn for you." I whirl to the girl, having forgotten she was there.

Heat spreads through my veins as I pin her with a glare deadly enough to ensure she will personally tell each staff member of my demand. "*No one* but me is to enter this room. *Ever.* Do you understand?" She nods, her wide eyes fluttering.

"Of course...my apologies, Ms. Mistaire," she mutters quickly, hurrying from my sight.

My shoulders drop as I shove the door closed a bit too forcefully. I stare at the simple bolt meant to keep others out. I've nothing to hide—in physical possessions, anyway—so I suppose it wouldn't matter if someone did enter.

I need to be careful, though. The king's attention is not all good, and the other assassins will likely try anything to fuck with me. Even if that means sneaking into my room at night to slit my throat.

I tap my finger before tugging on my umbral strand and weaving wards through the door. It's a risk I need to take, even if it means potentially exposing myself. I will not be here for long, and I doubt anyone of importance will attempt to enter my room.

I turn to face the window, grimacing at the beating sun shining through. A cold, cold shower is exactly what I need right now.

Chapter Six

Caspian

"Either you've lost all ability to weave since yesterday, or something's on your mind," Gavriel states harshly, obviously annoyed with my lack of effort. I sigh, swiping a hand down my face.

"I don't know." He gives me a look that says I'm lying. I shrug. "It's really nothing, just the new *guests* to the castle."

"Has one of them tried to hurt you?" He stiffens, prepared to go after this made-up attacker.

"No," I laugh as I shove his shoulder, walking to the table at the side of the training room. I gulp down a glass of water before continuing. "Nothing like that. Something just feels off...I can't explain it."

He nods slowly, considering my words. "Is it possible you're just uncomfortable with so many killers living amongst you?"

I should be wary of the many assassins that now walk these halls, but I'm not. I do not feel like talking about it further, though. "Yeah. But I think I'm just tired. I'll go rest for a while, then I'll be back to *best weaver ever* status." He barks out a laugh, and I roll my eyes at his disbelief.

I'm out of the room before he can say anything else, flipping him off and indicating I don't want him to follow. He should technically be on duty right now, but he gives me space when I need it.

Plus, he won't like where I'm headed.

My eyes widen as I take in the indoor training room provided for the assassins. I'm relieved it's empty, as my father has prohibited any castle staff or nobility from entering. Ridiculous rule, but I don't doubt any one of these competitors would tell him of my rebellion to obtain his favor.

Everything appears brand new. There are several mats for hand-to-hand, a wall of every type of weapon imaginable, and even sets of bars used for stretching and toning.

The accommodations are quite nice, which is interesting. I haven't known my father to go to such lengths before, especially for guests. I step into the middle of the room—onto a training mat—and take a deep breath.

"This room is for competitors only." I tense at the voice, willing myself to not immediately spin around and look guilty.

I turn slowly, facing my accuser.

Fuck me. Fuck the Angel.

There's only one person in the realm who's known to have that hair: the Silver Wraith.

She raises a brow, and I take in her features. Her long, silky hair is tied at the top of her head, with pieces surrounding her face. Black leathers cover her mouthwatering curves, and I bite my lip to hide my body's reaction to them. Her hands clasp behind her back as she stands contently, knowing she could certainly sink one of those blades on her thighs into my head before I blinked again. My eyes drag to her face, to soft lips curved upward slightly. Cunning, green irises glare back at me while a second brow raises, and I can sense the amusement emanating off her.

Shit, I was definitely not subtle in my perusal, and she watched me take in every inch of her body. I feel my dick harden and suddenly find the wooden bars interesting. Her head tilts in my peripheral; she must be highly entertained by how foolish I'm acting. You would think me no better than a young boy seeing a woman for the first time.

Who knew an assassin could be so breathtaking?

I clear my throat as sweat forms on my brow and a tingling sensation under my skin slides down my spine. "I am a competitor," I state quickly, though not with confidence. From the lack of recognition when I turned around, I do not believe she knows who I am. Maybe I can get out of here without her alerting my father that I broke one of his *rules.* She seems like someone who would enjoy doing that.

"Is that so?" Her voice is like rich, melted honey seeping into my pores. "Because you weren't at the initiation ceremony."

Stay calm. There were many people there; no chance she memorized them all.

"Been watching me, have you?"

"No." She walks toward me slowly, her hips swaying gently with each intentional step. Fuck, I should not be attracted to someone like her. Murder is not a quality I'd accept in a woman...though the tightness in my chest claims otherwise. "But I never forget a face. And yours was not at the ceremony." She stops a foot in front of me, her unwavering gaze causing my breath to hitch.

She's a frightening little thing.

She's also just a woman...I can handle her. I give her a charming smile. "Perhaps you just didn't see me. You're mistaken." Her eyes narrow slightly, one side of her lips rising—would she enjoy it as much as I, if I bit them?

"Perhaps. Or perhaps I should threaten to slice off your precious cock, and then we'll see if I'm still mistaken." Her bright eyes harden, and she smiles, though it's menacing as all traces of amusement fade from her face.

"You would fight me?"

"Without a second thought." She paces around me, and I follow her direction. I would be foolish to trust my back with someone who has a reputation like hers. "The rules state competitors may fight outside of trials—even to death—as long as the challenge is accepted by both parties...which you should know, since you're a competitor." She stops in front of me again, angling her head while her eyes roam my body as if she can't quite decide whether I'm her next kill or next fuck.

I'll take either.

My breath quickens when I process what she just said. I can't fight her...sure I'm trained by the best, but this woman is deadly. Savage. She wouldn't hesitate to behead me and bathe in my blood. "You're right," I stammer, unable to think of anything else to say. Maybe I shouldn't have told her I'm a competitor. She surely wouldn't challenge the prince.

But I'm also a little excited at the prospect.

"Do you accept the challenge, then?" How is she so fucking still?

"And what makes you think you could best me?" She actually smiles then, and I'm hypnotized. A small laugh leaves her; it's an evil laugh, but the sound goes straight to my dick. Her tongue darts out to caress her bottom lip, and I follow the movement carefully. I have never wished to be a piece of flesh more.

"Charming." Her amused voice shatters my aching thoughts as she raises an eyebrow. "I was actually thinking the same about you." Deadly and confident? My kind of woman.

"All right, I'll bite. What makes you think I couldn't best you?"

She makes a show of inspecting me head to toe, only to meet my gaze again with an unimpressed look. "A lot."

"Oh, you're good." I shake my head, knowing I have no choice but to spar with her. Well, at least it will be a spar for me; the look in her eye says she's hungry, and I'm her next meal. I suppose if she wanted to wrap her mouth around my flesh without using a blade first...

"I accept." I barely get the words out before she swings her leg to knock me on my back with a grunt.

I look up at her, still standing with both hands behind her, like this is just some silly game. Maybe it is to her. But now I'm pissed.

She waits for me to rise, not showing a single speck of fear or calculation. Of course she wouldn't. She's the most feared person in our kingdom.

I shouldn't find that hot.

"Play fair, wraith, or you'll be going against those rules you seem to love."

Nothing. No reaction. I thought the name would get to her, but I'm sure everyone she meets knows exactly who she is. Her hair is as unique as her face.

"Since you know of me, you must also know that I do not *play fair,*" her silky voice caresses every part of me. I unsheathe my sword and swing toward her waist, but she's no longer there.

A heavy blow hits the back of my knees and I drop to all fours, cursing myself as I sit back. I peer up at her smirking face and decide that this isn't such a terrible position to be in.

"Hm." She pushes a strand of my black hair off my forehead, grazing her soft fingers along my skin before continuing. "Maybe you aren't as useless as I thought...you could certainly do many things from down there that wouldn't require *that* sword." She pointedly looks at the weapon on the floor, her tone teasing. Aether, she's a bitch.

I snatch the weapon and stab forward with a speed that impresses even me. She catches the sword between her legs, not caring that the sharp steel could sever her limbs with little effort. I let go of the hilt and strike my fist into her gut, but she barely registers the hit. Instead, eyes of raw venom stare down at me, probably annoyed I could get a hit on her.

Leaping up to strike again, she grabs my arm and twists our bodies until our backs are touching. She bends forward and heaves my body through the air, forcing me to land on my stomach. Hard. I'm trying to get breath back into my lungs when I'm rolled over and her toned thighs wrap around my hips, holding me in place.

"Well, wraith, since the rules allow competitors to fight with consent, I would assume that applies to other things, as well." I smirk and run my hands along the top of her fitted leathers. Fuck me, she feels good...her legs stiffen, and I know she feels the evidence of my attraction to her violence. There's just something about a woman who knows her way around a blade, infamous murderer or not.

I shove to punch her gut once more, though she learns quickly. She grabs my fist—grabs. From mid-swing. As if the force of my intention was nothing but a small inconvenience. She twists my hand until my body is forced to follow, lest I leave here with a broken wrist. She scoffs, shoving my arm away and standing. I tilt my head back to meet her eyes; she watches me, bored.

"Again. But this time, quit being an idiot and put in effort." She sounds almost angry, as if I've offended her.

I roll and push to stand, grabbing my sword carefully as I watch her. "Or what?" I was already *putting in effort*, but I have a feeling she'd kill me just for admitting it. A brow raise—what would it take to get an actual reaction from her? I really want to find out. "Fine, don't answer. But when I win, you owe me something of my choosing." Not even a glimmer of humor flits through her eyes. She takes one step, tilting her head.

"And what would that be?" I open my mouth to answer, though I do not actually know...I didn't think that far. She doesn't wait to hear my confession, before flinging a blade in my direction, knocking into just below where I grasp the hilt of my sword. My hand flexes, dropping it, and she's in front of me slamming her foot into my cock before it fully lands on the mat. I stumble backward, resisting the urge to gag from the waves of pain.

"Fuck, give me a minute, will you?" She chuckles, shrugging as she continues advancing, though slowly.

"It's not my problem you're slow and unobservant." Why did I agree to this?

I tug on my kinetic strand, reaching for one of the blades on the wall and flinging it at her head before I second-guess the choice. She doesn't move—doesn't even flinch as she flicks her wrist and sends the blade backward just before it sinks into her skull. My jaw drops as I watch the weapon thud to the floor, clanking loudly. For a moment I freeze and consider how foolish it was of me to attempt such a thing, at the Silver Wraith of all people; but when I meet her eyes, there's a playfulness to them that wasn't there before.

She's not angry I just tried to kill her...

"That was better, though next time refrain from staring at your next move as you execute it." I roll my eyes, watching her as I throw nearly every weapon on the wall at her before my next heartbeat. Her hand snatches one from the air that nearly connects with her cheek, the rest maneuver around her and clamber into the mirror. I wince at the loud crack, willing the entire thing to not fall apart before I can find someone to fix it. The wraith throws her head back to laugh, spinning as she twists the small blade through her fingers.

She says something—likely an insult—though I don't hear as I rush after her and shove her body into the wall. I unsheathe a blade from my belt and press it to her waist as my weight smushes her front to the stone. She gasps when I press into her, my grip loosening from the barely perceptible sound.

She chuckles darkly. "You truly make it too easy," she breaths before her elbow connects with my throat—fucking bitch. I choke and push the uncomfortable sensation away as I block her next swing. We spar for several minutes, though I'm convinced she's hardly trying as sweat builds along my skin while she doesn't even look a bit worn. She pauses on a mat, a sinister smile spreading across her face.

"I know you're lying," she states as she circles me, looking like an ethereal predator. "You are not one of us."

"And why would you say that?" I follow her movements, trying to anticipate where her next advance will be.

"The Aether can hear your footsteps without strain. You've nearly tripped twice, which tells me balance is not part of your training regimen. And..." She fakes right and knocks a knee into my side. Before I can grab the area, she's behind me, holding me up with a blade pressed to the delicate skin above my rapidly beating heart.

"You leave your left unguarded. You're practically inviting me to come slit your throat." Her voice is pure sin, and my breathing speeds up for a whole new reason. I nearly lean into the sharp touch before I remember I'm not supposed to enjoy this.

"Fair. You win," I concede, not really paying attention to my words with the way her pelvis presses into my ass.

"No, I think you do," she purrs, and I almost groan. Aether damn this woman; of course the Angel would send me someone so unbelievably sexy but so off-limits. "I don't give advice for free; but your performance was pathetic, so I'll be lenient just this once." The lust fades from my mind, replaced with a burning sensation slithering up my neck.

"Are you going to lower your blade?" I spit, done with these teetering emotions I'm feeling.

"Don't let me catch you in here again. I won't be so kind a second time." She releases me, stepping around my stunned body as she sheathes her blade. I bite my lip at the sight of her striding out of the room, and stupidly find myself speaking again.

"I told you I'm a competitor."

She halts, peering over her shoulder and looking deeply into my soul. "And I told you I never forget a face...prince." She leaves me alone with my mouth agape.

I chuckle to myself, cursing my treasonous body. Finally convincing my legs to move, I hurry from the room before the wraith returns and fulfills her threatening promise.

Chapter Seven

Ariella

My eyes are unwavering as I stare straight ahead, focusing on the unscathed surface of the throne. Outwardly, I show no signs of stress. But on the inside, I'm a fucking raging storm.

I'm standing in the front line of the spread out competitors. There are six rows of three, with Isaiah to my right and Sivara to my left. She clearly has a fucking problem with me, because I can feel her eyes burning holes into the side of my face. The only time I've seen her before now was at the ceremony, so it must just be my reputation that has earned her animosity.

I won't give her the satisfaction of a reaction, though. We're not here to start drama, we're here to win.

And I will win.

I suck in a deep breath, the mixture of sweat, leather, and old perfume moistening the air. The throne room is large, with ceilings that seem taller than the castle itself, and walls spread so far apart, it would take minutes to walk from one side to the other. The tile on the floor is warm, giving the illusion of a comforting environment. But as I spot the hungry, excited gazes of the audience, I know it's anything but.

We're not guests. We're the entertainment.

The king may have claimed this competition was created under his generosity, but those surrounding me know the truth: he's bored and wants the kingdom's best fighters pitted against each other to amuse his curiosities.

The air is thick, making my breaths heavy and my heart beat fast. I hear its thumping in the space surrounding me, and I hope I'm the only one who can. I don't need the bitch next to me thinking I'm weak.

We've been standing here for nearly an hour, waiting for *his royal majesty* to make an appearance. The intermittent coughing and shuffling have become more frequent as the anticipation increases.

Mine included.

I'm nervous. I'm not scared to admit that to myself, though Aether damn me if I'd ever say it out loud. Heat scrapes the back of my neck, building sweat along my tingling skin. But I keep my breathing even and my face blank of all emotions except annoyance. I focus on the royal guards surrounding the throne, wondering how lo—

The large doors behind me swing open, though I do not move from my position. I know it's the king; the excited whispers and giggles tell me just as much. I also hear the prince's name drifting through the musky air.

I've tried not thinking about him since I caught him in the training room. He wasn't supposed to be there—I really didn't give a fuck, but the idea of cutting off his head was loud in mine. If I truly wanted to exact perfect revenge on the king, wouldn't it be appropriate to take away someone he loves instead of him? And who better than his heir?

It was the ideal opportunity, but not the right time. No...I need to wait a while longer. If I'm able to sway from my original plan so quickly, then it wasn't a good plan to begin with. I have to learn more about the

Blackwood family; their routines, preferences, secrets. I need to be smart about this, because I'll only get one chance.

A good place to start will be Caspian, though. Clearly, it won't be hard to get near him. He was practically coming in his pants the second he saw me; you'd think he's never laid eyes on a woman before.

Foolish fucking idiot.

It would have been so easy to strip him from this realm and send his royally stained soul to the Angel. But instead of being focused on his life, he was fixated on my ass.

Men.

The royal family themselves finally come into view, walking up the few steps to sit in their gilded thrones, draped in crimson finery. What I wouldn't give to toss my blade right at that bastard's head, rejoicing in the loud clank of his crown as it slides across the floor. It would be so easy—not one person in here could stop me before the blade sliced its way through the king's grimy memories and poisoned thoughts.

"People of Valoria, welcome to the first trial! Where you will witness the kingdom's brightest fight for glory!" I roll my eyes as he continues talking to the audience as if they're children seeing someone weave for the first time. And they're eating it up.

A prickle of awareness works its way up my spine and my gaze snaps to the king's left, where the prince leans back in his chair, hands grasping the arms while he glares at me. I allow myself a small smile. He's definitely pissed. I probably hurt his brittle ego when I showed him just how weak he was. I'm guessing no one in his life has actually fought him properly, making him think that he wins against every challenger.

Not me. I don't give a fuck how he feels.

In fact, I find his rage quite intoxicating.

I raise my eyebrow at him, and his eyes narrow even more, lip curling slightly. Yeah, this is going to be significantly more entertaining than I anticipated. But I have a job to do, and right now that's making it through this first trial; so I look back to the king, dismissing the prince and his loud silence.

"Competitors, for this trial you will be escorted to the forgotten tunnels under the castle." Interesting. "There will be no light to guide you and no one to help you. In this vast labyrinth, your task is to navigate your way to the center, where you will find various artifacts. Some are as large as my arm," he holds out the bulky limb, as if it's something we should be impressed by, "and some are as small as my hand. You are to choose only one artifact and bring it back to this room." His smile turns sinister as he looks down on the eighteen of us as if we're a mere game to him.

I suppose we are.

"There are no rules to this trial other than your task. Obtain the artifact and present it to me, no matter the cost. Because, you see, there are only fourteen." He laughs, the only sound in this heated room other than the rapid breathing of the man behind me. Gross.

Only fourteen.

Four people will not make it to the second trial. Good.

I plan while the king finishes his ridiculous speech. I'm familiar with the layout of the castle, including the service halls, though the tunnels underneath are news. There will be no light, which could be both an advantage and a disadvantage for me. I work best in the cover of shadows, but even those have small amounts of light seeping through.

Tunnels. I'm unsure how wide these will be, but I must assume that putting one at my back and walking sideways will be my best method. It may be slower, but it's important to protect every side, so it's necessary.

The tunnels will most likely be made of stone, which not only carries sound far, but it's also not the most quiet surface to walk on. I doubt there will be an orchestra down there, drowning out all sounds...and that means silence is my only ally in this.

But assuming I walk through enough tunnels, and stay alive long enough to get to the middle, how will I know when I'm there? I guess I should just hope I don't trip over an artifact and give my position away.

Fuck.

I'm frustrated that I never considered these tunnels a possibility. I will need to utilize all my training and make sure no one gets the chance to touch me.

"You will now be taken to your starting positions. Listen for the signal to begin." Excitement radiates off his wrinkled skin—he's too excited for a mere game of blind mazes. That thought has every sense heightening, preparing me to deal with anything the king throws in my path down there.

As royal guards step forward, each escorting one competitor toward the doors behind me, I glance at Caspian once more. Warmth slithers through my core when I see he's still glaring at me.

I can understand why so many girls whisper his name. He's attractive. His silver eyes contrast nicely with the strands of his hair, which are as black as my heart. He's strong, with muscles sculpting every inch of him. His presence exudes confidence, though he's very cocky; it's clear he expects the attention he receives.

I saw him up close for the first time at the king's competition announcement; there was a group of girls next to me giggling, attempting to catch the prince's eye. I nearly gagged when he looked over at them and winked, as if his attention is the Angel's gift to this realm.

Asshole.

Men who prey on women like that deserve the blades I sink into them. He better hope I don't learn of any unwanted advances he forces onto women, because I will no longer care about my business with the king.

His head will be mine.

But for now, I need to maintain my calm demeanor. So I smirk and wink at him, earning a heated puff of breath. My eyes catch the king as a guard moves to escort me away from the throne; Thalion looks between the prince and me for a moment before narrowing his eyes in my direction.

How easy it is to anger the male species. Let the games begin.

Chapter Eight

Ariella

Whispers of retreating footsteps greet me as my escort walks in the opposite direction. The darkness surrounding me is so thick I'm sure my mind will begin to form human-sized shapes in it soon. I nearly reach for extra fabric to cover my eyes, but I'm still unsure of how the artifacts are to be identified, so that could be a hindrance to my performance.

The guard who walked me down here—quite roughly—ordered me like a pet to stay put until a horn sounded, indicating the beginning of the trial.

"Do not move before you hear it," her grating voice deepens. "Unless you wish to be griffin dinner." Her hollow laugh follows those impressively light footsteps, dismissing my need for answers.

How in the Aether would they know if we began before the horn? Do they have a weaver who can map others' essence? That would require the Ethereal strand, and as far as I'm aware, the castle should not have any weavers of the sort. My jaw clenches. Of course they do…all the royals are good for is lying. Just another reason to remove their presence from the Kingdom.

I lean back against the wall, thankful for the cool touch of the stone along my neck. I remind myself to always wear this outfit to trials in the future, because I would have been thoroughly fucked had I worn my leathers. I run my hands down the soft fabric, sparking awareness along the curves that hide under the fitted material.

This is not the time for such feelings, so I focus on my surroundings. With my vision obsolete, it's easier to hone in on my other senses. Breathing slowly through my mouth, a faint mineral taste permeates the stale air. There's a muted scuffle in the distance; most likely a rat navigating these tunnels better than I ever will. But the sound of its small feet is surprisingly loud, and I tap my fingers along the hilt of my dagger at the thought.

This will certainly be more difficult than I imagined.

Especially because the tunnels are thinner than I had hoped. I took in what little information I could before the darkness completely engulfed me on the way down here. Dark, cracked stone makes up the entirety of this suffocating maze. I thought, just for a moment, that I saw claw marks along one wall. Though it's easy for the mind to play tricks when stressed.

If someone were to walk past me, we'd both need to be flattened to the walls to not touch. As much as I would love to dress in the brain matter of my fellow contestants, especially Sivara, that would be a waste of my time and too risky. I must use every bit of training I have to keep myself hidden.

The shadows will not save me here.

My eyes shoot to my left, where the sound of the horn echoes from. It is surprisingly louder than expected. Taking one last deep breath, I blanket myself in the words of my mentor.

Even in the darkness, a skilled hand guides.

"Thank you, Marek," I mouth, opening my useless eyes and taking the first step into this competition. Marek forced me to train with a blindfold for years, insisting that adapting to use all senses in any situation was important. I rolled my eyes at him more times than I care to admit, but it is in this moment that I understand the value of those lessons.

I walk slowly for several minutes, refusing to hurry my way through. Haste is a fool's mistake down here. My hand falls into empty space as I find a split in the tunnel. Inwardly cursing myself for not considering this, I feel around the space and learn there is an opening in each direction. Based on where the guard led me through the castle, I believe the tunnel to my right is the best option.

As I lift my foot to turn the corner, I freeze at the even breathing passing through the intersection. The individual pauses, probably noticing the choice that needs to be made. I breathe shallowly, not even daring to fully set my foot down. They walk closer, stopping just in front of my stiffened body. A hand inches toward my dagger as I listen to them think about their next move.

I will shove this blade into their skull if they make for the tunnel I intend to traverse; but luck must be on their side because just when I think they'll take a step forward, they turn to go in the direction I was walking. My hand relaxes, and I wait several minutes—until I'm certain they're far enough away to no longer be an issue until I start my path again.

I wind through several more junctions, mapping my decisions to the layout of the castle above me. I cannot be certain I'm still facing the direction I believe I am, though my gut tells me to continue. I mouth letters with every turn, memorizing the path I will need to eventually get out of here.

"Fuck!" I pause at the distressed voice, melting into the wall as grunts break through my concentration. At least two competitors grapple as they close the distance to me, forcing me to side-step a few paces to my left. They throw punches and kicks for a minute before one makes a choking noise, struggling to find the air needed to continue their fight. The other person groans deeply before a definitive crack fills the space, and my eyes widen at the sound of a body thudding to the ground.

The victor lets out a heavy breath, spitting in my direction. My nose scrunches at the gurgling noises they make, not at all trying to hide their location. Heavy steps run past me, my abdomen tensing when the lightest brush of their skin sweeps so close to my breasts. They must not notice because there's no pause as they continue running back the way I came. I stick my foot out as I move forward, not wanting to trip over the cooling body. I listen for a moment when I find them, making sure I'm truly alone.

Well, as alone as I can convince myself I am.

Crouching, I lightly pat the body. Obviously a man, I figure when my fingers graze his dick. I feel for anything useful, though it seems the only weapon this idiot brought was his hands.

And how did that work out for you? I think, rising to step over him.

I return to my place against the wall, keeping light contact as I navigate for what seems like hours. The hairs along my neck rise when my mind convinces itself someone's breath breezes over the exposed skin. I am not proud to admit that I must remind myself several times that the brain plays tricks when deprived of its senses.

I must be the trick, confusing my body instead, so it focuses its delusions elsewhere.

Eventually, I open my mouth to compensate for the thickening air. It's more difficult to stay silent, though I have a feeling that will not be my most significant problem soon. The tunnels shrink the closer I am to the center; and though I'm tense from the lack of space, it feels like encouragement. As if the eerily silent labyrinth is guiding the way to what I need.

My lungs stall when the sound of metal crashing fills every morsel of silence. Someone curses quietly, and from the noises they make, I believe they are rummaging through a pile of metal.

The artifacts.

I walk forward, my fingernails scraping the cracks embedded in the wall. When I reach another crossing, I peek around the corner as there seems to be some kind of light in this direction.

Are you fucking kidding me?

I run fingers over my slick forehead, scrunching my eyes closed. How in the Aether's fucking realm am I supposed to hide a glowing artifact all the way back to the throne room? I have encountered too many others already, but with an artifact I may as well run through the tunnels screaming the coordinates to my exact location.

Well, it seems I have no choice. The faint memory of the king describing the different artifacts comes to mind. The range in their sizes is enough to convince my feet to move swiftly—fuck if I'll become stuck with one of the large ones. I call to my shadows, silently thanking the Angel that it's too dark for any contestant to notice.

The idiot who was calling every being in the realm here with his noise jerks to his feet at the sound of my steps. I do not bother to hide the noise as he cannot see me, anyway. I watch his body shiver when I pass in front of him, scanning the artifacts with haste. The urge to sink my blade into his skull when he makes a whimpering noise and runs is strong. I don't, unfortunately. The oddly glowing objects in front of me are more important.

Looking through the dozen that are left, I bite the inside of my cheek when none of them appear to be the best choice. They are all various gilded items that seem to be illuminated from the inside; I'm unsure how they managed that, as the artifacts are solid and opaque.

Come on, Ariella. I cannot afford straying thoughts. Especially not when most of the other contestants have not been here yet. Something tells me they will be soon. I almost feel sorry for those who will be stuck with the large staff or chest plate.

My muscles become antsy after another minute, and I relent, reaching for the rusted candelabra when my fingers brush through a barely-there light. Carefully leaning forward on my hands and grimacing at the grainy texture, I look back against the wall where there is a hidden alcove. I see the smallest glow from inside, and against my every instinct telling me to not stick my hand in unknown places, I reach two fingers in. At first I feel nothing, but I stretch my knuckles, my hand cramping from the force. Something cool touches my skin. I drag it out quietly, and inwardly squeal when I see it is a ring with the same light the other artifacts have.

Well, fuck me...the Angel does listen sometimes.

I shuffle to a crouch, moving to slide the ring on one of my fingers but stop abruptly. I may need my hands to fight, and it would be difficult to guarantee their concealment the entire journey back. Before I can think further, I pinch the ring and reach down my fitted top, pushing it into the side of my bra. I ensure it's tucked snugly before springing to my feet and walking back toward my starting position.

The lack of other contestants and ease of navigating my way out of the tunnels is unsettling. The anticipation coursing through me turns my stomach as I wait with bated breath for *something* to happen. I'm several turns back, the space around me widening once again, and I release a relieved sigh.

That was mistake number one.

Mistake number two? Not being alert enough to quickly register the whooshing next to my ear. A hard object knocks into my cheek, though I barely register the pain as I immediately go on the defensive, crouching and silently unsheathing my blade.

"Where are you, little wraith?" I weightlessly tread so stone is at my back and wait for the best opening I have to end this with minimal damage. I do not recognize the voice, though clearly most of the other contestants here loathe me, so I suppose it does not matter who it is.

They're dead, regardless.

"Come on, kitten! Why don't you and I have a little fun before I cut your heart out? I can't wait to see the king's face when I present him the flesh of his favorite toy." Kitten? I grimace. "I know it's you...I can smell your brand of fear. You may as well quit cowering in the shadows." My lips thin as I bite my cheek hard to keep in a laugh. What a fucking idiot.

Those who need to use words to be intimidating are the greatest cowards. They have nothing but mindless banter to offer and hope that the sting of their utterances is enough to ward away enemies.

I close my eyes and focus my ears, wondering if the air down here holds a minute amount of sound. It's loud enough to cloud some of my attention, though I am still able to hear my opponent step past me. The moment his back is to me I stand and press my blade to his throat, satisfied with my estimation of his height.

"Let the Angel know I'll be seeing it soon," I purr into the man's ear, slicing through layers of thick skin until I hit the sweet spot that will drain his life away. My eyes roll at the frantic gurgling noises he makes, slipping on his own blood. His head must be what slams into the stone as his struggles cease immediately upon his fall.

I turn, spinning my slick blade through my fingers as I navigate the remaining distance of this trial with renewed energy. I am almost disappointed when I meet no other contestant in the tunnels before a sliver of light appears high in my peripheral.

Ascending the steps hastily, I knock twice on the thick, wooden door, wincing from how loud the action seems. The woman who escorted me down swings it open, raising a brow when she sees the blood coating my hands. Sliding my blade back in place, I follow the guard the unnecessarily long distance back to the throne room.

Chapter Nine

Ariella

The gilded doors make no sound as the stationed guards heave them open. Whispers instantly float through the large room as every single person in attendance turns their attention to me. I'm used to the scrutinization, so it is less than a thought to push their drama-filled nonsense out of my mind.

I saunter to my original position, taking my time to send the king a message. However he perceives that message is not a worry of mine.

When I stand before the raised thrones, inwardly groaning that there's only one other contestant here, my fingers twitch as they nearly reach for the artifact in my bra. I relax them again when I notice how the prince's questioning eyes look over my body, smirking delightedly when he sees no glowing object on my person. He sinks further into his chair, seeming oddly proud of himself.

I will leave the ring where it is for now. Bastard deserves a little humiliation in his privileged life.

Antsy fingers hover over my blade after an hour passes and nearly every other assassin has made it back to the throne room with an artifact in hand. Where the fuck is Isaiah? Even Raine made it back, and he had to carry a large pillow.

There are pieces of dangling fabric across the front, so maybe the pillow was not the worst idea.

I know I shouldn't worry. Isaiah can handle himself...I fight the prickling that taps against my spine at the thought of our incident. An incident that left him permanently marred and me with the only thing I will ever feel guilty about. My lungs fill deeply with air, willing my brain to push the thought away.

It isn't long before some of the other contestants begin complaining about standing here, which garners an eye roll from me. There's a group of the male contestants standing directly behind me while they not so quietly make comment after comment about my ass and what they'd like to do to it. I'm certain every person on this side of the room can hear them clearly, which does not affect me, though it's interesting to see the way the prince glares at them when they speak.

I've counted twelve sets of steps since I arrived, which leaves Isaiah and one other contestant. Sivara stands next to me again, eyeing the prince as if she's about to eat him for dinner. The one who keeps trying to befriend me—Ally—is next to her.

"No artifact, wraith? How sad for you," Sivara mocks, earning a few chuckles from the group. I cross my feet and spin in her direction, keeping my hands clasped behind me. Not a soul misses the insult of me willingly presenting my most vulnerable flesh without protection. Several snickers and coughs stir the tense atmosphere in the room. Her jaw clenches as she crosses her arms like a fucking child. "Well, you'll be kicked out of here in a moment, so I won't let that get to me."

I close the small distance between us, deliberately pressing against her arms. She drops them instantly, though raises her chin, refusing to step back from my advance. I reach a hand out and graze it over her breast where the ring rests next to mine. "Are you sure about that?" The entire room stills, not a single breath can be heard. I see the king sit forward in the gilded chair, resting his elbows on his knees. "Because if you're wrong, you just made your time here much more difficult."

She bristles, eyes snapping to the prince quickly before blinking a few times and meeting mine again. Her voice is impressively stronger than I thought she could manage. "I'm not wrong. I can see no artifact."

The bored mask slips from my face, replaced by an insidious smile. Hundreds of people watch our interaction, but my attention focuses solely on her unease. Her sweaty, metallic fragrance overpowers my own, and it is moments like these that I wish there was a strand of essence that allowed me to taste the fear of others. The amount of pleasure such a strand would bring me rivals every sorry fuck I've had the displeasure of experiencing.

"I'll show you mine if you show me yours." Her pupils dilate as she swallows loudly, though we're unfortunately interrupted before I can push this any further.

Jeth saunters through the room as if it's his throne he approaches. My stomach flutters when Isaiah enters a minute later, candelabra in hand.

Thank the Angel.

I stow away my relief, hesitant to disclose my relationship with Is in the instance someone wished to use him against me. My eyes find Sivara once more, a challenge in my gaze. She holds her position for all of five seconds before dropping her leer and stepping back.

Good. Perhaps now she will cease her hate-motivated advances. I nearly laugh, pushing my tongue to the roof of my mouth to keep it in. Of course she won't; she is too similar to Isolde, and that bitch has been at my throat for years.

"We appear to be missing two. One of you go find them—I am tired of waiting." Thalion's arrogant voice grates my ears, making me speak before I think any further.

"The absent *contestants* are dead." Footsteps halt as the king gradually shifts his attention to me, as if just looking at my face will cause him harm.

It might.

He purses his lips. "And you know this how, wraith?" The corner of my mouth lifts when I unsheathe my blade and spin it through my fingers to showcase the now dried blood. He stares at me longer than necessary, a wild energy flitting through his eyes. Interesting that he seems to catch himself off-guard, plastering a practiced smile on his features before continuing. "Well, it appears the first trial is complete! We have sixteen remaining contestants, though we must say goodbye to those who failed to retrieve an artifact."

The king sits back in his chair, clasping his hands together after gesturing to the guard at the foot of his throne. The tall male nods and faces our group. The red and gold uniform does nothing to soften his severe features. The angles along his face are so sharp I am sure I could see the ridges in his bones up close. He regards each of us with distaste, raw venom leaking from him in droves.

"Each contestant who recovered an artifact may present them now." The sound that leaves his mouth does not match his person in the slightest. He speaks with a high, almost whiny tone. Thirteen people step forward to set their artifacts at the guard's feet, and the tightness in my chest becomes less restrictive when Isaiah returns to his spot after securing his success in the trial.

I do not move, interested in seeing how the prince will respond.

"Now, will the fruitless contestants please step forward." There's movement in my peripheral, but I'm focused on the pompous, smirking prince in front of me.

He raises a brow, nodding to where the two unlucky assassins stand at the head of our group. I remain still, offering him the slightest smile that dares him to speak against me. His jaw works as he looks me over, clearly unsure whether saying something is worth the potential consequences.

"As unfortunate as it is to lose two additional competitors, that is the nature of the trials," the king announces, standing from his cushioned seat. "As such—"

"Wait." It is embarrassingly difficult to suppress my smile, a fluttering sensation working under my skin. The prince pushes off his imitation throne and stands next to his father, gesturing calmly to me. "The wraith did not present an artifact and must step forward for the pardoning."

Thalion's chest rises thoughtfully as he struggles to focus on me once more. "Ms. Mistaire, you will join your counterparts as Prince Caspian has dutifully informed me of your failure in the trial."

There are times when silence is as effective at carving open an opponent as a blade.

This is certainly one of those moments.

I had thought that having an audience through this competition would be maddening, though I am currently relishing their presence. Holding the prince's scathing gaze, I reach into my clothing and pull out the ring.

I raise my brows as I twirl the object around my finger before flicking it to the pile of artifacts, settling into my stance once more.

The clink of its landing is pure ecstasy as the prince's face blazes with heat. His fists contract, and I know that if we were in a different setting, he would be the one challenging me this time. Thalion glares at him like he's a child who needs lecturing before shaking the entire situation off and returning to his speech.

"What are your names?" he asks the two standing closest to him.

"Vincent."

"Saben."

"Ah, yes—well, it is unfortunate that we must part ways with Vincent and Saben." An armed guard quietly steps behind the two assassins, and a tingling chill swirls in my torso. "We thank you for your sacrifice."

Time stalls. The air surrounding me becomes electric. I can name the number of moments I have ever been shocked on one hand...including now.

There is but a second between the king's final word and the bodies of the two men dropping through the air. The thump of their heads penetrates the room, followed by the rest of their bodies. One of the men—Saben—falls in such a direction that the blood spurting from his gaping neck shoots across my waist.

Fuck's sake. These will need an extra washing now.

Screams radiate from the audience, sharp intakes of breath the only thing I hear from the other competitors. But it isn't the death that shocks me. No, it's that the king has shamelessly shown his true self.

To the people, he presents himself as a kind, generous ruler—one who punishes only in the name of justice. But I am intimate with who he is deep inside, and the man I see in front of me—eyes gleaming with child-like excitement at the death of two citizens—is exactly who he hides behind the facade.

Why is he doing this? How will this serve any purpose except to ruin his meticulously crafted image?

My eyes narrow, shifting to the prince. Did he know? Was he attempting to kill me by calling out my lack of an artifact? Those thoughts mute when his horror-stricken face turns my way, pinning me with his scared eyes. Is that regret I see?

I no longer care. I have no qualms about being killed in this competition, but I will not allow Isaiah to participate any further.

As I move to grab my friend's arm and drag him from the castle, several guards enter our space, one for every assassin still alive. My will shifts to killing the bastard breathing on me but I'm too stunned by the device he's clamped around my neck.

What the fuck is going on?

My hands immediately reach for the cool object and attempt to find its clasp. A few of the others curse, demanding to know what's happening. The people on the sides of the room are either running out or watching with hesitancy. I look to Caspian once more, promising the death of his entire family for this.

My threat does nothing as he doesn't seem worried about me, but instead worried *for* me?

Nauseating laughter forces my awareness to Thalion, who places a hand on his abdomen. "Oh, my! Did I forget to mention a few of the rules during the initiation ceremony? I suppose I did." He chuckles, shaking his head as if this was some slip of the mind.

"There will not just be one winner after the three trials, but also only one survivor. In this castle, your lives belong to me. The devices you now wear have been created specifically to track you. They are only removable at my touch, so you will not succeed in any attempt to unfasten them.

"From this moment forward, you will not step foot out of Valoria, and if you leave the castle grounds, you will return by midnight. Break either of those rules, or attempt to tamper with your devices in any manner, and their defensive response will ignite, leaving you headless."

Aether damn me as I am one broken thread of restraint away from advancing on the king right now and ending all of this here. However, given the circumstances, I know every competitor would most likely be killed. Including Isaiah.

Fuck, how am I supposed to plan the king's death while simultaneously ensuring Is wins the competition? Everything will need to be timed just right. I should have known better than to allow his participation, but that part of the past is negligible. I will ensure he wins these trials.

"No questions? Wonderful! Off you go, then." Thalion dismisses our group with the wave of a hand as he walks down to our level and leaves the room with a fully guarded escort.

I spare no one a last glance before striding through the center of the slick floor, leaving crimson footprints behind me as I head to my room.

Chapter Ten
Ariella

Bland walls and watchful paintings blur the more distance I gain from the throne room. Isaiah bolted after me as I left, insisting he join, but that intention was shut down instantly. He understands the frustrations that emerge when someone outsmarts me, but to have the king himself do it?

I am positively seething with a feral energy that I do not trust myself to hold in around him.

I have dedicated nearly my entire life to being the best. It's essential. Who else would seek justice for my father? There is no one else, so it must be me. And for so many years, I had convinced myself that the retribution required for what Thalion did was to take his life, but that would be the simple answer. I want to wrench the soul out of his body, just like mine was torn from me that day.

I could take the heads of queen Seraphina or Vespera, but he does not seem very fond of them. No, it's the prince I see by Thalion's side. The one he confides in and guides through all the ridiculous royal politics.

His heir. That is precisely the death that will wound him the most.

And when the prince is dead, I vow to claim the life of every heir he creates thereafter. There will be *nothing* left of the Blackwood name. The king will fear every moment of his remaining days; continuously peering over his shoulder, aware of my eyes on his every move. Scared to let anyone in, worried that I may decide to visit.

Tracking collars.

These must be commissioned from Lumarna, as I highly doubt the king would seek out the inventors in Auroria. Both cities are famed for their proclivity to push boundaries; wordlessly competing to be at the forefront of integrating magic with the latest technology.

And once I am done with everything I need to do here, I will find whoever made these and force them to regret creating the thing that threatened Isaiah's life.

The collar shifts as I stalk toward my room, and I reach up to feel it once more. It's rounded, no edges along any of its length. I do not recognize the material, either...it's cool like metal, though hard like glass—but it isn't either of those things. I search for the hinge, or a raised point where it would lock together, but there are none. The smooth surface wraps its entirety, leaving me unsure of how I'd get it off even if I did wish to try.

My steps halt at a corner when panicked breathing reaches my ears, along with periodic whimpering. I listen for a moment, walking into the next hall when there is no scuffling or other struggles to be heard. Ally leans against the wall, pressing a dirty rag to the side of her face as she quietly sobs to herself. My lip curls.

I mean to walk past her, but she notices me as I approach, eyes lighting up. "Oh, Ariella! I am so happy to see you...I don't know how to fix this." She removes the rag, and I hum at the deep gash that runs from her cheek down the side of her neck. The blood running over her clavicle into her shirt is a nice contrast to her dark hair and bright eyes.

"Have you ever heard of a healer?"

"Well," she scoffs, wincing as she presses the rag to her side once more. Disgusting—she's just asking for an infection. "I just don't want anyone thinking of me as weak for going to the healer..."

I blink. "Why the fuck would that matter? I'm sure they'd think you weak for dying from a healable injury, but that's your choice." I shrug, crossing my arms.

"Okay, fine! Will you take me? I don't know the way there..." She uses a hand to straighten from the wall, watching me expectantly.

"No." Do I have *kind and helpful* written across my forehead?

A deep groan. "Please? I'm not sure how I'd find anyone else in time!" I nod to my left and begin walking, if only to shut her dramatics up.

"You don't seem to know much of anything," I mutter when she catches up, her body swiveling with her feet as she's still holding her wound.

She giggles, sounding much brighter than she did a moment ago. "Yeah, I get that a lot. I shouldn't even be here...I think the mentors just sent me so they didn't lose the best of students." I say nothing, continuing to lead our way to the guest wing. For some reason only the Angel knows, she takes my silence as an invitation. "I mean, I can barely hold a blade. I trip over everything, and there's always bruises on my knees because of it. I'm not quick or smart. It almost feels like they wanted to get rid of me—and how lucky they are that this has become a fight to the death competition."

I sigh deeply. "I cannot imagine *why* they'd wish to be rid of you."

"You're a real bitch, you know that?" A laugh slips from me.

"Very aware." A finger taps against my blade, my skin becoming annoyingly itchy from the drying blood.

"Wait—I thought we were going to the healers?"

"I already told you I wouldn't take you there," I retort, quickening my steps. Just another minute before I'm free of her.

"Where are we going, then?" A desperate tone takes over her voice, and I have half a mind to extend her wound until she bleeds out completely. I march up to Isaiah's room and knock my fist against the door. He answers a moment later, eyes softening when he sees me, only for his brows to furrow as he takes in Ally.

"What are you doing here?" he asks hesitantly—he knows me too well.

"It seems your presence is required, after all. Isaiah, meet Ally. She needs your help to find a healer." He crosses his arms and leans a shoulder against the door frame, eyes narrowing at me.

"And you couldn't take her?"

"Do I look like a fucking escort?"

He smiles. "Do I?" I settle my hands on my hips and grin at him mockingly.

"Yes, you do." My best friend barks a laugh, shaking his head. He pushes straight, entering the hallway as his door follows until it's closed.

"Hello...dying here! Could we hurry up?"

Isaiah's eyes snap to mine, a playfulness settling in them. I give him a pointed look as if to say, *"do you see what I've been dealing with?"* He nods, shrugging agreeably.

"Yep, I got it," he teases, patting me on the shoulder before gently pushing Ally back down the hall. Something tugs in my chest.

I wait for them to turn out of sight before moving to my door, tugging on my umbral strand—

A familiar frame comes into view. "Shit." I lower my hand and lean against the wall; I cannot be caught weaving wards...especially not by the likes of the prince.

He and his friend have yet to notice me, so I unsheathe my blade to spin it through my fingers. The light catches on the metal and they both look up at the same time.

The guard that the prince was sparring before the initiation ceremony—and that is all it takes for me to speak.

"What business do you have in this part of the castle, prince?" I push from the wall, blocking their path. If he realizes just how thoroughly he drinks in my body, I'm not sure, but I will not stop his attention. It'll only work in my favor.

"What business is it of yours to know?" My lips threaten to curve—I don't let them.

"I seem to remember a certain threat I made the last time I caught you over here," I purr, spinning my blade faster. The prince's eyes scrunch closed, seeming as if he's internally cursing himself. The guard next to him looks in his direction, clearly confused. Interesting.

"When were you over here?" his rough voice demands; they must be close if he can speak in such a manner without repercussions.

"It doesn't matter, Gavriel," the prince says swiftly, crossing his arms. "That was the training room...I am allowed to walk these halls, you know."

I shrug. "Fuck if I care." My attention shifts to the man I really want to know about, who is currently glaring at me with a raging hatred that could match my own. "Do you stroll through the guest wing with random sentries all the time, or am I witnessing a special occasion?" Gavriel...the name sounds familiar.

"This is my personal guard." He still refuses to answer my question—why is he here...

My thoughts are stuck on one word. "*Personal* guard? As in, he follows you around? Protecting you from...what, exactly? Women of the court?" His cheeks redden, though it's difficult to discern how much in the dim lighting.

Gavriel speaks before his charge can. "Why don't you shut your fucking mouth, wraith, or you and I are going to have a problem."

I grin, feeling energized once more. "I love problems," I croon, dragging my blade over his crimson jacket. "Especially resolving them..." I think a spark of fear flickers through his dark eyes, though it's gone so quickly I'm not sure if that's what I saw.

"Okay, that's enough of that." The prince grabs my weapon and drags it to his own chest. What kind of foolish man claims he needs a personal guard, only to point a blade to his own heart? "You can hold this to me if you wish," he starts, holding up a finger when Gavriel moves to protest. "But only me." I study his silver eyes. I should *want* his attention—be thrilled that he's already giving so much of it to me. So why does it cause my stomach to churn?

I mutter something about how stupid he is before stalking away from them—I no longer wish to wash and sleep, with my nerves prickling wildly. Maybe I should have taken Ally to the healers, after all, and avoided that entire confrontation.

Chapter Eleven

Caspian

Angel, do I despise meeting with Varrick. I grimace, rubbing my palms along the dark pants I'm wearing, failing to remove the memory of Varrick's sticky, keen touch. The man shakes hands as if it is his royal duty, though I've never been enthusiastic about him.

He has served as my father's chief advisor for years; and though I have not witnessed him being anything other than kind, his lanky, pale demeanor seems to burrow under my skin.

Plus, he drowns in perspiration at just the thought of heat.

Gavriel chuckles, his bun shaking with the movement.

"You find my discomfort amusing?"

"Obviously," he mutters, grabbing the top of his breastplate. "Something must ail you from time to time. No one is as indifferent as you appear to be."

I pause just outside the castle, my brows rising as I stare at my guard for an abrupt moment. Does he always watch me so carefully? If I wasn't aware of his intense respect for his position, I may have suggested an alternate placement.

"Now!" a silken voice barks in the distance. I should check if she is well...I am duty-bound to ensure the safety of the contestants that remain a part of the trials.

That is the justification I provide my protesting mind as I turn from Gavriel and attempt to be subtle in my eagerness to visit the outdoor training grounds. I feel my guard's eye roll brand itself into my back—I must be terrible at feigning indifference, contrary to what he claims of me.

I curse at my feet when they quicken their steps at her intensifying commands. I finally crest the hill, looking through the activity below. I did not need to search, though. I would have spotted her with my eyes closed.

Ariella Mistaire.

I may have exploited Varrick's fondness of me to peruse the files he keeps of each competitor. After my father addressed her by name, the irritatingly obsessive thoughts would not cease until I knew the full thing. Surely I should address her as something other than wraith; that is the honorable thing to do, even if she does not adhere to the customs of how to treat royals.

She circles one of the others with the same predatory grace I witnessed the day I met her. Why does that bother me?

I falter on the other woman's name, though I recognize her slender form and black hair. I cross my arms and widen my stance when the wraith corrects the woman's form, scrutinizing her as if one hair out of place would not even be worthy of her approval. I'm captivated by her. Why would she agree to train an opponent, knowing only one of them will live? She must understand the victory is hers.

Unless she is planning to not win?

I haven't spoken with my father since the trial. I was not privy to his plans, and that is disturbing as I am tasked with organizing the trials. I never would have agreed to such barbaric practices, but he insists that their deaths are necessary.

"What do you think will happen if we send them home as failures? Assassins will not accept embarrassment, Caspian. They will come after our family in their vengeful states."

It was an absurd excuse for him to give, though I did not say that. Arguing further would have resulted in the termination of my presence in this competition. I would no longer have access to meetings or documents that could help me answer why he's actually killing them. I am not certain of why I care so much; these are assassins who live by killing others.

My eyes focus on the scene before me, and I sigh. I cannot fool myself...I do know why I care.

I study her toned body, aware of the stares I am receiving. Let them talk. I'd be foolish to not have my eye on her at all times—the deadly, exquisite creature she is.

She wears black shorts and a top with mere strings hugging her shoulders. "Ally. This is a basic skill...how is it you know *nothing* about centering your body?" Ally impressively does not cringe when Ariella glares at her—I can feel the heat of her stare from here. Or is that the blazing sun?

I shrug, biting my cheek. They're the same thing.

"I don't know! I shouldn't even be here!" Ally groans, clearly frustrated. She hurls her staff to the grass, running a hand through the partially remaining braid.

"Are you a fucking child?" One of my hands rises to cover my mouth and hide my smile. There is something about her venom that I find irresistible. "I am not here to coddle you, nor will I feel sorry for your situation. You asked for my help, so you will either pick it back up and continue, or leave. Think carefully, because I do not grant second chances." Ally wrings her hands, a look of pure concentration on her face.

"Wraith!" All heads snap to the voice, where another of the competitors stands in full leathers. Her brunette hair is pulled back into a tight bun, and she stands with severe confidence, brandishing a blade in each hand.

Ariella spins until she faces me enough that I can see the sinister smile on her face. She looks angelic as sweat glistens along her skin, damp hair outlining her features. She turns slowly to her challenger, as if she has all the time in the world and there are not dozens of eyes trained on her.

"Sivara." A tingling heat skims down my spine at the low purr in her tone—what would it take to have her say my name that way? She stands tall and waits with an eerie calm as her opponent approaches.

"Need a cloth, prince?" I shake my head and throw an elbow at Gavriel's side.

"Shut up," I mutter, refusing to look at him.

"Just offering. Don't think I've ever seen you drool before." He laughs loudly, tossing his head back.

"If you don't shut your fucking mouth, I'll assign you to a week in the pit." He silences instantly, clearing his throat. We're friends, though he knows I would follow-through on that threat with great pleasure. Maintenance and cleaning of the castle drains is not a duty anyone wants, though it would be entertaining to see Gav suffer through it for a week.

My skin cools at the dry breeze that glides through the grounds. I wonder if this is what it's like to live in the Cindara Desert. A heat that melts your bones from the inside and a dryness that leaves you parched no matter the amount of water you drink. The sandy terrain is not a part of the Eldorian Kingdom, so I am forbidden from visiting outside cities when not accompanying the king on political matters.

I do not travel often, as is, but would like to. I hope to open the borders between our lands and the outer cities when I am king. It is absurd to me—the separation laws. Just another thing my father will not listen to.

A sultry laugh interrupts my thoughts as the wraith's unnerving aura demands the attention of every individual on the grounds. The thought of her focus on me is tantalizing.

"A bit angry, are we, Sivara?" The woman could drop every man to his knees with a single word. If they could prove themselves to her, that is.

I will not allow them the chance, though.

"I challenge you, Silver Wraith. It is easy to fabricate a reputation, though no one has ever seen your true skills. You're probably a worse rival than your timid friend over there."

Ariella cocks her head, the movement bestial. The tension in the air is thick enough to touch. "Are you certain this is what you want?"

A finger taps against my upper arm; I turn my head, expecting to see Gavriel's questioning gaze, though he's watching the scene below. A few more taps, and I clench my fist when I see my finger is the culprit.

Sivara nods, and it seems to please the wraith, which causes the other woman to shift. "Right now?"

"Yes. You will not get another chance."

"We should go, Cas," I shake my head, barely looking at my guard before watching the women again.

"No, I want to see what she does." He mutters under his breath, something about how smitten he is with Faith—whoever that is. I'll question him about her later.

"Surely you're not being serious...you have no weapons or proper attire." Ariella shrugs, and I chuckle when she clasps her hands behind her back.

"You are the one who challenged me, Sivara."

The dark-haired assassin swallows, eyes skimming to the dozens that are watching their interaction. Did she not believe Ariella would agree to a challenge?

"Fine." The wraith smiles brightly. I get the feeling this is where she's happiest, if that's even a possible emotion for her.

Sivara attacks first, throwing herself skillfully around the mat, though Ariella avoids her attempts just as easily as she did mine. She almost appears to be having fun—I chuckle under my breath. She knocks Sivara in the face several times, her features brightening with each drop of blood she wrings from her opponent—who becomes more angry with each missed swipe.

Sivara stalks Ariella as she reaches her arms up to stretch like she couldn't care less about her opponent. Her groan is quiet, but it goes straight to my dick. Her opponent takes the moment to charge at the wraith's right, though her eyes look left.

"Watch out!" My judgment is disturbingly impaired in her presence.

Her head snaps my way for just a moment, but it's all Sivara needs to swing her leg and knock Ariella to the ground. She stands, fists clenched as she stomps to Sivara and kicks with an incredible amount of power. Her foot connects with her opponent's upper abdomen, sending her flying through the air. She grunts loudly as her back thuds against the stone surrounding their mat.

My mouth drops on a noiseless gasp, the mirror to every face here. Ariella's eyes flick to mine, her gaze spilling with murderous intent. I snap my jaw closed, raising my brows and brazenly running my eyes over her body. Gavriel shifts himself slightly in front of me, causing her to laugh under her breath. She grabs one of Sivara's blades from where it rests at her feet and straightens, her stare still on me.

I might possess the sense to be intimidated if she wasn't so fascinating.

I smirk; she's undoubtedly contemplating hurling that blade at me. Without breaking our connection, she flips the blade and catches it by the point, swinging her arm to fling it at Sivara. I lick my lower lip, smiling genuinely when she remains unmoving as her blade sinks into her opponent's left hand.

Fuck, that was arousing.

My eyes narrow, challenging her to bring that vicious attitude up here and see just what I'll do with it. It should not be possible, but her features harden further. I feel her curse me through our distance before dismissing herself, not once looking back to see what she did to Sivara. The woman cries, another helping her up the hill toward the castle.

I turn to my guard so that we may continue our visit to the city. His forehead crinkles as he manages to look down at me with false accusations. I sigh and shove his chest, leaving him behind as I move to the gates.

Chapter Twelve

Ariella

I jog down the steps of the guild, only a little upset that Marek and Jaxon couldn't think of any way to remove this fucking collar. My mentor wasn't surprised that this is the route the king has taken, but even his comforting presence couldn't reduce the amount of heat raging through me.

Adrenaline pumps through my veins, my fingernails digging into my palm so hard I feel the small tears they cause. I shouldn't be so angry—the prince was only trying to help. But it is not just that he didn't think me capable of seeing through Sivara's pathetic tactics, it's *him*. I didn't see him and Gavriel arrive, but I *felt* his eyes. I knew he was watching me...and that is exactly the desire from him I want, is it not? So why do I find myself so incredibly infuriated any time he's near?

I want him to get close to me, but I do not wish to be close to him.

Shadows cover me as I amble through the streets of Valoria, back to the one place I've longed to be for years but now want nothing to do with. I walk down empty paths, swiveling in a circle to study my surroundings. It's certainly dark enough...

Even just the thought is enough to make me groan. I tug on my umbral strand and coax my essence to the surface, sighing deeply when the dark tendrils seep from under my skin and caress me as if they know just what I need. Their cool touch is barely noticeable, but it's enough. I allow them to wrap around my body at their will for a few minutes, ignoring how wrong it feels to force them back inside me when a group of people pass by.

I pause at a familiar voice down the street, my nose scrunching when Jeth and Jaspar's irritatingly loud laughters echo through the chilly air. Light peeks from a building—a tavern by the smell of it.

"—only thing interesting about the wraith is that I don't know whether the hair on her cunt matches the hair on her head." I pause as several others laugh at Jeth's joke. I lean against the building, unsheathing my blade to spin it through my impatient fingers.

"You haven't fucked her yet?" I don't recognize the man who asks, but I'd bet my blade it's one of the other competitors.

"Nah, she's a tough one—but that'll make it so much sweeter when she does finally give in. And after I've fucked her until she's raw, I'd like to see what these ridiculous collars do when provoked."

Any sensible person would fear his obscene words—but I've never claimed to be such a thing.

No, I hope he attempts what he says. It's been far too long since I've sunk my blade into another.

My head rests against the damp brick as I count the stars.

I wonder if my mother is out there. I could use my spectral strand to communicate with willing souls, though the thought creeps me out. Fucking with the dead is dangerous and unpredictable.

Even with such knowledge, there is one question that continuously haunts my thoughts: what if? What if she is there and just waiting for my call? Is my father with her? Are they proud of me?

I huff a breath. Of course they wouldn't be proud. Their once sweet daughter has become the thing even nightmares fear. What is there to be proud of?

An acute awareness fills my senses. Someone is watching me.

I tug at my psionic strand and send out a pulse. One person—male—in the shadows to my left. They do not appear to be advancing; just watching.

I adjust my stance to lean on my arm. My head tilts down, allowing me to look ahead under the darkness of my hood. I nearly burst out laughing...does he truly believe he's hiding well?

I suppose I could have a little fun...

I spin on my heel to walk in the opposite direction. My head immediately clears when I leave the heady atmosphere of the tavern behind. Angel, he is such an idiot. Has he not trained to improve his footwork after I *kindly* informed him how loud it was?

I'll teach him just how easily the conspicuity could lead to his death.

I sharply turn a corner and run, weaving through different alleys. I'm fast enough to make him work, but not so brisk that he'll lose sight of me. Several turns later and I find the perfect spot to reveal myself. I slip into the abnormally dark alley and wait just beyond the corner.

The moment his body enters my territory, he halts from the blade pressed to his abdomen. This part of Valoria is quiet during the night, leaving only our heavy breaths to fill the silence. I say nothing, letting him peruse my face as I dropped my hood upon stopping.

"Mistaire." A wave of energy pulses through my body, the hairs on my skin rising. I bite my lip, selfishly pleased with the keen interest he shows in the slight movement.

"Been watching me, have you?" He grins predatorily at my use of the words he uttered to me weeks ago.

"You're hard to look away from." Bold. He's too comfortable around me.

"Why are you following me?"

He shrugs, tilting his head as those gleaming eyes burrow through my resolve. "I saw you on my way back to the castle and was interested in what you were doing."

"And why shouldn't I gut you right now? Especially after that stunt you pulled earlier—I've killed for less." He laughs deeply, leaning into my weapon. "You think that just because you're a prince, you are safe from my blade?"

His brows furrow. "Well, yes. You wouldn't murder the Eldorian prince."

"Oh, I don't discriminate," I whisper, slanting my head toward him as if I'm about to share a secret. "I'd slice open your throat without a second thought and sleep just fine after watching your life bleed out before me. And the next day? I'd carry your head around the kingdom, so there was no question about who killed the Eldorian Prince."

He groans, his eyes rolling as he shifts to lean against the wall. "Fuck, angel, that mouth of yours."

I pause. "Angel? Do I look like the Angel to you?"

He smiles, causing heat to rise along my neck. "The Angel is said to be beautiful, but cunning. Quick, yet silent. Disarming, but deadly." Silver eyes slide down to my lips, his fingers grazing the sharp of the blade until they surround mine against the hilt. "So, yes...you look exactly like an angel to me."

We watch each other. I search his eyes for deception, finding nothing but hungry sincerity. I sense no fear or hesitation. He is not oblivious to my dark habits and corrupted thoughts. He understands the consequences of someone with his status falling for someone with my reputation.

Yet, here he is.

How unworthy I am to have the genuine affections of anyone. Especially the target of my revenge.

Is this not what I wished for, though? I have teased and taunted the prince, knowing my calculated attention would garner his interest. All to get him close enough to me that I can follow through with my plans.

So why does something gnaw at my stomach when I think of pushing this blade any further?

I do not become emotionally attached to my subjects. I do not care for them or see them as anything but an obstacle to my ultimate goal.

I chuckle, the awkwardness of it foreign to my ears. "I'm sure you're used to women falling for such flattery—fuck, you probably don't even need to say anything to have them in your bed—but I am not the one, prince.

"Truthfully, I'd consider yourself lucky enough. No one has *ever* followed me and lived long enough to tell the story." My threat does not have the desired effect. Rather than seeming concerned, he grins boyishly at me. I hold my breath, if only to hide just how his attention truly makes me feel.

He purses his lips as if he's attempting to withhold a laugh. "What?" I snap, thankful that the darkness covers the flush in my cheeks.

The corners of his eyes crinkle, his gaze brightening mischievously. "You—the Silver Wraith—just admitted that you find me attractive." There's a little bounce to his stance; he seems too excited about something I definitely did not say.

My brows furrow as I ignore the tingling heat spreading through me when his hand squeezes mine playfully. "Is that—" I scoff, seeking for something to cover my loss for words. I settle for storming off. "Fucking delusional," I mutter to myself as I pull my blade back to sheathe it, smirking at the conversation he has with himself before jogging to walk next to me.

We travel in silence for a time, and it's curiously pleasant. That is until he speaks again.

"I'm sorry about the trial—the collar and new rules. I had no idea my father was planning that."

"Of course you didn't. Your father does whatever the fuck he wants." I'm only a little surprised that he heard me, with how quiet my words were.

"I know. It's just—"

I halt and spin to him. "*Do not* defend your father to me. I don't fucking care how great you think he is." I continue, faster this time, leaving the wide-eyed prince sputtering.

"Wait!" I don't. He catches up, anyway. "I wasn't going to defend him." That gets my attention. I look over and raise a brow, and he surveys the surrounding area in response. "I was going to say that I cannot change his rules, but I don't agree with them, either. What he's planned for you all is not right."

I study him. The square of his jaw that wraps around to a soft point, connecting to plush lips. His dark lashes are thick and feminine. The way his hair frames everything...curling at the top, only to part at the right angles to accentuate the lines of his face.

But it's his eyes that speak to me. The silver irises that somehow match my own anomaly and see much more than I've ever been willing to give.

"You're staring," he whispers, clearly amused.

I shift, swallowing thickly and berating my incessant curiosity. "Only because I'm trying to figure you out."

He makes a surprised noise. "What's there to figure out that I haven't already shown you?"

"Are you seriously asking me that?" I turn my head to him once more, somehow not shocked that he's being sincere.

"What?" He asks when I stare longer than is considered acceptable.

"You do realize that you are the fucking heir to the kingdom...and you're associating yourself with the likes of me. Why in the Aether would you willingly allow others to see us together if not for malicious purposes?" I breathe deeply, confusing even myself. When he doesn't answer, I flick my eyes his way, though he's no longer there.

I look over my shoulder to where he stands in the middle of the street, shoulders slumped while his face says he's trying to keep me at a distance. I've hurt him.

My chest squeezes.

I unsheathe a blade and spin it through my fingers while I wait for his internal crisis to pass. The emotions flitting through his features pique my interest. Do others always feel so deeply?

I think I used to—when my parents were alive. After my mother's death, I stopped smiling as much. The colors around me dulled, temperatures were more unbearable. I began asking myself why I ever enjoyed any of my hobbies...we only live to die, anyway, so what's the point? What about that knowledge makes anything about life enjoyable?

But then my father was killed and my heart was no longer empty. It was overflowing with anger; a rage that could level both realms. I no longer enjoyed doing anything, choosing to focus all of my energy on training for the day I would kill the bastard that took the last of my family.

But Marek saw the struggle within me, as I warred with needing to feel nothing but being forced to feel it all.

"Ari, sometimes the hardest battles we fight are within our souls. It's a lonely journey to find a companionable peace, but you will fail at every turn if you do not train your mind as you do your body."

"It's useless! My head is too messed up—I can't do it!"

"Okay. Then we're done here." He stands, leaving me alone on the floor.

"What? Why?"

He looks pointedly at my fists. "I cannot help you if you're unwilling to try." He crouches before me, the intensity in his eyes a little frightening. "I see you, Ariella. I know why you train as hard as you do. Why you fight to be the best. You have a fire in you that I have not seen in a long time, and if you would allow me to help, I will make sure you are every bit the warrior your heart demands you to be."

The prince exhales, running a hand over his chin. He moves, meeting me several feet away, the heat of his body cracking the icy exterior I've forced. "I know you wouldn't tell me if I asked why you think you're *so* unworthy of affection that you accuse me of being malevolent when I give you a touch of mine—so I will not ask. I'm unsure why you think so poorly of me, but it's clear I've failed you in my duty to prove otherwise." He pauses. "Well...maybe I do understand. I did try to get you kicked out of the competition not too long ago."

A laugh escapes me, and I clear my throat to mask it.

"Did I just make you laugh, angel?" Figures. The arrogant bastard grins at me, a wild gleam forming in his eyes.

"No," I claim weakly, spinning to continue the walk back.

"You have three strands, right?"

"Yes." That is technically the truth—not that I hold any qualms about lying. Especially to the prince.

"And from two different affinities? That's not very common," he remarks suggestively. I won't ask what he's alluding to, nor indicate there's anything more than what he's stated.

"You've read my file, I see."

"Of course I have—I want to know everything about you." I laugh mirthlessly, raising a brow at the two men eyeing us from ahead. They continue to watch hungrily the closer we get.

I throw off my hood and step around the prince, daring the men to continue with their advances. The taller one sputters at the sight of me, jerking the hand that holds a cup, covering himself in a foul-smelling liquid. The other pushes at him, both stumbling as they run in the opposite direction.

I tilt my head back, feeling his eyes on me like a blazing flame. When I face him, I frown, sucking my teeth. "Where is Gavriel?" He blinks several times, brows creasing.

"I sent him back when I saw you."

"Fuck's sake, prince. Have you no sense of self-preservation?" My head throbs.

The fine clothing he wears—black trousers with a silken top covered by a vest that was clearly made with the highest quality leather. I will not even comment on the brandishing of the royal crest that he proudly displays on each collarbone.

"What could possibly be wrong with my clothes?" He exclaims when I look at his shirt for the third time. I will never admit it was his arms that snagged my attention.

Not even the Angel could pry such confessions from me.

"That's the problem—nothing is wrong with them." His head tilts. An insult rests on my tongue. "Those men were just about to do things to you that you couldn't even imagine exists. You're a walking target for fools like them." I gesture to his outfit.

His lips twitch. "Careful." He takes a deliberate step. Another. "Or I'll start thinking you care about me." Silver eyes dare me to deny it.

But he has a point...why did I step in between them? I could have easily stopped any assault they attempted, but I didn't allow it to go that far.

"Let's go." His answering chuckle irks my patience.

One last corner and we're finally upon the castle gates. I do not give the guards satisfaction by acknowledging their curious stares—let them talk. The prince can make his own choices, and if he is unconcerned with his name being associated to me...that is not my mess to handle.

I walk through the front archway, a bounce to my step. It's as if my body knows how close we are to sleep and is just as desperate as I am. Turning right toward the guest wing, I do not concern myself with parting words for the prince.

If he needed someone to coddle him, he should have stalked one of the noble women instead.

But it's not just my steps I hear. My head snaps to the prince, eyes widening when he continues to walk next to me. "What do you think you're doing?"

He grimaces, scoffing at whatever his expectations were left wanting. "Walking you to your room."

It's my turn to scoff. "As if I need an escort?" A heavy gust of air blows from his mouth as he shakes his head.

"People can do nice things for others outside of predetermined obligations, you know. They can also want to spend time with others just for the sake of their company, and not because they're scheming.

"Not everyone is a product of your world."

A rebuttal sits on my tongue, though my traitorous lungs will not grant me enough air to say them. I tap a finger against my thigh as we stroll to my room in a comfortable silence.

Maybe his company is not so bad.

It's unfortunate he will be dead soon—I may have enjoyed his friendship.

My shoulders drop when my door comes into view, and I mutter a goodbye to the prince before releasing my wards and turning the handle.

"What the fuck was that?"

I freeze. Never once have I failed to conceal my forbidden essence.

I half turn, contorting my features in a way that hopefully hides the blood-souring nausea wrecking my insides. "What was what?"

His eyes narrow, and he saunters forward, inspecting the door thoroughly. "How did you do that? Those were wards, were they not?" Observant prick.

"How could I possibly have wards, prince?" My hand drops from the cool metal, only to hover over another form of it on my thigh. "What are you suggesting?" The challenge in my tone is clear: s*ay the words and see what happens.*

His gaze skims over my face before landing on the collar. His fingers flutter as if he means to touch it, but holds himself back. Something gloomy passes through his eyes before he meets mine again.

He smiles, this one crooked and soft. "Keep your secrets, Ariella," he whispers before spinning on his heel and disappearing into the shadows.

Chapter Thirteen

Ariella

What must be hundreds of people stand in silence as guards draw open the throne room doors. All eyes turn to our group, the excited atmosphere potent. Far down the path we are to walk, the king, queen, prince, and princess sit in their respective chairs, waiting stoically.

I slide a foot to begin the ridiculous journey through the room, to Aether with the dramatics of the salivating audience. I despise being made into a spectacle. I'm not two steps in before a palm latches itself to my chest with a force that means for me to halt. I look down slowly, debating how important it is that the fool who dared touch me keeps his hand.

"Slow down, wraith." Jeth's nasally voice overpowers the whispers. "Someone as hot as you should be walking next to me. We're the best here, so it only makes sense." I refuse to meet his arrogant eyes.

"Remove your hand." I weave as much venom as possible into the words.

"Or what? Nothing wrong with a man testing out the goods of a woman before he fucks her. Plus, I don't believe the shit they say about you. You look harmless to me." He chuckles, looking over his shoulder at his companions who follow suit.

"If you do not remove your hand, it will not be the only appendage you lose tonight." My eyes flit to the prince's white knuckles as he watches the encounter.

"Ooh," Jeth mocks, his fingers dangerously close to their end. "The feisty ones always suck the be—" I lunge to grab his wrist, folding it until I hear the snap. Jeth screams as I twist his body, unsheathing the sword at his back before kicking him roughly. He stumbles, arms flailing as he falls—a satisfying thud greets my ears when he lands roughly on his back. The audience next to him backs up when I swing the sword around and plant a foot to his shoulders.

"No, no, please! I'm sorry, it was just a joke!" I push harder, enjoying when his groans turn to wheezes.

"Jokes are meant to be humorous, and yet I'm not laughing." I rear the sword back before sending it through his wrist. A clean cut.

I hum, stepping over his writhing form to avoid soaking my boots in blood and dropping the sword on his abdomen. His sobs lessen, and my eyes find the prince, who is not attempting to hide his pleased smirk. I raise a brow at the men in the crowd that have moved to cover their women.

As if that would stop me from taking them.

Not that they wouldn't come willingly—I'd fuck them better than those feeble pricks could ever dream to.

"You stupid bitch!" I stop, a wicked smile tugging at my lips. The prince looks at me expectantly, his eyes gleaming brightly. *"What now, angel?"* his gaze challenges.

Before he can blink once more, I snatch one of my blades and spin to fling it at Jeth. It makes a delicious noise when it sinks into the man's cock. His eyes become unnaturally wide as he looks between me and the blade, frozen in place. Eventually, his gaze lands on me again, a torrent of emotions darting through him.

"I warned you."

I turn and saunter the final distance, ignoring that fool's childish wailing. Perhaps it was imprudent to maim another contestant right before the second trial, but he was asking for it. I'll leave him my blade as consolation; I've no desire for it back, anyway.

My fingers flex before I clasp them behind me and peer at the Blackwood family. Vespera wrings her hands together, worrying her lip as she attempts to look anywhere except the bloody scene I've created. Her blonde hair is woven into a braid, draped over a tense shoulder.

She could be salvageable yet.

Seraphina lounges in her seat with an outward air of boredom, though her eyes speak different tales. Their calculating leer matches the severe angles to the queen's face. Her jaw appears carved out of stone, while her lips are thin and endlessly framed in sincere distaste.

Nothing will ever be good enough for such a woman.

Interesting, though, that her contempt is only aimed toward her people and not the mutilated contestant behind me. Deep brown hair surrounds most of her head, with a brighter piece at the front from where it catches the warm light.

I should not look his way, nor give him any more of my attention, but my disloyal eyes betray me. My abdomen flexes when my body registers the all-consuming heat of the prince's stare. His clothes seem finer this evening—where he often wears trousers and a button-down top, tonight his tawny skin is covered by a crimson doublet that is threaded with gold. The griffin within the royal crest stands proudly over his heart.

He certainly portrays the image of nobility.

The corner of his mouth rises when he notices my perusal. His eyes flick to Jeth before meeting mine again, and he raises his brows as he nods slightly. His nonchalant composure nearly breaks at the unimpressed look on my face.

He knows I do not seek or care for his approval.

I itch to play into his ongoing attention and secure his loyalty. It will be so much sweeter to know the king watched me take his son from him emotionally before I kill him. Though I'm not sure I even need to pretend anything...the prince is quite taken already.

The musky air fills my lungs when an awareness builds behind my neck. Curiosity drives my eyes to the king, who glowers at me as his jaw grinds side to side. I offer the slightest acknowledgment, curving one side of my mouth before ignoring the Blackwoods once more.

Jeth's sobbing fades until he can no longer be heard by the entire realm. I assume he's been taken to a healer, though I've little care to confirm. Thalion rises, his light hair swaying with the precise movement, and raises a thick hand to silence the audience.

"People of Eldoria, and contestants, welcome to the second trial! This particular trial will test your stealth and strategy. I do hope you've donned proper clothing, as any small mistake could leave you caught and eliminated from the competition." He chuckles darkly, and several people in the crowd follow along.

"This trial is simple. You will be given a riddle to solve, where the solution reveals the location of your trial. You are to bring back the hidden artifact at your location." Gold and crimson decorated guards shuffle from behind the thrones, each taking a position in front of the thirteen assassins.

I survey the features of my guard, a patronizing comment resting on my tongue when he will not even look me in the eye. Despite being the same height as me, he manages to lift his chin enough to focus his eyes over my head and ignore my presence. His nose bends to the left, making his face appear tilted. He looks nice, though. Soft.

He reminds me of Isaiah a few years ago.

"I realize it is after the dinner hour. However, do not fret. Your devices will not ignite at midnight. Ah-ah," he chides at whatever he finds disappointing behind me. "It is just for tonight's trial. You have until the break of sun to return with your artifact and move forward in this competition. If you do not return by midnight tomorrow...well, you are not foolish enough to think there is a way out of your fate."

The guards raise an arm, passing each of us our riddles. To my left, Sivara scoffs at the contents of her paper. The riddles must not be difficult, then. A glare from the king's gilded crown skips over my eyes, and I blink, finding His Majesty watching me intensely.

"Your trial begins now. Do make haste—you do not wish to be snared in the claws of the night when you are so close to the final trial."

It's as if we're the only two present in the room. I almost hear the echo of his deep voice as he says the cryptic words only to me.

A threat. One I'd do well to heed.

The king may be a bastard, but he is not foolish. The Blackwoods are the family in power for a reason, and Thalion is the embodiment of their viscid disposition.

I snap my gaze away, pocketing my riddle and turning to Isaiah and Ally, who huddle together, whispering amongst themselves. My stomach clenches. Is always seems to know when I'm watching him; he looks up at me, and I raise a brow. We communicate well without words. He nods slightly, waiting for my returning one before focusing on Ally once more.

The remaining competitors stare at their riddles, silently mouthing the words as if that will change their meaning and help solve it. Ignoring them, I stalk through the group and swiftly out of the doors. Guards stiffen when I pass, their fear palpable. I grimace at the mustiness of their sweat encased suits.

How often do they fucking wash their clothes? The answer is undoubtedly nauseating.

I reach for the paper as I walk beyond the doors of the castle. There's less light here, but I will not chance someone reading the words. The king's obvious interest in me earlier pricks the back of my mind, and my instincts warn me to increase caution. Something in the way he eyed me...the underlying threat was no mistake.

I suspect the king does not make many mistakes.

I shiver. Aether fuck me, it grew cold quickly. I pinch the paper and roll it open.

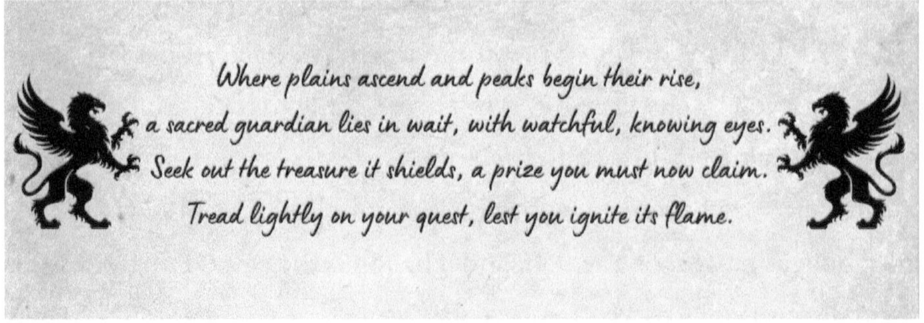

"For fuck's sake." This cannot mean what I think it does.

A sacred guardian in the mountains. Obviously a fucking griffin...it is the only lawfully protected species in the realm. Harming a griffin—even in self-defense—is punishable by lifelong imprisonment or death.

But that is not the thought that bristles the hair along my arms.

No one encounters a griffin and survives. They are territorial and vicious. I've heard stories in passing; mere rumors, though I scour each memory I have of them.

"It don't matter how clever you are. They see you and you're dead—just your presence pisses them off." The round man spills his drink as he cackles, soaking the fabric of his shirt that's barely holding together as is. I can't make out his next words, his slurring increasing by the second.

"No way that's true! They wouldn't be sacred if they killed everyone they see."

"Is true!" The first man screams, his face growing purple. "My grand told me it happened to him!"

The three others burst out laughing, one gripping his abdomen when he can't stop. "And did his fucking ghost tell you that, Ter?"

"Course not—I don't have the spectral. Besides, he hasn't died yet." He coughs, my nose scrunching at the wet sound.

"Then how can he claim to have seen a griffin and live if he says they kill everyone they see? That's fucking stupid, Terry."

I tilt my chin back, basking in the chill. Every story I have collected about griffins has been the same as my memory of those senseless men. They're killers. Savage. Unforgiving beasts.

I still before snatching the riddle back into focus. Fuck me.

There are an undetermined amount of nests on the Elysaran Mountains. The mountains span weeks worth of travel, and I've not a single clue as to where I will find the one I need. I groan, my head throbbing. I doubt the artifact will be conveniently displayed...I'll need to see the nests to know.

The likelihood of me surviving long enough to inspect even one nest is nearly zero. My fingers tap against a blade, and I shrug.

I've defeated worse odds.

Bone-chilling wind whips my tied hair around violently, obscuring my vision every few seconds. This is going to be a very long night. I've already wasted an hour running to the base of the mountain—to the only safe ascent point that I'm aware of.

I am foolishly relying on the presumption that someone must have given the artifact to a griffin, and likely would not have traveled far or deep into the creatures' territory. And they surely couldn't expect me to travel far, steal from a fucking griffin, and return to the castle before dawn...my jaw clenches hard.

I am going to gut the fucking prince and feed his innards to the king.

I'm not meant to return. They created an impossible trial knowing they could behead me for failing if the griffin did not first. Why? Do they see me as such a threat that the prince fabricated an inevitable death?

My fingers twitch to rip the collar off and get it over with, but the raging heat inside my body demands more.

I begin the steep climb, the ground hardening while my breaths become visible. Eventually, I veer off the path that others use for transport. It's perceived as the safest route through the mountains, as it avoids as many threats as possible. I know the griffin territory is west, most likely centered around the part of the Weaver's Torrent that travels through the mountains.

When I'm high enough that snow crunches under my boots, I pause. They'll hear me approach if I'm not careful. I chew on my cracking lip, cursing the Angel for providing me the worst possible weather tonight.

Not the worst, I suppose, though I've never claimed to lack dramatics.

My pyro strand would prove effective—but I am not convinced there isn't someone watching me. Did the king send a spy to ensure my death, or is he convinced I will certainly not live through this encounter?

I have no choice but to risk the exposure. The use of this strand could be explained easy enough if I manage to radiate heat from my lower half without sparking flame.

I tug on the strand and silently enter the griffin territory.

Chapter Fourteen

Ariella

How long have I been crouching here? If the state of my limbs is any indication, a fucking month. There's a griffin nest thirty feet ahead, and the beast herself sleeps curled in a way that makes her appear smaller. But by the Angel, the single foot I can see looks to be the size of my head.

She's beautiful. Her white, feathery exterior would completely blend with the snow if she were not in her nest. The mixture of sticks and foliage are a pleasing contrast to her color, which made finding her suspiciously easy. I can just make out the sharp point of her beak, most of it hidden within the tufts of her mane. I see no evidence of the artifact, though I pray to the fucking Angel the person who brought it here threw it at the first griffin they found and that it was her.

My tongue attempts to wet my lips, but my mouth is too dry. It's a futile effort. I glance at the snow and focus on the small river my feet have created. The flowing water taunts me, whispering enticingly and hoping I'll break my concentration to swallow it.

I fear that would be too loud—Griffins have impeccable senses. My nose scrunches as an uneasy feeling settles in my gut. I am uneducated in the minute details of the creatures, leaving me no choice but to assume she cannot detect me at this distance.

I'm stalling.

Fuck the king and his son; I need to succeed in this trial if I'm to ensure Isaiah's victory. The reminder dissipates a small amount of the tightness in my throat. It's easier to do everything when it's for him, as I've no regard for my own survival. The only objectives that flit around my thoughts at all times are to murder the prince and ensure Isaiah lives through this competition.

I inhale a deep breath and relish the burn in my lungs before silently releasing it.

Rising until my knees are just slightly bent, I tug on my pyro strand once more and begin melting the ground beneath me until it is soft enough to dampen my movement. Weaving myself into the shadows would be the best method of obtaining the artifact, though the itch in the back of my mind keeps returning, signaling that I am indeed being watched. This effort will be for nothing if I'm caught using essence I claim to not possess.

My feet inch forward, slow enough to remain soundless, though fast enough that I'll be able to grab the artifact and make it to the castle before dawn.

If the artifact is even here.

If nothing were to go wrong...like her using those frighteningly large talons to slice my face apart.

I barely blink as I stalk the distance between us. She remains still, aside from the shallow breathing that disrupts her top feathers with each inhale. My legs pause just a few feet in front of her. If it were not for the heavy wind, I've no doubt she could hear the rapid beating of my heart. I open my lips, nearly groaning when I finally get enough air.

I need to calm my body down or it will give me away.

My fingers dig into my thigh hard enough to bruise when she shifts. Is it her sleepy movements or the faint glow under her belly that is making my hands tremble?

I'm going to vomit.

Biting my cheek, I dip further into my stance and inch the remaining space with every skill I have. Walking back to the castle would take less time than this. I become paralyzed when something falls through my vision, and it takes me several agonizing moments to notice the amount of sweat running down my face.

Too soon am I standing directly beside her. My only reprieve is that her face is hidden beneath a leg while her breathing remains steady. I meticulously melt the snow that prevents me from kneeling, careful to avoid heating her body. Would she wake from that?

I lower to the ground and lean on my hands. There is a slight gap from the curve of her abdomen that will allow me to reach into the nest. The artifact isn't large—the one fucking thing that has been kind to me today—though it's in the shape of an egg. A griffin-sized egg.

I'm concerned with my ability to pull the gilded object out with only one hand, but there is no other option at this point.

If I am honest with my scrambling thoughts, getting the egg out will be the easiest task in this trial. I cannot gauge the weight of it, but the artifacts in the first trial were gold, so it's not difficult to imagine the egg is not just merely painted that repulsive color. It will be heavy and loud. If I allow even the lightest clink to its side, I'm dead.

I never thought there would be a day that I'd miss Jaxon and the fanatical workings of his mind—he would have an answer right now.

Clamping my lips together, I reach under the griffin and feel for the egg. A feather brushes against my forehead, and I strain my arm, stretching it past its natural allowance to avoid touching any other feathers. One of my nails taps on the metal, the sound barely audible to me, but I freeze all the same.

One. Two. Three.

I count to thirty before I realize I'm no longer breathing, and my vision darkens at the edges. She has not moved, nor has the rhythm of her breathing changed.

Perhaps the Angel doesn't loathe me.

The sweat covering my body has cooled, creating a sticky layer over my fingers. They complement the surface of the egg, practically fusing the object to my hand. This was a needed development as the egg is larger than I'd anticipated.

I grip the artifact firmly and slowly lift it from the nest, careful to avoid the sticks and feathers. The uncontrollable shaking in my arm does me no favors, but I still manage to slip the egg out undetected. I set it on the damp grass and scrunch my eyes closed, taking several measured breaths before focusing once more.

Pushing back, I pause in a crouch and bring the artifact to my heaving chest. Fuck me, I've nowhere to store it. I'll need to switch hands often if I'm to avoid losing one to the incessant cold. My eyes flick up briefly before I flex my legs to stand.

There is one other moment in my life I can recall my vision contradicting what my mind desperately wishes to be true.

Nine years ago, Marek decided I was ready to complete an assignment without his nosey self peering over my shoulder. Under one condition: Isaiah must join me.

His mistake was overestimating my capabilities.

My mistake was agreeing.

Is and I found our target—some foolish man accused of stealing coin from his boss. The owner of the shop commissioned the guild to punish the man for a crime we did not have evidence of.

As is the case with many of our assignments.

Some may call me an abominable murderer, and I'd agree. They spit obscenities about me in the perceived safety of their homes and shops, as if I should fucking care about ensuring rightful punishment at all times.

But when the assignment fought back, I was unprepared. None of the previous targets had quarreled, though Marek had the reputation I dreamed of at that moment. Of course he retaliated—he found it amusing that the guild had sent two *children* for the job. So when he swung his blade at Isaiah, I froze. There was ample time for me to block the strike, but I failed.

My best friend screamed as he was sliced open, the horrid sound allowing me to move. It was a mere moment before the man had a blade in his heart. My eyes flicked to Isaiah, who lay motionless on the ground.

I may not have wielded the blade that struck my best friend, but I did not intercept it. There was no difference.

My vision claimed he was dead. My mind could not grasp the truth of such a thought—the same issue I am currently experiencing.

I stare wide-eyed at the ground as my breathing shallows. I must be imagining things…I've been in the cold far too long to be thinking clearly. That is surely all this is, and I am panicking over nothing.

My gaze inches up slowly, sliding over thick fur, a dark, aggressively curved beak, and finally meeting bright, scalding blue eyes.

"Oh fuck."

The griffin cants her head at my trembling voice. We watch each other for several moments while I silently threaten the Angel. I whimper when she leans into me, brushing the firm, smooth surface of her beak over my temple.

If I reach for my blade and kill her, the king would execute me for harming a griffin. But if I don't, I'll likely be her next meal.

Her hot breath fans across my face, and I instinctively lean away, struggling to swallow when she reacts with a low clicking deep in her throat. She pulls her head back, studying me curiously before her pupils dilate as she discerns what I am holding.

The hardening of her eyes dissolves any opportunity I had to live through this encounter.

My feet finally unlatch themselves from the ground when the griffin growls loudly, the chilling sound shifting to a screech. It could be sweat or blood running down my neck, though I've no desire to know which. I spin and sprint in the direction that will take me back to the castle, forcing my body to nearly glide over the packed snow. Wings shuffle behind me as another screech grates my ears.

She's pissed and preparing to hunt. And this time, I'm the target.

"Shit!" My heels crunch as I dig them into the snow, attempting to avoid slamming into the creature that landed before me.

She spreads her wings to their full length, swinging them in my direction aggressively. I stumble back, my foot catching on something and forcing me to my ass. My breathing is erratic while my stomach flips in all directions. I frantically scan for an opening, but she's too fast. Her claws swipe at my torso, catching the fabric above my knee when I hug the egg to my chest and crawl back on one hand.

I need to stand. I am too vulnerable like this.

Her eyes somehow become more crazed before her abnormally large body rears back. I roll in time to avoid being flattened, only to blind myself with small bits of ice. I turn my head to find her blurry form descending on me.

Holding up a hand, I scream, "Wait!" My eyes scrunch as I pitifully attempt to shield myself. It is several moments before I comprehend there was no impact and my stuttering breaths mixed with the piercing wind are the only things I hear. I peek to the side where the griffin stands with her gaze locked on me.

I slowly push to my feet, not looking away from her. "Listen...this is not your egg." I hold up the artifact, gesturing to it as if she can understand me. "I am not stealing from you. I need this, okay?"

My reputation would vanish if anyone in the kingdom knew I was trying to placate a fucking griffin.

I'd label myself as a fool if it didn't feel necessary.

The air vibrates with her rumbling chest as she steps toward me. "Please, just look! You must see this is not your egg..." My words end on a whisper when she lowers her head until our eyes are level. My tie snapped at some point, causing my hair to blow straight back when she huffs a breath.

I search her impassioned eyes, finding everything I feel within myself but refuse to acknowledge. Rage, hunger, determination, emptiness, loneliness.

Have we seen the same things in our lives?

Her white, feathery fur ripples in the wind as she tilts her head and blinks questioningly at me. Her eyes flit between mine and the egg a few times, and I hold my breath, my muscles unbearably tense as I wait. I haven't a second to process before the skin on her head scrunches together as she screeches, swinging claws at me once more.

This time, she doesn't miss.

I fly through the air, landing roughly on my back. My lungs struggle to inflate, and my hands press against my chest, only to slide off from something warm coating me. I groan at the intense pain that shoots through me when I lift my head. Hot blood cascades from four deep, fatal gashes.

"Fuck!" I grit through clenched teeth, my vision blurring at the edges.

I tug on my vital strand, coaxing it to the burning wounds and gasping when another wave of blood gurgles from the openings.

Someone is watching you.

My eyes search the landscape, marking the griffin that stalks me. I see no other person, though their presence is practically inevitable, so I cannot risk it.

I pull a small amount of essence forward, using my hands to cover any light that would seep through the wounds. I can heal the most life-threatening parts of the griffin's attack, though it will fucking hurt to walk back to the castle like this—if I survive long enough to walk again.

The bleeding slows to an amount I believe will be fine until I'm back in my room. Only there could I heal fully, claiming to have seen one of the castle's healers if there's a person foolish enough to question me.

I can think of one.

I cough, barely managing to spit the rising liquid out and settle for it draining down my jaw. The griffin hovers over my shaking body, and I briefly wonder if I did slow the blood down enough. Against my conditioned judgment and all of my training, I let my arms fall to my sides and soak in her warmth. Fuck, am I tired.

Her head drops to my chest, and she runs her beak over the shredded skin. I cry out, my hands jolting to grab her face. Her eyes widen at the touch as she leans in closer.

I'm going to die today.

The king will win. I will not get my revenge. Isaiah won't make it through the last trial without me.

I stubbornly tuck the egg into my side, wincing. The griffin watches the artifact carefully, desperation flitting through her gaze. "You truly believe this is your egg, huh?" I mumble, my brows furrowing at the foreign tone of my voice. She lifts a claw and taps the egg lightly before looking back at me expectantly. "I don't—wait, what?" I scoop my hand under and mimic the griffin, tapping a fingernail on the surface. My eyes snap to hers. "It's hollow. This *is* actually yours, isn't it?" She blinks once, watching me carefully.

I'm going to be sick.

I laugh wildly and choke on the movement. "You can have my life." She pauses, tilting her head until I can only see one calculating eye. "Just promise me one thing...kill that fucking bastard for what he took from us."

I let my body sag into the snow, enjoying the only moment of peace I can remember experiencing since my mother was alive. Will I see her?

For as many years as I've planned for my death, I have yet to consider what will happen when I die. Stories suggest our souls travel through the Aether Realm and live on as one of the beings that inhabit their lands. Others claim there is nothing after death, though I will not admit I know that is false.

I once summoned the spirit of a boy, not much older than I was at the time. I sat in my room, without a single clue of what was soon to come. I may have held onto my mother a little longer at night.

She and my father spent much time alone those days—they behaved as if things were okay, though I could hear their arguments. The amount of times my father would say, *"Valyria, please don't do this! Think of Ariella!"* Followed by the same words my mother uttered over and over... *"I* am *thinking of Ariella!"*

More than twenty years later, and I still cannot discern what I did to make her end her life.

Just before her tragic accident, I had felt lonely and needed a friend. A young boy appeared and sat with me, though we never shared a word. My mother found us and screamed for him to leave me be, ignoring every protest I'd made. She explained what he was and how he was there, but that is not the part that poisons my dreams.

I think that boy was her breaking point. The reason she finally ceased fighting with my father and shoved a blade through her heart.

My surroundings come into focus when the griffin presses her beak to my chest. I groan loudly as my hands fail to grip the snow. She opens her beak and...scoops blood from the wounds, rotating her head as she licks it clean.

Dying I can accept; but *eating me alive*? My blade no longer seems like a bad idea.

The griffin chirps, rubbing the smooth of her beak against my swollen cheek. The rumbling soft noises vibrate my head, but those are not what catch my attention. The majestic creature steps back and looks piercingly into my eyes before nodding once. Her wings lengthen and she pushes to the air from her feet, shifting the ground beneath me. I tilt my head back, watching her reversed form fly over the nest into the darkness.

I watch until the stark white of her feathers disappears.

"Fuck me...I'm alive," I mumble to myself, no longer caring for whoever watches me.

My teeth grit as I stand, pausing until the dizziness passes. I look to the sky, noting the positional change of the moon. It will be dawn soon. I force the pain down and jog back through the mountain, wondering which circumstance will claim me first: my wounds or the beheading from losing this trial.

Chapter Fifteen

Caspian

Hard armrests press against my palms, their intricate carvings only slightly painful under my tight grip—a small discomfort amidst everything else. The vast throne room stretches for hundreds of feet before me, red tapestries and gold lighting setting the warm tone, broken up by some in the audience who chose to wear something other than the royal colors. Flashes of blue and purple are the most prominent, contrasting oddly to the unending crimson.

The tapestries along the walls flutter, their crinkling noise barely perceptible above the low murmur of the people. The audience is split into two groups—as usual—as they crowd along a blood red rug that paves the walk from the doors to the thrones.

I stretch my neck and chew on my lip, the hushed whispers and occasional clank of hands clapping or guard uniforms shifting grates on every bit of my nerves. Twelve of the competitors stand to the side of my family, all having successfully completed their trials—though I do not care about them. Two of them are still missing, one of whose absence is spinning the fuck out of my stomach.

Where is she?

I'd chosen each location and artifact for this trial, hers having been some noble in the upper district. She should have been one of the first competitors back...I swallow around rising bile.

Murmurs hush as the room's doors slide open, my mind instantly focusing on whoever is entering only to be let down for the thirteenth time. Jeth, that bastard. Grabbing her as if they're familiar—as if he's owed the privilege of even being near her. My veins heat again, and I close my eyes to remember that Ariella can handle herself...and she did. But that doesn't lessen my need to make sure he never thinks about her again.

I smirk at the blood still coloring his hands and shirt. He appears to have changed his pants after she sunk a blade into his cock and—

I bite back a groan. The glimmer in her eyes when she pinned me with a heated look, demanding me to watch—as if I'd ever look away—has forced me into quite an uncomfortable position these last hours. Attempting to hide the bulge in my pants from my father and the rest of the audience, without making it obvious...it has been a struggle.

"It doesn't appear the wraith will be joining us for the remainder of the competition," the king breathes, his eyes flitting from the large windows to the doors. It's nearly dawn, plans to alter the rules skimming through my mind as I try to think of *anything* my father will listen to...

The doors burst open, though it is not the guards or another assassin on the other side this time.

Ariella.

My heart skips. She is the embodiment of rage as she stalks toward the throne, her eyes leveled on my father. Blood is the new decor choice in the castle, so it is not until horrified gasps come from every direction that I see it. Them. The gashes running from her left collarbone to her right ribs.

Pieces of her fitted suit swing with her confident movements, revealing much more than just the outlines of her breasts.

"Sit down, Caspian," my father spits, loud enough for only me to hear.

I don't listen. I can do nothing but stare at the blood that oozes from her wounds. It's smeared over her face and down her jaw; and as she walks closer, I can spot the difference in the deep crimson and the black trousers she wears.

So much blood. How in the fucking Aether is she alive?

I lower myself on a step when she sees me. Those striking green eyes narrow, and I'm almost certain she's cursing me and all of my ancestors.

The thought betrays my indifference, and I smile. Just for a moment before her dire wounds snag my attention again. She rolls her eyes, but I see the exhaustion. She's barely holding herself together, yet insists on facing the king with the level of confidence I would expect from her when she's healthy. Not dying.

She stops before the throne, father's guards blocking her path. I nearly trip down the steps to shove the guard away; he does not need to be so close to her. She raises a brow and watches me scrutinize the injuries. The cuts are deep and large...this was not the work of some random person.

"Who did this?" My voice is quiet, but severe.

I shouldn't care that she's hurt. That is the nature of these trials: kill or be killed. Win or die. The wounds our healers care for each day speak to the brutal nature of these contestants. Something like this should not be a shock, nor should it squeeze my chest so tightly.

But it does.

The moment I ensure she is safe and offers me a name, Gavriel and I will leave for the city.

"Why don't you ask your father?" she remarks loudly enough for part of the audience to hear. My brows furrow as I turn to the king and give him a questioning look. He doesn't acknowledge me, but he also does not appear surprised at Ariella's pronouncement.

"What is she talking about?" That snags his attention, the rest of my family turning their eyes to me.

"You'd believe the *wraith* and accuse your own king of such transgressions?"

"I've accused you of nothing, father. However, you assigned me to coordinate all three trials. I wrote their riddles myself, and I am certain Ariella's would not have led to such wounds." I gesture to her chest, snatching my hand back when the warmth of her body shocks my fingers. She watches me thoughtfully, searching for an answer to whatever preconceived conclusion she held before storming in here like a vision in red.

She holds out an egg-shaped object, and I note the tremor in her arm. My eyes widen as I lean forward. It has the distinct casing of the artifacts we distributed, though I inspected each of them and this egg was not among the rest. It curiously is not the pendant I picked for Ariella's trial, either.

"Don't worry, *Your Majesty*, I was sure not to harm the griffin. No laws were broken."

"Griffin?" I exclaim loudly. My jaw slacks, and she nods imperceptibly at me before a predatory smile cracks the dried blood along her cheek.

She speaks softly, rage threaded through every word. "My sincerest apologies that your plan to kill me did not succeed, Thalion. Thanks for the challenge, though." Vespera sucks in a breath, a hand slapping over her widened mouth. Ariella's eyes flit to the pile of artifacts, causing her to press the egg at her side and raise an eyebrow to my father. "This will remain in my possession."

She turns on her heel and saunters through the massive audience without being dismissed. Even after facing a griffin, she still holds herself as if it were a trivial matter.

The reality of the situation slams into me then. She stood against a fucking griffin and lived...and the egg? She must have gotten it from the griffin's nest—

She's fucking incredible.

I watch as her form turns the corner, silver flicking through the air is the last I see of her. Why am I so shocked? Of course she survived a griffin encounter—there is nothing that wicked woman cannot do.

Except heal herself.

Does she know where to find the healers? Before I can consider the consequences, I'm running away from my father's throne. He yells for me to return once, not embarrassing himself with a second command when I do not even acknowledge the first. I'll likely be punished for this later.

The intrigued whispers of the audience are blurry streaks at the edge of my vision. The men stationed at the doors look to the king as I approach, standing down at the dismissal he most likely gave.

He abhors creating familial drama in the presence of his people. A quality I am currently thankful for.

Flashes of Ariella's tired eyes, heavy breathing, and trembling arm push me faster. Perhaps it is cruel to hope she fell unconscious so that I may carry her to the healers. I'm certain she'd drive her blade into me for doing so, but the thought only makes me smile.

It would be worth having her fury directed at me.

The fire in her eyes is intoxicating on the worst of days, but when she focuses those burning intentions on me?

"Fuck." It's quiet, but I relax slightly at her voice.

I peek around the corner of a dark, unused hallway to where she leans against the wall with her eyes scrunched closed. It may be the lack of light, but her skin appears more pale than it was several minutes ago. She was certainly concealing the dire nature of her wounds, and they are much worse than I had thought. Something claws at my chest, imploring me to rush to her.

"Ariella." Her name is a whisper on my lips, the taste of it warm and reassuring. She tenses but doesn't open her eyes.

"Fuck off, prince." I press fingers to my lips; now is not an appropriate time to tease the wraith. I pause next to her and drink in her presence.

Only one person may win this competition. I need it to be her.

It's a relief to find the clarity I've been warring with.

It is also a comfort that she's coherent enough to snap at me. "You need to see a healer—"

"No."

"These are not mere scratches, Ariella. Please let me take you to Elowen; she is our best and—"

"I said no, prince." Her eyes open this time, pinning me with a glare that dares me to ask again.

I nod, caught in the depths of burning emerald. It's a strange realization to know I would do anything she asks. These feelings are too intense to think of, so instead I take a different approach.

"How can I aid you, then? Surely you do not want others finding you in the hallway struggling with your wounds?" That captures her attention. Her heavy eyes search mine as she chews on that damn lip.

"If you utter a word of this to anyone, I will kill you." I smirk at the threat.

"You'll kill me either way, angel." She is not impressed with the humor. I level her with as serious a look as I can summon. "You have my word."

I can practically see the conflict she's struggling with. I cannot imagine she accepts the help of others very often.

"Fine. I need to get back to my room." I open my mouth to protest, but her expression forces me to abandon the words.

"Okay, here." I offer my hand, quietly appreciating the lack of hesitation before her fingers wrap around mine. I bend under her arm to take her weight, pausing when she winces and presses the egg harder into her side.

"I'm fine, just go."

We're lucky that no one sees us as we walk to her room. I should call for Elowen...she can heal Ariella in her room if the wraith refuses to go to her. She leans into me more and more as we move, her hand squeezing mine tightly over my shoulder. Her breaths shorten, and I'm amazed she's still standing when we're finally at her door.

She twists a hand and pulls back slightly; the movement shifting something in the door. I fucking knew it...those were wards she unlocked a few days ago. I want to ask how, but keep the questions to myself. She's barely conscious as we step into her room, and my forehead creases when I survey it. No, not *her* room, but *a* room. It's so impeccably clean that

I do not believe she stays here; even the air smells of fresh linens, lacking her usually sultry fragrance.

I set the egg on her bed and lead her to the bathroom, pulling her toward the shower. Warm water should help while I fetch Elowen.

"No, stop," she commands weakly. I reluctantly allow her to pull from my hold, but hover closely as she leans against the vanity.

Her face is contorted as if she's in much more pain than she's willing to show. Blood still seeps from her wounds. She must truly be the Angel, because the amount of blood she has lost and yet lives? Impossible. Her skin is nearly gray, and I shake my head, stepping from the room. I do not fucking care if she doesn't want a healer. I'll deal with her wrath when she's no longer in death's grip.

"Don't you fucking dare." I could act as if I did not hear her near-silent words, but I pause and look over my shoulder. She leans against her hands, smearing blood along the stone. Her head falls back, and it takes everything in me to not bolt from the room.

"You're dying, Ariella, let me get Elowen!" The hint of a smirk graces her face.

"Shut the fuck up, Caspian. I need to concentrate." I step back into the room; the warm, metallic scent evidence of her draining life. I will give her one minute before I go for the healer. I shouldn't even wait that long, but the tinge of worry in her voice is enough to keep me here.

Her arm lifts, and she stumbles. I reach out, my hands far too eager to have her in them again. She rights herself only to begin weaving. Her fingers tug on invisible strands as I watch her carefully. Those movements...she couldn't be...

"By the Angel," I breathe when warm light glows from the gashes across her torso. I watch as her skin stitches itself back together and color slowly returns to her face. This is unheard of. To possess essence for all affinities...I feel uneasy. Not from her secrets, but understanding why she keeps them. She would be targeted for her essence. Exploited or killed—because that is the law. Enforced by the king.

My eyes snap to her face, which thankfully looks better with each passing minute. Is that why she hates my father so much? Does he know her secret, and she was right to accuse him of attempting to end her life?

What the fuck is going on? Clearly, I have been willfully ignorant of the greater happenings within the castle. I will cease with blindly trusting others and pay more attention to the things that occur when I turn around.

Ariella groans. My body reacts, jerking forward to help, but she doesn't need it. I want to give it to her regardless and will hungrily accept whatever punishment she sees fit for the misbehavior.

I am captivated by the woman in front of me—blood and all. Not even Elowen could have closed her wounds in just one session...but Ariella has healed them to meager scratches. She slumps, her body completely giving out. I rush to catch her, ignoring the heat that spreads from each place our skin touches.

She sighs when her cheek touches the cool tile, and I briefly wonder if I should try to wash some blood from her. But my lip curls and closes that path of thinking. I am not interested in violating unconscious women.

When she awakens is a different matter entirely, however.

I scan her face as if I've not yet memorized every piece of it before releasing her and sliding to the wall behind me. It takes just one breath for me to rationalize staying with her. She seems healed enough, though I cannot be sure. If she won't allow Elowen here, then I must watch over her. I'd also worry about another entering her room, as she didn't replace her wards—whatever she risks using them for must be important.

I chuckle at how ridiculous this is. I know she will be okay; I also know she will be pissed if she finds me here. When was the last time someone sat with her who didn't want to use or kill her?

The drying blood on her hands smudges against the tile when she shifts.

A reminder.

Of things I shouldn't care about, but do. I haven't fought this curious fascination that keeps tugging me toward the wraith. But...I do not want to. Who she pretends to be, or what she does outside of this castle—none of it matters. I want to know her. Be near her and soak in the confidence she exudes. And if all she'll ever give me are harsh words and blades to my throat? I want that, too.

I cross my arms and swipe a hand over my mouth, watching the even rise and fall of her breathing. I do not have the nerve to question my father outright, but he must know something. The memory of his cold, azure eyes haunts me. I know that if I fuck up again, he will see it as a threat to the king rather than disobeying my father.

I need to be careful, but this is too important to overlook.

Someone had sent her to a griffin...never mind that she was brilliant enough to be the only person I've heard of to survive such an encounter, but what was the purpose? Had someone truly intended to kill her, or perhaps they assumed she just wouldn't complete the trial?

I chew on my lip, the corners of my mouth tugging upward. Stubborn woman.

If she were anyone else, she wouldn't have even attempted to search for the griffin.

But she's not anyone else. An unusual warmth grows from my chest, and I take a steadying breath.

I'll begin with Varrick—aside from me, he is the only other person with access to my design space. Where I keep the valuable pieces of the trials hidden until it is time to deploy them. My head throbs, and the exhaustion I've ignored catches up to me.

I look once more at Ariella's sleeping form, deciding she will not be waking any time soon. My head falls back against the wall, filled with thoughts of messy politics. I'll deal with them tomorrow.

Chapter Sixteen

Ariella

Unforgiving lights shock my eyes when they flutter open. My hand snaps up to block the sting, and I assess my body.

My chest is sore—though the gashes are nearly healed—and my clothes are stiff from the copious amount of dried blood. I am surprisingly okay, otherwise. My essence feels drained, and memories of the previous night resurface.

Facing a griffin. Challenging the king in front of his court. The prince walking me to my room. Healing my wounds—

The prince. He brought me here against his wishes, as I vaguely recall his insistence that I see a healer. I sit up too quickly, my muscles protesting such movement.

He watched me weave strands I should not have...an affinity I've not claimed to possess. I pause to listen for his presence; it's just me here. He must have taken the first opportunity he had to inform the king.

My nose scrunches from an awful rotting smell, and I look around the bathroom before realizing what it is—me. I pull at my top, grimacing at the way it lifts my skin with it, and bring the material to my face. The smell is positively revolting.

Even my head objects when I stand, forcing me to grab the vanity until the wave of dizziness passes. Food. I need food.

Shower, eat, murder a king—in that order. My stomach rumbles painfully at the thought. Will I make it to the dining hall before the king's guards descend on me? The prince could not have left too long ago, as I wasn't attacked in my sleep.

I blindly reach for the brush when my fingers graze a rough texture I don't recognize. I peek through my eyes and lean to switch the light off before lifting the folded paper. I open it too quickly, dismissing the flutter in my abdomen when the prince's name for me appears. The only light is from the window in my room, but I'm still able to read the words clearly enough.

> Angel,
> I wanted to stay until you woke, but my presence was required elsewhere. I've asked Gavriel to stand watch outside your door. I know how important your wards are to you, so be assured that no one but myself entered your room while you were sleeping.
>
> p.s. you're cute when you snore

I scoff, rubbing a hand over my throat as if it will relieve the dryness inside. "I do not snore."

Perhaps he's waiting to tell the king until I'm already surrounded and have no chance of fighting my way out.

My head hurts too much for this.

Peeling the remainder of clothes that melted into my skin feels like a punishment, but I tear them off quickly and toss them to the side. I have never appreciated a hot shower more, and I'd kill to remain here all day, but I hurry through the motions until I'm certain no blood remains. I dress in a comfortably fitted set of shorts and a top.

I still—my reflection in the mirror shows a woman who is tired and lacks the determination that usually resides in her eyes. If I look this worn now, I'm sure I was a vision last night.

I disregard why that seems to bother me.

The urge to find Isaiah suffocates all other thoughts, and I march to my door, only to pause as my hand reaches the gilded handle. The prince said he's had Gavriel on watch...does the man ever have a moment off? I'd think he was the prince's shadow if it weren't for the displeasing attire he's made to wear.

I straighten and swing the door open, raising a brow at the guard examining something. He shoves it into his pocket before I confirm what it is and pushes off the wall with a foot, crossing his arms.

"Ah, finally the wraith awakens," he announces with a tone that knowingly exposes his disdain for being forced to guard my door.

"Why are you here?"

A finger taps against my thigh, his eyes catching the movement. "Trust me, I wouldn't be if the prince didn't insist."

"Well, next time you can tell him I don't need a fucking babysitter."

He throws his head back as he bellows a laugh. "You think I didn't? I tried to tell him—even offered to take the pit for a few days. He wouldn't hear any of it."

I step through the threshold and saunter in his direction. He shifts, clenching his jaw. A hint of hesitation glimmers in his deep eyes when I still a mere foot away. "The prince must not care for you. He knows my proclivity to slit the throats of those who interfere with my life; and yet...he still sent you here."

"Save your assassin shit for someone who cares. And while you're at it, stay away from Caspian. I don't know what the fuck you've done to make him so preoccupied with you, but it stops now."

I study him for a moment, a genuine smile forming on my lips. "Is that a threat, Gavriel?"

"You're damn right it is. You will do nothing but hurt him, and I won't sit back and watch." That stung.

Sunlight streams down the hall when a door opens, though I'm too focused on unsheathing my blade to hear Isaiah approach.

"What's going on?" My hand hovers over the cool metal for a heartbeat before I tap against it once more.

"Nothing—Gavriel was just leaving to tell his prince what a *good boy* he is for following orders." Something resembling a challenge crosses his face, but I've no desire to deal with him any longer. "Go on. I'm sure Caspian hasn't had his ass kissed all morning in light of your absence."

"What was that about?" Isaiah questions when the guard stomps out of sight.

I wave my hand, dismissing his concern and gesturing for us to walk. "That's not important." I pull out my blade and mindlessly spin it through my fingers. "Someone tried to kill me in that trial." I don't mention the king. Yet.

He nods, considering. The other competitors were present when I arrived—they saw just what I was put through. "Fuck, Ari, I didn't know what to do. The prince chased after you before I could, and with the way the king seethed when he ignored commands? I figured I should keep my head, as the prince probably took you to a healer."

I halt, blocking a woman's path. I do not move as she mutters curses about me under her breath. I focus on my friend; he looks tired. Worn. I haven't been as here for him as I should be...especially considering I *will* have him crowned victor in this competition.

"I would have beheaded you myself for doing something so mindless. You know not to worry for me, Is. I am more than capable of caring for myself."

He pins me with a disbelieving expression. "I know, but you shouldn't always have to. The prince—"

"The prince took me to be healed, that is all." A half-truth. The small piece that I can offer him, lest I begin sharing my secret with the entire realm. "Isaiah, I—" I, what? The reality of our future remains unspoken, neither of us wanting to discuss what we know happens next. He will not accept my aiding him in the final trial...and that renders the conversation pointless.

I study his dark eyes before sighing. "I'm hungry. Let's stop at the dining hall." I'm feeling too weak to be comfortable. He gives me a disappointed smile as we continue.

It's disturbing the amount of paintings the king has of himself and his family. It seems that Thalion's greatest admirer is Thalion. The staff must clean these portraits daily, as not a spec of dust resides on their surfaces. I scoff—he takes better care of these than he does his own people.

"How are you doing? Do I even want to know how you managed to escape a griffin attack?"

I laugh and shove his arm. "I didn't escape. She just stopped advancing and let me walk away." I don't miss the several intakes of breath from those listening to our conversation.

"She?" I meet his questioning gaze, wondering the same myself.

Shrugging, I twirl my blade in the other hand. "I didn't examine under her feathers to confirm. It just seemed like a female."

"And your wounds?"

"Barely visible. The healer fell unconscious stitching them together, but they appear as just a bit of red skin now." Another half-truth.

He questions me about the griffin as we eat, while those around us pretend to not soak up every word. The next trial is not for several days, so we do not rush through the morning. Ally joins us, and I cannot discern why I feel uneasy with how comfortable she is around Isaiah. I suppose that's my fault.

I remain aware, my eyes flitting to every guard we pass on our walk to the training grounds. I've yet to be attacked by the king's men...

"What are we working on today?" Ally questions excitedly, smacking her hands together as we walk down the hill toward the sparring mats. The Angel must love her because I am unsure how she's lived so long on her own. The woman has zero survival instincts.

"Is and I will go a few rounds, and I want you to watch the more advanced techniques we use. Assess how our movements were built from the basic skills we've been teaching you."

She groans at whatever upsets her this time. I could tell her that I do not plan to train her at all today—I am not in the giving mood.

"It's cool, Al," Isaiah starts, sharing a pleading look with me. I roll my eyes as I trudge ahead and listen to him coddle her. He is too good for this realm. "I'll work with you after and we can go over some more complicated steps." My nose scrunches at the little squeal she breathes.

"Pathetic," I mutter to myself.

The sun exits the clouds, my eyes protesting the sudden brightness. The ache in my head had improved after eating, though now it seems my efforts were wasted. I stop at the edge of the mat and face the outer wall as I stretch. My shoulders protest every movement, but I grit my teeth through the pain and force them to succumb.

I am in my head as thoughts of princes, essence, and politics fight for my attention when Isaiah and Ally's conversation halts. My eyes snap open to a scowling best friend and a smirking Ally, both focused on something behind me.

"What?" I don't look—I already know what they see. His essence is a beacon that warns me of his approach.

"I thought you said there was nothing going on between you and the prince?" My forehead creases at Isaiah's shadowed tone.

"I believe I said it wasn't important, but there isn't anything *going on.*"

"Are you sure?" Ally chews on her thumb, struggling to hide a giddy smile. "Because he's walking over here, and his eyes have not left you once."

"He's likely just checking on me. I was quite wounded." They blink at me. That was a pitiful attempt at redirecting their unvoiced questions...not even I believe my excuses.

I spin when his boots sound against the mat and study him for a moment longer than necessary. He looks so...mundane. Loose, sapphire pants adorn his long legs, while a white top flaunts his broad shoulders.

I cross my arms as I clear my throat. "What do you want?" He doesn't answer, inspecting every part of my body before he reaches me. A breeze drifts by, carrying the scent of worn books and the kind of lavender I enjoy in my tea.

"How are you feeling?" His concern means nothing.

"Aside from annoyed that your bitter guard was stalking me earlier? Perfectly fine."

He purses his lips before mimicking my stance. "Bitter, huh? That is exactly what he said about you."

"It's my room—I can behave how I please. He was there uninvited."

"I invited him," the prince remarks, a challenge in those playful eyes.

"Interesting, because I don't recall inviting you, either." Bantering is not something I usually enjoy, but I find it amusing with the prince.

"Would you like to?" I blink once and bite my cheek as if I'm truly considering such an absurd question.

Of course I wouldn't—I'm forced to see him enough as it is.

Yet...I find myself blurting, "And if I say yes?" He steps close enough that I have to tilt my head to hold his gaze.

"Then allow me to escort you." He sweeps a hand out, offering. "I'm quite eager for a tour—I was a bit preoccupied last night."

I throw my head back to laugh, tensing when I lift and meet his wide eyes. I look away, finding the texture of the mat quite interesting. "Not happening, prince. I do not allow anyone into my room. Ever."

He opens his mouth with what I'm sure is an enlightening retort, but thinks better of it, nodding. "A challenge, then."

"You wish to challenge me? Have you no memory of the last time we sparred?"

He chuckles, snagging his lip between his teeth. "Oh, I remember." His smile turns sinister as he clicks his tongue. "I remember how easily you had me on my knees for you. The way your thighs squeezed mine when you pinned me on my back. How *warm* your—"

"Fine," I spit out, wanting nothing more than to punch his ridiculous face. "I accept. But I did go easy on you the first time—it will not be the same today."

"You think you'll win against me again?"

"I've no need to think about it; of course I will win. You, on the other hand, should start praying."

"Pray," he lilts. "To whom, exactly? An Angel I'm not even sure exists?"

"No," I drawl, closing the distance between our tense bodies. I look him in the eye, a wicked smile tugging at my lips. "You'll be praying to me by the time we're done here. For a mercy I will never grant."

His answering chuckle sends a shiver down my spine as he tilts his head to the clouds. He swallows heavily, and I inwardly curse myself at my body's heated response. "I don't see the problem, then. We both know I'm more than willing to bow at your feet. I can think of *many* ways to pray in that position..." He bites his lip, and I watch the movement carefully as he leans in to whisper, "Shall I skip the embarrassment of you winning and get started now?"

I narrow my eyes at the moonlit aura of his; it's more difficult than it should be to maintain an indifferent facade.

"Choose your blade, prince." A predatory smile pulls at his lips as his tongue swipes over them.

I walk to the center of the mat and wait with my back to him—foolish to do in any other scenario, but highly entertaining right now as his heavy footfalls stalk toward me. He likely believes he's being quiet, arrogant prick that he is. Though they are more forgiving this time...maybe he listened to my advice, after all. His steps skip just behind me, and I twist to catch the leg he swings at my waist. My blade presses over his femoral artery, Caspian freezing when he realizes my target.

"You wouldn't." I hum at his words, pressing until my blade jerks slightly from the give of his skin. He winces.

"Would you bet your life on that theory?" His eyes bore into mine, and I will forever be haunted by the way he successfully distracts me enough to curve his leg in and twist our bodies until we stumble. I flip the blade so that the tip presses into my forearm as I fall, grunting as his weight drops on me. Before I can defend myself, he's straddling me as he presses down on my crossed arms.

He leans down until he's close enough that I can map the ridges of his irises, where different shades of silver blend together seamlessly. He glances at my lips before smiling, the heat from the sun *nothing* compared to the fire burning every place he leans against. "We should really start training together daily. I'm finding it very...beneficial." My thighs clamp together at the raw desire laced in his every feature, and he smirks, having noticed the slight movement. "It's okay to admit you want me, angel. I won't tell anyone just how badly the Silver Wraith *aches* for the prince she claims to hate," he breathes in my ear, the wetness pooling between my legs a traitorous reaction to his words.

"You'd do well to get off me before I make you regret it," I say quickly, swallowing around the thickness caught in my throat. I need to remove myself from this position before I do something positively foolish like admit the truth of his claim.

"I'd love to see you try—" I slam my head into his nose, swinging my knees up to shove him over my body. By the time I'm standing, a horrified crowd has gathered as he remains on his back, laughing deeply. I step forward and stare down at the bloody mess of his face, my brows scrunching. "Fuck, you're incredible," he breathes to himself before opening his eyes to realize dozens of people are watching him do...I'm not sure what, exactly.

He pushes himself up, and we continue like that for hours. When it turned from a challenge to me training him and correcting his many mistakes, I'm not sure, but all at once the reality of our situation soaks back into me.

"Why haven't you told anyone?" His eyes flit to our audience for a moment before he snatches the opportunity my line of questioning has presented. He takes one step in my direction—and another—until the heat of his chest warms my own.

He smirks when I lose my focus in the near touch of our bodies. "And convince my father to take you from me?" He drags his blade lightly over my abdomen, delicately curving it around my breast until the tip presses into the base of my throat. "I don't think so." I cannot let him inside my head. I have things to do here, and he is not one of them.

But the longer I'm in his presence, the more illogical my resolve seems.

"He couldn't take me from you—I'm not yours to steal." That is precisely what he hoped I would say.

"We can change that," he whispers, his tongue clicking on the final word as his eyes slide to my lips. Lavender breath kisses my skin, and I realize one of us has leaned in further. "I wouldn't wish to be deemed a liar, after all."

"I'll pass. I've had enough disappointing partners to last the Angel's lifetime." His gaze hardens as he purses his lips. I remain still when the blade nicks the skin above my pounding heart.

"Clearly those *partners*," he spits, giving me the sense that he wouldn't mind knowing their names, "did not understand how to tend to such treasures."

"And you do?" A flare of wild hunger appears in his intense eyes.

"Why don't we go find out? I'll let you decide." There's amusement laced in each purposeful word. I smirk and press into the blade.

"I have a better idea," I purr, delighting in the way he clings to my unspoken proposal.

The prince waits eagerly, barely inclining his head toward me before I drive my knee into his cock and slide the blade from his hand. Breath hisses through his teeth as I step to his side and kick the backs of his knees, sending him to the mat. My hand grips his hair and jerks him back until his wild eyes find mine.

The sharp steel presses under his chin, forcing him to tilt his head until it rests against my lower abdomen. I ignore the thrill that travels down my spine when he laughs and my blade yields to the movement.

"This was quite the effort just to get me on my knees, angel. I believe I told you earlier I would do so willingly."

I hold his gaze, neither of us daring to be the first that looks away.

"What the fuck is this?" The connection remains a moment longer before my eyes track up, landing on an exasperated looking man.

Curly, dark hair bounces over rich skin as he jogs in my direction. He wears tailored pants with a white, half-buttoned shirt, and a black vest adorned in red and gold jewels.

He halts several feet away, holding his hands up as if to placate me. "Please do not hurt the prince. Name your price—anything you wish for—and it's yours."

The blade in my hand bounces. "Anything?"

"Yes!" His dark eyes dart around wildly as he silently questions why no one else is helping the prince. "Whatever you want, just don't do this."

A smile tugs at my mouth, and I study the man before me. My left hand strokes Caspian's lush hair—a warning and a comfort—as I press the blade harder into his skin. "And what if the only thing I wish for is to kill your prince?"

The man's jaw drops, garbled noises falling from his gaping mouth. "Fuck off, Bastian, she's fine."

Bastian. The name doesn't suit the sputtering mess before me.

"Fine? Caspian, she has a fucking blade to your throat!"

I drag the tip lightly over his skin, faltering when he shudders. "So observant, Bastian," I taunt, flattening the blade again. "Shall I demonstrate how to use it?"

His eyes fly over my features, widening when they notice the thing that makes every cowardly man piss his pants.

"You're the Silver Wraith." I chuckle, enjoying the way Caspian hisses when I tighten my grip on him.

"Amazing...nothing gets past you, does it?" I crouch, my knees surrounding the prince as I rest my chin on his shoulder. "Who is that?" I speak for only us to hear while glaring at Bastian.

His body relaxes into mine slightly, and I allow him to turn his head enough to look at me. The close proximity I've put us in hits me hard.

"That would be my cousin." I hum, pursing my lips.

"Should I slide the blade across your throat just to see his reaction? He's quite interesting—it's pitiful." I look over when he doesn't answer, only to find him smiling at me. "What?"

I should be the one making *him* uncomfortable, not the other way around.

"You are very beautiful." The words dance from his tongue and settle heavily in my stomach.

His confession means nothing.

So why does it hurt? Why does every memory of someone telling me I'm beautiful resurface, and why does my chest feel like it's suffocating when I realize there's only one?

Two, now.

He watches my reaction, and his brows furrow as his eyes whisper things I cannot accept. He moves to speak, but I release him and stand before my next heartbeat.

"We're done here," I state coldly. Sheathing my blade and stalking away amidst the call of my name.

Chapter Seventeen

Ariella

Afternoon light creates deep shadows along the edges of shops and houses. I stare at them longingly as I pass, suddenly feeling the weight of the realms on my shoulders.

Just one day.

One day to not think about the endless tasks I must fulfill before I take the prince's life. A finger taps—I could resume my original plan to eliminate the king...I sigh, stretching my sore neck.

One day to not be seen as the Silver Wraith, or to not have groups of people whisper amongst themselves as I walk by, because I decided to not cover my hair.

My eyes flit to several men huddled together as each of them touches the terrified woman they surround. Ordinarily, I would not bother to interfere with the shit that happens on Valoria's streets, but my training earlier was not nearly enough to stave the raging heat in my gut. My hands itch to play.

I turn on my heel and saunter to the group. They are standing in front of a darkened dress shop that has a large display window with a hanging paper that indicates it is closed. I stop just behind one of the men who's about my height, my nose scrunching at his musty clothing and greasy, matted blonde hair. None of the six men notice me at first, continuing to taunt the now-crying woman.

It should be against Eldoria's law for women to not be trained in defensive strategy during their schooling—because abhorrent men like this exist, and the day a woman willingly fucks someone like them is the day I meet the Angel.

I nearly gag as their shifting movement reminds me just how many people in this city do not understand how to use a bath. I almost regret involving myself, but flashes of the prince's words invade my mind and I clear my throat loudly enough for each of them to quiet and turn toward me. The one closest to me jolts back, pushing the rest into the window. The woman peeks around the ones still surrounding her, her eyes widening before she retreats, as if to find solace in those that were threatening her not a moment before.

If looks could kill…

"What is it you boys think you're doing?" My voice is sweet. Inviting.

The others look to the musty one for an answer. Pathetic.

"Nothing—just having a little fun with our friend here." He grabs her arm and jerks her to the front. I chuckle, unsheathing my blade and twirling it idly through my fingers. My eyes find the man who whimpers—*whimpers*—and I study him. His hair is cut flat to his oblong head, receding at the front. He wears brown trousers with a cream top that is poorly tucked in.

"What is her name?" I question lightly, my tone non-threatening while my eyes suggest otherwise.

The leader frowns, blinking several times. "What?"

I offer a saccharine smile and nod to the one in question. "You said she was your friend." I take a step forward, one of the cowards attempting to run, but an arm blocks his path as another demands he not move. "So, what. Is. Her. Name?"

"Lila," the woman mutters quietly, casting her eyes to the cobblestone.

"Did I ask you?" She swallows loudly, shaking her head. "Did you want to be near them?"

She peers up at me. "What?"

"Fuck's sake, are you all truly so mindless? Did you want to be near them or not? Do not make me repeat myself again." Lila hesitates before whispering no, though she stands still, as if she's not sure which direction is safer.

"That wasn't so difficult." I look to the grimy men, curling my lip. "Leave before I decide to render you all cockless for the rest of your miserable lives," I command darkly. They foolishly block each other's paths and trip over nothing as they run down the street. Lila hugs herself, eyes flitting from me to the street carefully.

"Learn how to use a blade, will you? Because if I catch you in such a position again, you'll be the first to meet mine." I spin on my heel and stalk away, wiping sweat from my forehead.

The thick air replaces the slick along my skin after only a moment, and I curse the Angel for whatever the fuck it did to the seasons. I pass dozens of wilted plants and gardens as I walk, almost feeling bad for how neglected they appear.

I finally arrive at the guild and ascend the steps, tripping over something on the last one. I hop on one foot to right myself, my eyes searching for whatever caught it, but there is nothing there. My forehead creases—I *know* there was something...

Two floating green circles appear on the top step, and my hand slaps to my chest as I laugh deeply. "Myst, you sneaky creature. Don't you know it's rude to trip a trained killer?" The eyes rise, and her short fur shifts from a grainy black to a pretty orange—the same color as the setting sun. She stretches before rubbing her face along my leg and sauntering to the door.

I watch with a raised brow as she sits next to the entrance, waiting like a princess to be serviced. "Ridiculous cat," I mutter, stalking to the door and sweeping my arm for her to enter ahead of me, lest she complain to Marek that I'm abusing her. "Where's Marek?" Her eyes flick toward his office before meeting mine. "Can you fetch Jaxon?" She huffs but trots down the hall that will take her to his room.

I nod to Eva—one of our more reserved students, who is painting the sunset next to a window—as I walk to my mentor's office and knock, shoving the door open the moment he answers. His head snaps up, ready to reprimand whoever dared to be disrespectful, but his deep-set eyes soften when they spot me. He assesses me like a worried father before settling into his chair, crossing his arms.

"Where's Isaiah?" I drop into one of the seats opposite him, leaning my head back over the edge.

"Probably fucking his new admirer." That was more bitter than I'd intended.

"Ari," he sighs, swiping a hand over his chin, pinning me with a disapproving look.

I wave my hand and stare at the ceiling. "Whatever—I haven't much time, and I came here to talk to you and Jaxon about something."

"Talk to me about what?" I bend back further, taking in Jaxon's reverse, tall form. "Thanks, Myst." He bends to scratch her head, dismissing the now-gray cat and closing the door softly.

"She tried to fucking trip me earlier," I announce, muttering about how bitchy she is under my breath.

"She was just having fun. Scouting has been quiet lately, and she's bored."

"Well she can cloak somewhere else—I'm not in the fucking mood."

Marek looses an even heavier sigh. "All right, what's going on?"

My finger taps on the arm of the chair as I explain events that occurred in the second trial and my suspicions about them. Jaxon will likely need a healer with the way his jaw remains unhinged, though Marek's expression remains stoic.

"You must be lying...there is no possible way you survived a griffin attack!" I tense, my head slowly panning to Jaxon.

"Are you certain you'd like to accuse me of lying?" He gulps, licking his lips twice before looking to Marek for help.

"Ariella, enough. I understand you're angry, but killing him will help no one."

"Killing me?" Our strategist shrieks, shrinking into his chair as I remove my glare.

Marek chuckles, eyes creasing as he leans on his elbows against the desk. "Don't threaten her if you can't handle the same, then."

"Threaten her? When did I threaten her?"

"Jaxon. If you're alive, you're a threat to her—you know this." My eyes get lost in one of the two dimly lit lamps, the men's bickering stirring feelings from earlier.

I need to move.

I stand abruptly, swiping my hands over my hips. "As enjoyable as this is, I only came to tell you that I am being targeted." They both snap their mouths shut, focusing on me. I turn for the door as I continue, "I'm unaware of any attempts on Isaiah, nor am I privy to any plans to attack the guild. If you hear of *anything* happening outside the castle walls, look into it."

"And you?" Marek questions softly. I breathe deeply before looking over my shoulder.

"The person behind this is bound to slip up when they realize I'm not easy to kill. And when they do slip, it's my blade they'll fall onto." He nods, dismissal enough for me to rush through to the front doors, ignoring the way a group of students quiets when I pass.

My chest heaves as I step into the cooling air, droplets of rain beginning to fall. My head tilts back, and I allow my shoulders to slump.

I'm not frustrated that he called me beautiful...I'm frustrated because of how closely he's had to watch me to notice.

He already fucking knows of my unreported essence, which blares the question: *what else is he seeing?* Does he know of my plans to kill him, and that is the rationale of why he's as preoccupied with me as Gavriel claims?

"Shit," I groan, pushing my feet forward to hurry back. I dropped him and stalked away when he complimented me—that rejection could be enough motivation for him to run off with my most closely held secrets.

My mind slows as I breathe in the distinctly appeasing smell of the rain. It is easy to feel watched by every eye under the Angel's sun, but when it rains like this? It's as if I am encased in my own little realm, where I am invisible and untouchable.

It's freeing.

I turn into an alley—a shortcut and refuge. Despite the night just beginning, the shadows are heavy and meager light creeps into the space. I tug on my umbral strand and call the familiar tendrils to my hand, the hint of a smile forming when they emerge. They are like an extension of me. I need only call to the strand once, and they are mine to control without additional weaving. That is not how the other strands behave—

Something pierces my thigh as I walk, and in the next heartbeat my blade is across the alley, sinking into the assailant's heart. I have but a moment to look at the arrow jutting from my leg before another whizzes past my face—so close the end brushes the tip of my nose. I pull the shadows over me and step back to the sleek brick wall.

"Where did she go?" one shouts over the pouring rain, squinting his eyes at three of his friends entering from the other side. I cannot help the giddy laugh that bellows out of me, causing the remaining six attackers to pause.

It doesn't matter if they witness my use of forbidden essence...their mouths will no longer work by the time I've had my fun.

And this *will* be fun.

I run to the left, only letting the shadows go when I maneuver up against the wall, pushing off and swinging my foot into the closest man's head. The hit sends him careening into the brick, where a distinct crunch overpowers the rain, followed by his brain matter draining through the cracks.

My eyes find the one who shot the arrow, giving him a maniacal smile as I practically bounce on my eager feet. Grabbing the intrusion in my thigh, I rip it out and toss it to the side. "You shouldn't have done that."

Their eyes widen before battle cries sound, all five charging in my direction. I duck as a sword aims for my neck, kicking the knees out of another, forcing his body into the path of the sword. He screams when it separates his torso and hot blood slaps my face.

I unsheathe a second blade, planting my feet to take the blow of a shoulder to my abdomen. The man slams me back against the wall, my legs wrapping around his waist to hold my body steady. It proves difficult, as the fabric of his thick pants does not soak in water properly, making them slick.

I cannot see his face, but his panting breaths graze my cheek as I bare my teeth to his ear. "All this trouble just to get between my legs?" He stiffens, gripping my hips hard enough to bruise. "Though I think you'll find I'm too expensive for you—because the price is your life...and I collect payment up front." Strangled noises abandon his throat when I shove my blade into the base of his spine and clench my jaw as I drag it up through as many vertebrae as I can manage before the three remaining men yank his body from me.

My feet are quick to catch me, and I throw my arms in the direction of their gurgling friend. "Oh, come on, boys! Can't a girl have a little fun? I was almost at the top!" I cackle, noticing for the first time red masks covering their faces.

The bulkier man looks to the others as they stalk closer. "Let's just go! She's dead, anyway!" They hesitate.

"Oh, I'm not the one dying here tonight," I purr, taking a single step forward, smiling sweetly. "But it's cute you think I'll allow you to live."

The man to my right swings, his arm blocked by mine as I tilt to kick the one to my left. I do not watch his back meet the ground, instead grabbing the wrist touching me and twisting sharply. He cries out, his shoulder following the movement. One moment he's whimpering in pain, and the next he wears his head backwards.

From my peripheral, the man I kicked scrambles to stand, slipping repeatedly. I spin and thrust my fist into the last assailant, rendering him unconscious. I'll deal with him later.

I tug on my psionic strand, intending to stop the attacker running down the alley. Nothing pulls.

I try my umbral strand. My brows furrow—no pull. I cannot grasp any strand.

The squeak of his boot grabs my focus once more. "Fuck," I mutter as I reach down to pull my blade from another's spine, twisting to fling it into the neck of the last one standing. He grunts, falling forward, and I frown as his skin slaps against the puddle.

Impressive, actually. He made it to the head of the alley before I got him. I almost allowed this pathetic excuse of a life to slip through my fingers.

Unacceptable.

I reach him, rolling my eyes when I hear his violent sobs. "Are you fucking kidding me?" I reach for his jacket and pull him back to his knees, stepping around his shivering body to crouch before him. "You're seriously going to cry during your last moments in this realm? *You* attacked *me*...that's fucking pitiful."

He attempts to hold back, his lip quivering from faltering breaths. Saliva begins foaming around his mouth, and my nose scrunches hard. I shake my head, waving a hand in his direction. "Actually, cry all you want. That's disgusting." His eyes begin to gloss over—I'm running out of time. "Who sent you?"

He focuses on something over my shoulder, forcing me to snap my fingers in his face to garner the attention I seek. "Who. Sent. You?" I demand, not kindly.

"He'll get what he wants. He always gets what he wants," he breathes, coughing blood from the movement.

"What the fuck does that mean? Who?" He slips before I finish asking, splashing into the puddle once more.

My fingers tap against each other as I look up, barely able to make out the shapes of the other six men. I stand, snatching my blade and marching to the unconscious one. I shove it through his chin, ignoring his last hissing breath when a speck of gold peeks from under his black, oversized jacked. My hands rip the buttons open, pausing when—even in the dark—the red and gold of the royal crest sears into my eyes.

I tug on my luminal strand, needing to confirm what my mind tells me I'm seeing. I still cannot tug on that, or any, strand. My fists clench to the point skin tears from the pressure of my nails.

There is only one reason I can't access my essence. One reason why my leg does not hurt in the slightest after being penetrated with an arrow.

I reach to dig my fingers into the wound where a thick, oily substance coats the tips. I hold them up, narrowing my eyes—there's no need for any light. I would recognize that deep blue from a realm away.

"Fuck me!" I slice the crest from the royal guard, pocketing the palm-sized fabric. I waste no time grabbing the arrow that pierced me and sprinting back to the castle.

I take stock of my body, cursing when I'm unable to tell if I'm cold because of the weather or the poison. I have maybe an hour before it infects me with permanent damage.

My stomach flutters. There is only one person I can go to this with...he holds all my other secrets. What's one more?

I reach the castle quickly, my vision beginning to blur at the edges. I pass several guards and staff who stare with their mouths agape—I'm certain I look terrifying, dripping with endless water and blood.

I enter the prince's hallway, Gavriel immediately pushing from the wall and blocking my path to the door I need.

"Move or meet the Angel," I demand, stopping in front of the version I think is the real him from the two standing before me.

"Fuck off. Thought I told you to stay away."

"Let me see him. Now." We study each other, and I am so close to shoving this arrow through his infuriating eyes.

"No."

"Gavriel, I swear to the fucking Angel." My shouting is certainly reaching other wings of the castle. Fuck if I care—I feel as though I've drunk several bottles of wine. A poison that makes you enjoy dying—at least the king had good taste. "You will let me see him right now."

"Are you fucking drunk? You can't even talk straight. You're absolutely not getting near him." I'm not confident I'll hit his face if I try, but that does not deter my attempt. I swing my fist and he catches it easily, to my utter confusion.

"What is going on, Gav?" A door swings open, the prince's eyes widening when he sees me. He rushes over, taking my hand from Gavriel's. "Ariella...are you okay? What happened?"

"Is—it's not my—mine," I stutter, scrunching my eyes closed at the intense wave of dizziness swimming through me.

"Are you drunk?" My eyes slowly snap open, meeting his concerned gaze.

I think I shake my head. "No—fuck, I'm dizzy," I giggle—*giggle*—and pull out the arrow I tucked under my arm. "Hallow. I don—don't have saida."

He pales. "By the Angel. Fuck. Gavriel, get Elowen." I murmur something about him being a good boy and listening. "You," he tugs me gently through an open door, "are coming with me. You'll kill me if I let anyone see you like this."

I laugh, groaning at the pain in my chest. "I'm will kill you any—way, dear prince," I sing, pressing a hand to my ribs.

"Stop talking, Ariella. Fucking Angel, your fingers are turning blue already. How long ago did this happen?" Who does he think he is to question me?

"Be—fore I came got here." He huffs a breath, pulling me down onto something soft.

I fall back to my elbows, sinking lightly into the fluffy material. Something is...is not right. I cannot ascertain what he says next, but the room shifts and I'm covered with what seems to be every blanket in the realm.

"No," I drag out the word on a whine, weakly attempting to push the inferno off. "So hot." Hands grab mine, their touch warm but comforting. And a reminder.

I'm dying.

"I know, angel. But I need to keep your body temperature up." I wince at a loud noise, followed by shouting. I attempt to tell them to turn the damn sun off, though my traitorous lungs are barely working.

"—must drink—the saida will neutralize—" A woman's voice.

My head is lifted as someone pleads with me to swallow the vile substance they pour into my mouth. I do just to get them to shut up, reaching for my blade when they don't. My hands do not listen.

But the lack of my body's response is not what alarms me.

Several voices and blurry figures surround me as they rip my pants off against my every protest before forcing more revolting shit down my throat.

"Caspian, calm do—next to her and hold—back to her room—"

"No. She stays with me." The prince's declaration replays over and over until there's nothing.

Chapter Eighteen

Caspian

Ariella's lips are slowly—too slowly—shifting back to their natural rosy pink. I roll her hands between mine, as I have been for three hours, willing them to warm enough that their blue hue fades. She's ceased shivering, though her skin feels too cold to be safe.

I *will* know who dared poison her with Harrow. They will pay deeply for this.

The tightness in my chest dissipates the heat when she shifts—I must remind myself of her progress. She's no longer wheezing, her color is returning, and she's not dead.

There is no other reason for my puffy face and worried, bleeding lips than I care more than I should. Flirting with the beautiful assassin is one thing...but the manner in which my heart immediately fell from my chest when she held up the poison-tipped arrow? How I was scolding Elowen for not bringing the saida tea quickly enough? The realization that I was trembling so hard I couldn't be certain whether it was her hands or mine that shook more? All of it was immensely out of character for me...innate reactions to watching her succumb to the poison.

This woman whom I barely know, but desperately want to.

There is so much she hides, though I have the distinct impression that no one has ever cared enough to find out exactly what.

Namely, her essence. To possess all three affinities...how long has she kept such a heavy secret to herself? The isolation from truthful relationships is lonely.

Something I intimately understand.

My hands squeeze hers—not a comfort for her, I realize. My eyes search her unwitting face; the delicate curve of her nose that connects to slightly parted lips. Dark lashes that oddly do not match her illustrious hair. From the moment I saw her in the guest training room, I've wanted to run my hands through the silken strands—much like the grasp she had on mine earlier. I chew on my lip.

She'd held onto me so confidently, molding my body to the exact position she desired. It is almost shameful how badly I want her to do it again.

My head turns at voices outside my door. Much to his blatant disagreement, I'd ordered Gavriel that *no one* is to enter, so the sounds eventually disappear. I allow myself to relax next to Ariella, fighting my heavy lids as I continue massaging her hands.

Warm skin brushes lightly over my lips, stirring my exhausted mind. I shift and groan at Gavriel to leave me alone. I'm not in the mood to train this morning; especially after the previous night's events.

An amused chuckle shakes my head. "I am not concerned with what you and Gavriel do in the evenings, but if you mistake me for that brute again, you will no longer have the appendages necessary to continue."

I jolt up, my eyes fully alert and scanning the bemused woman I'm...currently sprawled across. "Shit, I'm sorry—did I hurt you? How are you feeling?" I carefully push away from her abdomen, heat rushing my neck at the imprint of my head.

"Fine. Though I do not recall seeking out company last night...so how the fuck am I in your bed?" The heat spreads to my cheeks and her emerald eyes narrow threateningly.

"What's the last thing you remember?" Her shoulders drop as she crosses her arms, covering the taut nipples I absolutely did not notice before...

I drink in this version of her as she thinks. Her bright, mussed hair rests politely over an exposed shoulder; she purses her lips, wetting them with her tongue.

I should have chosen a less flattering shirt...only a few of the buttons are fastened, dangerously close to exposing the lines of her breasts.

"I left the guild. It started raining on my walk back to the castle, but it was interrupted—" Her eyes widen, and she shoves at the bedding, exposing her midriff and black panties. I swiftly avert my gaze, clearing the thickness in my throat. "The arrow. I was poisoned and I...I came to you?"

I nod, suppressing the satisfaction that I was the one she sought out for help. "You did. You were quite...contentious with Gavriel when he wouldn't allow you to see me."

"I see," she murmurs, lost in her thoughts once more. After a few silent minutes, she tilts her head and looks down. "And why am I dressed in this shirt—yours, I presume?"

I raise my palms as an uncomfortable object swirls around my stomach. "I swear I did not touch you." Her eyes flit to where I was indeed just touching her—I'm fucking this up. "That was not intentional...Elowen insisted on changing your clothes. By the time she treated you, your body temperature had cooled immensely. You were soaked from the rain, and it was worsening the effects of the Harrow, so Gavriel and I waited just outside while she dried and changed you."

I expect a fight, but she only nods and chews on her lip. Not even a bratty rebuttal? Why does it bother me so much to see her look so...sad? I suspect she's not aware of how vulnerable she appears.

"I need to know what happened," I blurt, my disloyal mind too desperate for an answer. Her eyes meet mine, lacking their usual hardness. She mercifully decides to explain the events and—by the Angel—I didn't think it was possible to be more attracted to someone.

I cringe at my internal distractions.

"Wait—" She pauses with her mouth open. "*Seven men*?" Her lip curls, and she blinks at me as if I just said the most daft thing she's ever heard. "How in the Aether did you best seven men...amidst being poisoned, no less?"

There she is.

Her features sharpen and she appears as though she's contemplating my death, unable to decide which method would be most efficient. I smile as I lean on a hand and wait.

"Okay," she states, shaking her head—I may be a little disappointed that she doesn't follow through. "It was your father's men that attacked me. Sentries." I wish I could claim that information surprised me...

"I suspected."

"And I don't fucking care if—" she halts, her eyes snapping to me as her brows furrow deeply. "You believe me?" Why wouldn't I? She has no reason to lie.

"Of course I do," I echo my thoughts, warring with my need to ensure he cannot attack her again, and upholding the duty I have to this family—regardless of their transgressions. "I will make sense of this."

"Fabulous," she mutters, swinging her legs off the bed to stand. Her hand darts to the mattress to steady herself when she rises, and I tense, prepared to aid her. Her face scrunches before she straightens and taps a finger on her barely exposed thigh. I'll need to obtain smaller shirts...that is far too long on her. "I'm leaving."

She spins and saunters to the door, looking exactly how I imagined she would leaving my bed. I manage to swallow the groan that appears in my throat.

"Wait—" She pauses, peering over her shoulder. "Wearing just that?" Her eyes trail down until she focuses on the minimally buttoned shirt.

Perhaps it's not long enough...

"Would you like it back before I leave?" Her tone is tantalizing as she reaches a hand up to playfully unlatch the highest button. I clear my throat, rubbing a hand over my heated neck.

"No," I blurt too quickly. Fuck, I really am pathetic... "I have bottoms you can wear—if you'd like."

She smirks, humming as she takes agonizingly slow, deliberate steps toward me. "I'm fine. Though I wouldn't wish to be caught stealing from the prince..." she trails off, another button popping open. If she undoes the final two, the Angel will have an unexpected visitor today.

"You can keep it." Please give it back.

"Are you sure?" she taunts lightly. One button left...the sound of my thudding heart nearly vibrates my entire body. She reaches the bed, lifting a knee to it.

This annoyingly irresistible woman holds my gaze, a mischievous glimmer filling her eyes. She pushes forward until she's sitting on her bent leg, while the other remains to the floor...just a fucking breath from my reach. The dryness in my mouth assaults my senses as I struggle to speak—or move.

"I'm sure." An utter lie.

Her answering smile confirms that she caught that slip of truth. I jolt when her heated fingers graze my cheek, my eyes flitting to hers. "You don't sound so sure..." I'm certain the evidence of her effect on me is filling the space between us, though I do not dare look away from her scrutinizing gaze. She barely leans forward, her lips a moment from mine.

This must be what it feels like to meet the Angel.

"Do I make you nervous, Caspian?" Her alluring whisper coils around my dick—it's too difficult to breathe.

"Yes, though not because of any reason you're used to." A shadow passes through her eyes before her head tilts.

"Why? I could snap your neck before your next breath."

"That's exactly why...you *could*, but you haven't. Yet. And why is *that*, angel?" My fingers reach to twirl a piece of hair that hangs between us. "I think I make you just as nervous. You're unsure of how to handle the truth that I wish to *bathe* in every depraved part of you—or the extent in which I seek out your blade as I do my next breath.

"I'm an anomaly to you...but I think you like that, Ariella—don't you? You secretly relish how I've seen *every* part of you, and instead of deterring me, it makes me want you more."

Her breath no longer warms my skin as we examine each other. The anticipation between our bodies nearly breaks me, but she sits back before I have the courage to push this further.

She peers down at the one button still holding the shirt together and smiles playfully. "Actually, I think I'll keep this." She makes for the door again, grabbing her boots and torn clothes from a chair before turning the handle.

She's partially through the doorway when she looks back, her brows furrowed deeply. I wait, thoroughly interested in whatever could make the Silver Wraith speechless.

Her throat clears as her eyes flit to my desk before focusing on me. "Thank you." A genuine smile tugs at my lips, and I nod before she closes the door behind her. She and Gavriel share words before she's gone—walking through the castle...wearing only my shirt.

I allow myself to drop and breathe in the warm, sultry scent embedded into my sheets. No one will clean these until I say otherwise...

Before I get lost in her memory, I roll from the bed and swap my shirt for a less wrinkled one, running a hand through my hair as I walk into the hallway. I cannot focus on how I look at the moment—I need answers.

"You look like shit," Gavriel mutters as I close my door. My mouth opens with an immediate retort, but the words halt when I see the dark circles under my friend's eyes. He gives so much of himself without complaint, so the least I can do is not tease him for it.

"Take the day and rest. I need to go speak with Varrick, but there are no other pressing matters that require your attendance." I nod to his room down the hall and slap him on the shoulder before stalking in the opposite direction.

Varrick should be in his study, which is conveniently located at the center of the castle next to the throne room. He may be my father's political advisor, but there isn't a single thing that happens in these walls that he doesn't know about. The chance of him not knowing why royal sentries attacked and fucking poisoned Ariella...

But I cannot just march in there and accuse him or my father of anything. No, because if either of them are to blame and they suspect I'm suspicious of them, I'm not sure what they'll do. I don't know just how far Varrick's opinions influence my father's decisions, but the man has never truly liked me, so it's not a risk I'm willing to take. Especially when I have Ariella to worry about.

Should I go to my mother first? She and my father do not have the greatest relationship, though he is still her king. She defies him in her own ways, but it's only ever been petty things like the color of her gowns or her attendance at certain events. She has never spoken ill of him, nor has she fought against any of his decisions. She may be queen, but my father has never seen her as his equal—one of the many things I wish to change upon my claim of the throne.

I shake my head and rub a hand over the back of my neck. As much as I'd like to confide in her, I don't know if I can completely trust her not to tell the king everything. I know she loves Vespera and me, but that love has always warred with her duty as queen. It would be best if I didn't mention this to her, if only to spare her from having to choose between me and the king. And Vespera is too young to be forced into dealing with any of this...

It seems Ariella and Gavriel are the only two I can trust.

I snort—what an ironic fucking statement. The prince who can only turn to a royal guard and a famous assassin.

I should never trust her. I should hate her for what she does, what she is...and yet, I don't. I can't seem to explain these feelings even to myself, but the moment I saw her for the first time, I knew she'd mean something different to me than anyone else. I've yet to discover exactly what that is, but—

I jolt when someone clears their throat, my head snapping to the left, where Gavriel walks tall next to me. "I thought I told you to go rest." He mutters something under his breath before focusing on me.

"I will not allow you to visit your father's advisor alone—I trust you with *her* more than I do Varrick."

"What do you think he's going to do, Gav? We've known him for years...he may be a little strange, but he wouldn't dare harm me," I say quietly, nodding to a group of people that we pass. We're in the main part of the castle now, where many ears listen for any amount of information they could use to their benefit. Gavriel doesn't respond, just as wary as I am to speak around others.

I step quickly around three women, muttering a kind hello when they call for me, and knock on Varrick's door before one of them insists on a moment of my time. I do not wish to entertain them any longer. A muffled call to come in sounds, and I give Gavriel a pointed look before stepping into the study and closing the door behind me. A large, wooden desk is positioned to the left, resting on top of a deep green rug—I've always thought that was an interesting choice, especially as it clashes with the reds and golds of the tiles and walls. Though maybe he finds comfort in the color. The paintings lining the walls, each of different types of forests, speak to his love of the greens in nature.

But it's the painting behind him that tugs at my attention each time I visit. The background a mix of blues, pinks, and purples that suggest either the start or end to a day. Instead of a landscape, however, the scene is painted in the sky, where there are miles of clouds so realistic I feel as though I could touch them. On the clouds—not above—is a forest made of trees that match the colors of the sky. Most have pale pink leaves with white petals that fall from their burgundy branches. There are several crimson trees in the mix, their existence appearing like seeping blood.

I squint my eyes, noticing...noticing something I've not recognized before. The red trees are not that at all—no, they're the same as the rest, where the pink hues peek through the crimson in a few places. The red does flow like blood, though it seems to soak into the bark rather than fall from it, as if it's feeding the tree.

"Just one moment," Varrick calls, waving a hand as he continues writing whatever is so important he cannot be bothered to greet his prince properly.

Not that he does, regardless.

"Expecting someone else?" His head snaps up, eyes widening momentarily before he stands and shoves several papers together until they're folded over his current work.

"Well, I was certainly not expecting you, Caspian. What brings you here?" I have to drag my eyes from where his hands rest almost protectively in front of something. His lengthy, black hair rests in a knot at the top of his head, while he wears clothes that are far more disheveled than mine.

Deep breath. "I wanted to speak with you about the attack last night," I say carefully, watching for a flicker of *anything* in his features that would confirm what I wish wasn't true.

He blinks, forehead creasing as he crosses his arms. "Attack?" I almost laugh.

"Yes, it seems one of the competitors was attacked outside the castle grounds."

A shrug. "You know how brutish those people are—honestly, I'm shocked they haven't all killed each other off yet." It's a struggle to keep my features relaxed enough; he's not going to give anything away.

"It was an attack by royal sentries, not another competitor," I mutter distastefully, sliding the arrow Ariella brought from under my jacket. At least I had the foresight to wrap it, instead of coating my clothes in Hallow. He rears back when I toss it to his desk, studying it for only a moment before his deep-set eyes meet mine once more.

"Where did you get this?"

Something prickles under my skin, telling me to lie. Or at least withhold that Ariella brought it to me. "It doesn't matter—what's important is that it is an arrow from our guard and it is laced in Hallow. I want to know why the fuck one of the competitors is being targeted." Fuck, I need to control my rage; I cannot allow him to see what she means to me.

Of course he doesn't miss the slip.

"Ah, you mean the wraith? She was the one attacked with this arrow?" I nod, not trusting my words just yet. "Well, I am afraid I do not know why she was attacked, however I cannot say I am either surprised or disappointed." A barely perceptible smirk appears before he masks it.

"And the second trial? You've no clue how she was sent to steal from a griffin, of all things?"

He tilts his head, eyes narrowing. "What are you suggesting, prince?" A reminder of the lack of power I hold compared to the king.

I walk forward, pocketing my hands. "I do not believe I've suggested anything," I drawl, already cursing myself for what I'm about to say. "Though I coordinated every part of that trial, and aside from me, you are the only other one with access to my design office. Or have you forgotten?" His jaw clenches, though he shows no other sign of his anger.

"Of course I haven't. But I'm uncertain what these attacks on the wraith have to do with me?"

"They have everything to do with you, Varrick! Is it not your job to protect my father?" He moves to speak, but I continue. "There is someone in this castle who was capable of tampering significantly with the second trial and organizing an attack by royal sentries who were given no such orders to fulfill. Why is this not a priority of yours?"

"Of course it is—I take such threats very seriously, though only in regards to the crown. I do not care that the assassin was targeted, though maybe next time they'll actually succeed in killing her. Angel knows we'd be better with her—" I slam my palms against his desk before he can continue.

"Finish that sentence or speak of her again, and I won't care who you are to my father." There goes every plan I walked in here with, though the heat coursing through my body couldn't care less. I turn and walk out of the office, ignoring his triumphant stare.

Gavriel follows me back to my room, neither of us daring to speak until my door slams closed. He listens as I tell him of the conversation with Varrick, his brows scrunching further with each word.

He studies me for several moments after I'm done recounting my stupidity. "You need to stay away from her."

"Excuse me?" I surely did not hear that right...

"We will keep looking into whatever the fuck is going on, but you don't need to be near her to do it," he says harshly, holding his hands up to stop my retort. "Whoever is trying to kill her will likely keep trying, no? If you are placing yourself in her path, you're the one who will end up hurt or dead. I can't let that happen."

The muscles along my jaw ache from the tension I've put on them over the last day, but I don't feel the pain as I clench my teeth together so hard I'm certain they'll crack. I want to tell Gavriel to fuck off. Tell him that he knows nothing of her, and he has no right to speak to me like I'm some ignorant child. Of course I fucking know who she is and the risks of wanting her. I do not need him, of all people, treating me as if I'm so blinded by desire that I cannot separate her from everything else.

I want to spit all of it and more at him, but the tightness in my throat softens the red haze in my head—he doesn't deserve such obscenities when his demands come from a place of fear.

I scoff, running a hand through my hair. If only I was scared for the same reasons.

Chapter Nineteen

Ariella

If this is Ally's personality at the guild in Meridian, I fully understand why they sent her to the competition instead of another, better trained student. It is unfathomable to me how it is possible for one person to be so irritating. I'd choose a day with Isolde before this...at least she doesn't talk *as* much.

"Oh! And then she jumped from the bow—*jumped*! As if those creatures were not swimming below us!"

"Wow...that's the most frightening thing *you've* ever done?" I bite my cheek at Isaiah's question; he's certainly becoming as annoyed with her as I am. Fuck if I'll say anything, though; he wanted her around, he can tell her to leave.

"Well, yes," she mutters uncomfortably. "I nearly fell unconscious right there!"

I shove her voice from my mind, focusing instead on the large group of women ahead of us. Each donning a different colored dress, all pastel. The bright colors wash out the royal gold and reds nicely—

"And he said hello as he passed!" One of the women squeals, the others huddling closer and giggling. My fingers flex. "Angel, he is the most kind and handsome prince...and to have his attention on *me*?" She sighs deeply, sweeping dark hair over her shoulder. It is moments like these that I am thankful for the amount of restraint I possess...I doubt the king would allow me to walk away after shoving my blade into her skull, which would inadvertently affect Isaiah.

The thrumming in my chest demands more than an excuse, but I cannot give into it.

"Ms. Mistaire." The three of us pause, my abdomen clenching at the king's voice.

I cross my feet and spin, clasping my hands at my back and raising a brow to Thalion as he saunters in my direction. He stops just ahead of me, his assessing gaze heating the blood rushing through my veins.

Fully ignoring Isaiah and Ally as they bow and mutter, *"Your Majesty,"* like good little minions, his icy eyes find mine. "I wondered if I might have a word." Not a request—an order.

I deign him no response, glaring as he smirks and turns to walk in the opposite direction. I nod to Is before following the king, keeping an adequate distance between us. I've an idea of what he wishes to discuss, though I still do not trust he wouldn't ambush me—but only the hint of dusty surfaces greets me as we turn several corners before he pulls a key from his crimson jacket.

He pushes open the door, turning to gesture me inside first. When I refuse to move, he scoffs as if I'm a disobedient child and disappears through the doorway. I follow cautiously, looking down each direction of this poorly lit hallway before disregarding every instinct and walking into the room.

My face remains impassive as I take in the space, though my heart thuds heavily against the walls of my chest. Painting after painting line the walls, the colors less vibrant the older they are. Dates under each appear as far as two hundred years ago, though I'm certain there are many more that I do not see...the room is a hallway in its own right. Crowns displaying various designs of ruby and gold sit upon pedestals, under what I assume is the respective painting of their owner.

Further down, worn armor stands proudly against a large tapestry of the royal crest. The golden background, with a standing griffin stitched in black fabric, outlined in red, serves as a reminder.

It is the same crest I gave to Caspian after his father's men attacked me. The entire reason I am here. To kill this bastard's son and watch his kingship burn.

I face the monster himself, who regards me with a serpentine smile while his hands rest inside large pockets. His broad torso blocks the path to the now-closed door, though I refuse to feel caged in. He is but one weak man standing in front of the killer I've created just for him.

Curious that he feels safe enough to lock himself in a room with me...

"Ah, well, I will not waste time with formalities." He sucks on his teeth as I remain still. "I have a request for you, wraith."

He chuckles when I manage to look even more bored, tilting his head. The way his eyes drink in the lines of my body is nauseating.

"I can see why my son is so smitten with you." That...is not what I expected him to say. The hairs along my neck rise at the bite of his words. "Truthfully, you are stunning. However, as much as Caspian wishes to fuck you," he spits, shaking his head as if the very idea disgusts him to his core. "I will not allow it."

I smile and take one step, the movement predatory. "Is that so?"

He straightens his chin, an attempt to feel as tall as he looks. "He will tire of you the moment he gets what he wants—that is just how young men are. But he will not be getting what he wants. You will deny his every advance." He waves a hand at nothing. "Break a limb, if you must; I do not give a fuck. But you will not touch him." Fuck's sake...did he and Gavriel sit down and discuss ways to keep me from the prince?

"Is that why you're trying to have me killed? Because you do not wish me near him?" Humor dances in those calculating eyes as he strolls through the room.

"No, though that is a benefit I'd considered."

I hum, sighing deeply as I tap my finger on a blade. The king's eyes focus on the movement as he walks; he's smart to not look away from me. "While I've quite enjoyed your *assassination* attempts, you'll need the entirety of your pathetically trained military to have a mere chance of killing me." He chuckles, nodding as his fingers caress the darkening gold of a used crown.

"So I've noticed. Which is the reason I've brought you here. Whether you are dead or not truly is unimportant to my objectives. However you choose to live your final days means nothing to me, as long as we are clear that you keep your blood-stained hands from my son." He turns to cross the room where the large tapestry rests.

I should not entertain more conversation, but the words fall from my mouth, anyway. "And why does it matter *so much* to you if I fuck him? As you say, he will tire of me the moment he leaves my bed."

He shakes a finger, malicious eyes finding mine for a moment. "That is precisely why it matters." He studies the tapestry longingly as an agonizingly silent minute passes. "If I may speak so candidly...I know his past affairs were but a night of fun, though he is different with you. I have a feeling he will become more attached upon having you.

"If you were any lady of status, I would not bother—but we both know that is not what you are." *What*, not *who*.

My jaw clenches, and I blink at the ache behind my eyes. "Of course...the woman you hire to kill your people for you is not good enough for your son. Completely logical thinking, I must admit."

He chuckles, facing me. The buttons along his silky gold top stretch as he breathes deeply. "Do you know why I brought you here, Ariella?"

"I'm sure you'll enlighten me." He smiles warmly at the paintings he gestures to.

"This is the Blackwood lineage, as you've certainly surmised. You see, these are the elite of the Eldorian Kingdom—the kings and queens that have ruled these lands for thousands of years. Then, of course, there are the noble houses that walk these halls with an unwarranted sense of superiority. Followed by the greater essence citizens who live closest to the castle grounds." He halts a foot away, a queasy feeling settling in my stomach.

"Then, as you know, there are the lesser essence citizens that reside in the outermost parts of Valoria. But you see, Ms. Mistaire, the lowest tier of citizenship lies within the guilds." It is an immense struggle to remain still when his smirk turns sinister. "Those who have no families. No homes. Who are only worth their meager skills with a blade.

"That is you, Ariella. You are nothing. You are not suitable for even my son's bed, because he belongs here...and you are not even worth a thought."

My gaze hardens, a clear, nefarious threat settling in my eyes. "Not worth a thought, yet I'm the one you request when you hire the guild. You arranged for me to face a griffin and sent several soldiers to kill me when that plan failed. You even had me impregnated with Hallow...that is quite the difficult poison to obtain...

"Then you personally escort me here, to the sacred memories of your family lineage—the *royal* family lineage—just to tell me not to fuck your son. Truthfully, Your Majesty, you seem to be confusing my worth for someone who *isn't* the subject of your every thought." He sneers, his fists clenching until the knuckles lose their color. I spin and walk to the door, the king expressing last words just as I turn into the hallway.

"Do heed my warning, Ariella."

Chapter Twenty

Ariella

It seems the closer I am to my goal, the less tolerance I have for such mundane activities. I do not wish to sit upon the browning grass as I eat and listen to pointless conversation.

And yet, here I am.

Rather than claiming the prince's—or king's—life, I've been dragged into talk of the upcoming ball. One in which I would never willingly attend—but that's the thing...I do not have a choice. The collar around my neck ensures my attendance *and* finest behavior.

Too many times have I considered using the ball as my final stage; delighting in the horrified faces of those in attendance as they watched me slide my blade across their king's throat. I've never enjoyed—or tolerated—an audience during my assignments, but this is different. It's the very moment I have trained for the last twenty years...the sole objective my life has revolved around, and the reason I am the best killer in this realm.

But I cannot follow-through yet.

My eyes flit to Isaiah as he tosses his head back to laugh at whatever Ally said. She bites her cheek and watches his movements with pure adoration in her gaze.

It's possible I've been too harsh in my judgments of her. My opinions and desires mean little when I know my life has a quickly approaching expiration. He is the only one of us who will live, and if he wishes to spend the remainder of this competition with Ally, it is certainly not my place to tell him otherwise.

Even those thoughts are not enough to assuage the roaring hunger inside me. I want to scream at them—shake them until they grasp that dresses and dance partners are among the most trivial matters to worry over.

They still would not understand, however. I've never even whispered my plans for the royal family...losing my grasp on the ultimate goal will only tarnish all that I worked for.

So here I sit—under a sweltering sun as I pretend to care about the upcoming ball.

"Ariella?" I suck in a breath, focusing on the two sets of eyes waiting for my answer to something I didn't hear.

"What?" My voice is clipped, but I do not feel like dealing with this topic any longer. Or anything else today.

Ally's eyes flit to Isaiah before she repeats herself. "I was wondering what you plan to wear?" I lift one of the hands I am leaning back on, gesturing to the only clothes I ever wear.

They're practical—though I'll admit they are of little use against the heat.

"You wacky woman," Is mutters, chuckling under his breath. "You cannot expect the king to allow such attire at the *ball*."

"You seem to be under the impression that I fucking care what Thalion will allow." We study each other, a darkness passing through his eyes. I know what his instincts demand him to say—to implore me to just follow the king's orders, because he'll kill me otherwise.

Then his rationale approaches, where he once more realizes that we will both not survive this, anyway, so it is pointless for him to argue. He chuffs, rolling his neck back; I salute his dismissal and slice another piece of apple with my blade, sighing when the tangy juices coat my tongue.

"Well, I personally think you should wear a dress...oh!" She waves her hands, lurching upright. "You would look so pretty in one that had silver beads woven into the fabric! Actually, in Meridian there's a dress shop that is inspired by the Ebelan ocean! Many of the dresses are a deep blue or green, but some are even orange, like the sunsets that reflect off the water. Each dress is made of a silken fabric and stitched in a way that it looks like waves swimming over your skin. And the owner's specialty is placing small diamonds throughout, so when the wearer moves around, the light catches the jewels in such a way that their body appears just like the sparkling waters beyond the coast!"

My lips thin as I nod absently. "That all sounds brilliant, though I will not be buying anything of the sort."

Silence follows, prompting my eyes to find Ally's. She chews on her thumb, deep creases formed next to her eyes. Fuck's sake. "What?" I bark, earning a glare from Isaiah.

"It's just..." she hesitates, mouthing something silently to herself. "Well...don't you want to look nice for the prince?" Is doubles over in a coughing fit, his eyes sparkling when they meet mine.

His head shakes frantically as he waves a hand at Ally. "I am not helping you with that one." Another cough before he focuses on his food.

"Why in the Aether would I wish to look like anything *for the prince*?"

I glare into her eyes, nearly at the end of my patience when she begins sputtering. "Um—I just thought...you know...I thought you two had something going on?"

"Something going on." Not a question, though my tone is cruel enough to warrant an answer.

She looks to Isaiah for help, who pointedly ignores her—the rejection is oddly gratifying. "You can't be serious, Ariella?" she exclaims breathlessly. I raise a brow and remain very still. "I see the way you two look at each other..."

My jaw clenches; either she's too perceptive, or I am not avoiding him enough. "And how is it you think I look at him?"

Her mouth forms an 'o' before she wets her lips, her throat bobbing. "Well, it's how he looks at you, really...it's sweet. His eyes find you the moment you enter a room, and it's like he can't blink until you're out of sight. His focus on you is so intense it makes *me* blush!" She sighs dramatically. "I wish someone would look at me that way..."

So she is too perceptive, *and* I'm not avoiding him enough.

That must be what the king has seen—enough to prompt him to threaten me face-to-face. I had wanted Caspian's attention originally, but I did not plan for his brand of infatuation. It's fucking with my head.

"What do you guys think the third trial will be?" Ally's quiet voice interrupts my silent seething. "There's still more than a dozen of us, so I'm sure they're planning something big."

"Hopefully nothing with a damn griffin," Is mutters, pushing to his feet when I do.

"You're bleeding." My eyes slide to Ally at the prince's unwanted voice, who is practically beaming with a not-so-casual *"I told you so."* She grabs

Isaiah's arm and violently drags him toward the city, chattering about her need to find a dress immediately. He peers over his shoulder and pins me with a pleading look. I shrug and wave sweetly, chuckling when he slides a finger across his throat before relenting to Ally's mission.

A force grips my wrist and tugs, my head snapping to the right just as the prince's mouth wraps around my finger.

The unrelenting confidence this man possesses...

It's a nauseating struggle to remain impassive as I raise my brows—another twenty years of training could not have prepared me for this moment.

My eyes narrow as he sucks, swirling his tongue around thoroughly. My abdomen clenches when his teeth graze the sensitive skin on my fingertip as he pulls it out. He smiles wickedly at whatever he sees when scorching eyes meet mine. The air shifts as he rises to his full height, examining my finger closely.

My lungs burn—a reminder that I need to breathe.

When he's satisfied, he drops our hands, both of his still wrapped around mine. "That's better," he teases, his smirk one of a prince who has never been told no.

"I don't recall granting you permission to touch me." Ignoring how breathless I sound, I attempt to draw my hand back. He doesn't allow it.

The air between us thins as his feet take one step—he chuckles darkly, pressing our coiled hands into his stomach as he leans forward.

"Trust me, I am painfully aware...because if you had," he whispers, his eyes trapping me. I couldn't move if I wanted to—do I want to? "We'd already be in my room. No one would see us for *days.*"

I swallow thickly around a laugh, allowing my lips to curl slightly though they beg for far more give. "You truly think so highly of yourself." His thumbs stroke my palm as lavender and something I cannot place settles over me.

"It's difficult not to when *the* Ariella Mistaire looks at me the way you do." The fantasy—whatever this is—shrivels into nothing and exposes the reality I lost focus of. I straighten and snatch my hand back, the prince finally letting go.

"What are you doing here?"

His lips purse, eyes searching mine before he shakes his head. "Ouch," he mutters, and I have the sense that I wasn't meant to hear it. "Well, I was hopi—"

"Silver Wraith, how wonderful to see you again!" Bastian saunters over to where the prince and I stand too close. I step back, tilting my head toward the unwelcome visitor.

He wears cream, tailored pants that button around a muddled shirt; it's as if he lazily tucked a few parts in and donned a navy vest before leaving the castle. His charming smile appears strained as he waits for me to speak.

"Is it?" He nods, clasping his hands behind his back.

"Her name is Ariella," Caspian grits out, his tongue expertly curving around the final word.

Bastian's eyes widen as he licks his lips. "Right—my apologies, Ariella. I meant no offense."

I hum, crossing my arms. "Then what *did* you mean?" He shifts, clearing his throat. The sun's light brightens momentarily, highlighting his lingering eyes.

"Actually, I had come here to ask you something." I blink. "Yes, well...if I may speak with you privately?" His gaze flits to the prince, though his high-pitched tone tells me everything I need to know—Caspian will not like what his cousin wishes to say.

Perfect.

"He stays, or I leave. Ask your question." The prince smirks, deciding I've kept him here for a very different reason.

Bastian smiles politely, bowing his head. "As you wish. I was hoping you'd allow me to accompany you to the ball."

"What?" the prince and I speak in unison.

I study the sweating man before me, though it takes not one heartbeat before an idea invades my mind.

"Of course she wouldn't go—"

"Yes," I interrupt Caspian, his head snapping toward me.

"You can't be serious?"

I face him fully and narrow my eyes. "You'd accuse me of lying?" He rears back, scoffing loudly.

"Of course not...but you truly wish for this?" His words say one thing, though his eyes maintain a different story—feelings that are not mine to care for.

"I belong to no one, prince. You'd do well to remember that." I turn on my heel and stalk away from the dramas of men, directing my stride to the castle.

The sun sinks into my exposed skin, succeeding in overheating every part of me. I did not desire to attend this pathetic ball, though I suppose Bastian has given me an opportunity...this is what I needed to effectively push Caspian away.

So why does my stomach hurt?

A finger taps against my blade restlessly, the click of my nail providing something to focus on.

"Damn—now I know how you've stayed alive for so long." I halt at the arrogant voice, willing the Angel to grant me even the semblance of patience, lest I drastically decrease the number of living contestants today.

A calm facade slides over my features as I pivot to Sivara's smirking face. Thalia looms just behind her, arms crossed as she feigns a kind of superiority she'll never truly experience.

"I mean, I thought it was curious how much time you and the prince spend together...but now his cousin, too?" she taunts, gesturing to the two men who stand several feet away, watching our interaction closely. From my peripheral, Caspian's hesitance at intervening begs me to fling my blade at him. "You must know how to use your tongue well, because it's certainly not your personality that has them falling all over you." I smile malignantly and draw closer to her, studying her upturned eyes.

"Would you like to find out just how well I use my tongue, Sivara?" The tops of her cheeks redden, and her feet shift as her eyes barely dart to her companion.

"Why the fuck would I want to know that?"

I shrug. "I just assumed so, considering how often you talk about me. So if that's not what you want, then why do you care so much about who I'm fucking?"

"Because you're getting advantages that the rest of us aren't!" I burst out laughing, unsheathing a blade and pointing it at Caspian and Bastian before I spin it through my fingers.

"Look at them..." She does, her forehead creasing. "Do they truly look as if either of them could provide me with any sensible benefit?"

"We can hear you..." My attention slides to the prince's cousin as he winces, running a hand through his styled hair uneasily.

"You were meant to," I state coldly, focusing on Sivara again. "If you wish to bring him to your bed, I won't stop you. The prince's cousin is an idiot, but maybe he could be useful for something." I wink before stalking away.

The king...the ball...Isaiah...the prince...my head throbs.

Chapter Twenty-One

Ariella

Isaiah bangs against the door for the fourth time. "Come on, Ari…we have to be there. I'm sure you look just fine."

Says the man who doesn't have to wear a dress.

Also says the man who isn't obligated to dance with the prince's cousin.

"I know I look fine," I retort, swinging open my door. Isaiah leans against the frame, lifting his head when I exit. "I just do not want to go…I'd rather march up the mountain in this outfit and face the griffin again."

I pull the door closed with a hand behind me, tugging on my umbral strand to ward it discreetly.

A wasted effort because Isaiah would not have noticed, even if I'd announced it. He stands frozen, mouth agape as his feet become rooted to the bright tile on the floor. I glance down, grimacing at my choice of dress…I'd convinced myself that it would infuriate Caspian the most, though I now fear it may garner the opposite reaction.

To the amusement of the shop owner yesterday, I'd chosen a floor-length, black dress with slits along the sides that reach my waist. Each step highlights my hips down to the silver heels I've donned, along with a color-matching jeweled belt cinched at my waist—it rests just below the slit between my breasts, leaving most of my skin exposed.

And the best feature? The third slit that divides the fabric curving down my back...the top of it ends just a breath away from fully exposing me.

"You're a dream." My eyes flick to Isaiah's as he slides his hands into the pockets of his suit pants and tilts his head. "Though I recall you mentioning your aversion to the prince's attention..." His suggestive eyes narrow as a smile trails his lips.

I step forward with my left leg, fully exhibiting the blade attached to it. "What are you suggesting, Is?" He barks a laugh as he raises his hands placatingly.

"Absolutely nothing...are you ready?" He holds out an arm—one in which I would refuse any other day. But I smile genuinely as my hand wraps around the hard muscle, my fingers immediately tapping against his smooth maroon jacket.

"Are you still *accompanying* the royal cousin?"

"Unfortunately." He chuckles.

"I know you don't want to hear it, but I recognize how difficult this will be for you; so if you need saving, I'll be there." He's right, I did not wish to hear that.

But I mutter a barely perceptible thank you just as Ally turns a corner, creases etched deeply throughout her face.

"There you are! I swear I've run this entire castle twice looking for you!" Isaiah stiffens, and his response is but a muted sound as my gaze finds the ballroom entrance.

It's pathetic how tense I am.

I refocus on Ally when she squeals, covering her face with both hands. "By the Angel! Ariella, you look so beautiful! I cannot believe you wore a dress..." I nod.

The tulle of her gown sways with each movement, and she tosses her sleek, black hair over a shoulder as she reaches for Isaiah's other arm. He smiles brightly when she settles on his right, straightening his back dramatically.

"It seems I am the luckiest man in the castle tonight to have the two most beautiful women escorting me to a royal ball." Ally giggles as my head shakes.

The click of my heels is deafening as we step up to the entrance, a royal guard stationed on each side. They do not address us as we approach, though I *feel* their eyes on me all the same. Their faces lurk behind the same crimson masks that made a feeble attempt at my life; strange as I've not seen them worn in the castle before.

Their uncanny features raise the hairs along my neck—a clear message. A warning.

My eyes widen as we step into the ballroom, my senses assaulted by the opulence of the scene before me. The walls are adorned with luxurious red velvet drapes that cascade down to the polished tile floors. Every surface shimmers with golden accents—from intricate carvings on the ceiling to the embellished frames of mirrors that line the open wall—illuminated further by the crystal chandeliers that hang boldly over the guests.

The air is thick with vases of fresh flowers and overused perfumes. The room is so large that I can just barely make out the musicians at the back, next to the throne, but their symphony envelopes the space as if they were next to me. The violin's thoughtful melody overpowers the other instruments, as if they are just meant for support.

Hundreds of people mingle and dance throughout the space, laughing and drinking with no intensity to their gazes. As if the only thing in their life they must worry about is how drunk they can become. Foolish are the ignorant.

“Don’t look now,” Isaiah mutters in my ear; well above a whisper, lest I miss his every word. “But I believe the prince spotted you the moment you walked in. It appears he’s prematurely ended a conversation with the Lumarnian nobles to walk over here.”

My eyes threaten to find Caspian regardless of my friend's instruction. “Is that so?” He hums. “And how would you happen to know all of this?”

The only person in either realm who could live after grabbing my shoulders so freely is very fortunate I’m in a forgiving mood. “Must I spell it out for you, Ari?” I raise a brow at my best friend, and he groans as his hands squeeze. “Fuck, sometimes I just want to wring your neck.” He emphasizes his words with a light tug on my collar.

I lift a shoulder, smirking. “Try it, and see what happens.”

A toothy smile. “Listen—that man clearly adores you, and he is certainly not afraid to show it. Maybe...” His face scrunches as he drops his hands from me. “I don’t know, Ari, maybe give him a chance?”

“I do not give chances.”

“Yeah?” I nod before he gestures to the space between us. “Then what’s this? Why are you my best friend?”

A playful smile burns my cheeks as I force it down. “Charity.” He bellows a laugh, catching the attention of a few guests. They look us over before returning to their conversations.

“Angel, I can’t fucking stand you sometimes,” he remarks, attempting to sound serious, though it’s half-hearted at best.

Fingers tap against my blade, snugly resting against my thigh in a pliable, black sheath. My stomach flutters when lavender encases my senses, a heartbeat before the prince enters my peripheral.

"Prince Caspian," Isaiah bows his head, snatching Ally's hand. "A pleasure to see you again—Ally and I were just headed for a dance, so enjoy your night."

"We were?" Fuck's sake, I'd no idea it was possible to be so dense.

The prince chuckles, nodding as his hands descend into his pockets. "You as well." He faces me fully, not bothering to hide his meticulous perusal of my body. His jaw clenches.

"Something to say, prince?"

Nodding, he swipes a thumb over his lip. "You are breathtaking...but I'd make a liar of myself if I claimed I wasn't infuriated that everyone here will see you like this."

My eyes widen perceptibly—the audacity. "Excuse me? You'd have me change because I'm showing more skin than the court prefers?" He chews on his lips as he moves one step closer.

"No, I wouldn't have you change. Because if I'd known this is what you were wearing, you would not have left your room with it in the first place." He's deadly serious.

"Such brave words from the same prince who has gotten his ass kicked multiple times by me."

A shrug and a haughty smile. "And I'd take a thousand more just to be the only one that saw how beautiful you look tonight." Those silver eyes blaze with the sincerity of his confession.

What is it about him that roots itself under my skin and shifts every resolve?

I flex my fingers—when was the last time I released essence?

"Why do you do that?" My eyes snap to his. He studies me.

"Do what?" I know what he'll say, but I question it regardless.

"Shut down..." He reaches for a strand of my hair. I let him. "Every time I compliment you, or tell you how I feel, it's like you become this entirely new, unfeeling person."

"Don't compliment me, then." He scoffs, dropping my hair. I keep allowing him too close...

"Dance with me." Not a question—a request. For me to give in to whatever the fuck is happening between us. He offers a hand, failing to notice the amount of people watching our interaction.

An awareness settles in my throat, and my gaze flicks left to where the king sits on his throne. I cannot see his eyes from such a distance, but I feel him watching me. Watching Caspian.

"I'm supposed to be accompanied by your cousin, if you remember."

"That is not something I will ever forget—but he won't show until much later. Probably already drunk, if his past escapades are of any indication."

I look to Thalion again, and whether it's to defy his orders or appease the fluttering under my skin, I cannot be sure...

I set my hand in the prince's and lead us to the center of the ballroom. Guests scuttle from our path, creating a wide space under a chandelier. I spin, a fragment of my dress curling around Caspian's leg before slipping back to mine. He smiles coyly as I secure my open hand over his shoulder.

This is a performance. For them. The prince and the assassin—dancing for the entire kingdom's witness.

But it is also for us...a production long overdue. The prince —caught in a deadly game that has succeeded in blurring the line I created between revenge and desire.

My fingers find the lapels of his vest as we begin our movement. Our feet find a steady rhythm, weaving together skillfully. We spin and my eyes catch on Isaiah, who leans against the wall with a drink and pins me with a look that certainly says, *"I was right."*

He'll pay for that later.

The assortment of perfume is heavier here, mixed with the aroma of lingering sweat. It's not unpleasant, though I'm certain that is due to the prince's scent masking a majority of it.

"Tell me something about you," the prince insists, my abdomen clenching at the words.

"Like?" The hand on my waist presses in until our clothes brush, and sweat begins to bead against my neck.

His eyes remain connected to mine, as if there is nothing else in this room for him to see. "Something no one else knows."

"I'd argue that you already know more about me than any other living person." His brows dip. If he wishes to know the meaning of my words, he doesn't ask. Instead, he watches me with an unimpressed look, and I realize I *want* to tell him something no one else knows.

"My favorite color is purple—not bright purple, but the soft kind."

"Like lavender?" he whispers, his lips molding the word perfectly.

"Yes."

He pauses our dance as his fingers trail lightly down my waist, over the sensitive skin at my hip until he grips my thigh just above the blade and lifts. I arch into him and grasp his neck as he dips me back. I attempt to steady my breathing, my collected mask slowly dissolving. The silk of his hair cools my tingling hand, and I'm certain the Aether can hear the pounding of my heart.

A finger taps against the blade—not mine.

"You have yet to threaten my life with this today...that must be a record," he teases, raising my body as he pulls my leg further over his hip.

"Why don't we rectify that?" I grab his neck with my free hand, sliding the other down his chest until it covers his. He smiles boyishly as my fingers push under his grasp and wrap around the hilt of my blade, dragging it up my thigh. It scrapes lightly against my skin, though the prince doesn't allow for anything else as he tightens his hold.

His gleaming eyes remain on mine as I position the blade just over his throat, being irritatingly reminded of our audience when the whispers begin.

Have they not been whispering this entire time?

"I'm beginning to think you enjoy when I do this," I admit breathlessly, the tone of my voice foreign to my ears.

He leans closer. "I'll enjoy anything you do to me..." A challenge.

My breath hitches when the music changes to a fast-paced tempo that procures many new dancers.

"Sil—Ariella, there you are. I—" Bastian pauses, registering the scene before him. "Am I interrupting something?"

"Yes."

"No." Caspian's gaze hardens, a shadow passing through his stormy eyes. I pull my blade back and continue holding my leg against his hip when his hand releases, sliding it down his pants after sheathing the weapon.

"Well, thank you for keeping my date company, cousin." My head snaps to Bastian as my nose scrunches.

"I am not your anything—I'd get that through your fucking head before I become your killer." His half-smile falters, the color of his cheeks lightening.

The prince laughs deeply, slapping Bastian on the shoulder. "Don't be scared, cousin...she'll only bite if you ask nicely."

Men.

I pivot to walk in the direction I last saw Isaiah, thanking the Angel when he's still leaning against the wall. He hides his smile behind a drink as I approach, snickering to himself.

"Fuck off, Is." I jab him in the throat, forcing him to hold out his drink to avoid spilling it. He laughs through a cough, smacking his chest.

"I don't know what's more amusing...seeing the hearts in your eyes when you danced with the prince, or watching them disappear the moment your *escort* arrived." He's prepared for me this time, quickly sliding from my attack.

I snatch his drink and finish it off, grimacing at the overly-tangy cider he chose. "Where's Ally?"

He sighs loudly. "Bathroom—though I'm worried she's lost by now." I lean a shoulder against the crimson tapestry, studying his profile.

"You really like her, don't you?" His lips purse to poorly hide his answering smile.

"You don't..." A question and a statement. His expectant eyes slide over to me as I shrug.

"It doesn't matter what I think...you know that," I mumble, tapping the compact prison around my neck.

Another song begins playing, the happy tone a deep contrast to the looming conversation. It hurts—what he's thinking. This man would impale himself on a blade before allowing me to die in this competition.

The reality of our truths squeezes my chest too tightly.

He'd surrender his life to save me. I will do the same for him…the difference being that I planned to die, anyway. It was my fate before the competition was even announced. But if it wasn't, what would I have done?

I sigh, a finger tapping against my chilled thigh. I know in my soul that I'd have made the same decision either way. Though he will certainly blame himself for my death—unless I tell him of my plans.

I need another drink.

"Ari, I know what you're going to say…but just hear me out, okay? I—"

"No," I interrupt sternly. "No, I will not fucking talk about this with you. This will not be an argument; I've already decided what will be done, and that's final."

His shoulders slump as his head falls back on a heavy groan. It may be the first—and only—time that I am grateful for Ally's presence. She saunters to our tense bubble, looking between Isaiah and me cautiously.

"Everything okay?" Her hands clasp in front of her as she squirms in place. "I can go if you need…"

I push from the wall and straighten, donning an emotionless mask once more. "Not necessary. Is was just mentioning how he'd like another dance with you." Her face brightens, and she reaches for Isaiah's hand as he threatens me with a look that says we will be discussing this later.

We certainly will not.

The high-pitched notes across the ballroom deepen, slowing to a calm, sensual song. My lip curls at the dozens of couples smiling fondly at each other.

I could leave…I'm sure it has been long enough that my head will not be blown from my body if I walk out those doors. The guests have all feasted their eyes on the Silver Wraith and her fellow competitors, which is all this absurd ball was for. I chew on my bottom lip, assessing the risks.

"Might I have this dance?" If I ever meet the Angel…I whirl to Bastian, pinning him with a dense glare. He bristles, though manages to keep his hand out. "Just one? You did say yes, if you need reminding."

I take one step. "Did I?" He nods irresolutely. Pathetic, really. "And why is it you presume that because I said yes to some ridiculous fucking question days ago, that you're owed the privilege of my company?" Another step. "As if my decisions cannot change? As if your desire for my attention is greater than my contempt for you?" His mouth gapes before he clears his throat and straightens his offensive gilded jacket. He studies me for a moment before scoffing, sneering to himself as his head shakes.

"Who knew you were such a fucking tease?" This—his anger, his retaliation…this is where I thrive. I smile, the darkened haze in my mind easing.

I unsheathe my blade and spin it lightly through my fingers, counting the number of veins bulging from his neck. "Truthfully, Bastian, you'd have to be the realm's most daft person to not know that. I've hidden nothing…you just constructed a different version of me in your head. Likely because you wished to fuck me and needed to delude yourself into thinking I am not the killer everyone believes me to be. That was your mistake—not mine."

He laughs, his gaze darkening into something depraved. “You’re right. I am undeniably owed something.” Faster than even I can comprehend, his hand reaches up to squeeze my cheeks as he leans forward to slam his lips against mine. His grip is so tight, I’m certain I’ll need to heal bruises in the morning.

I bend my wrist to shove my blade through his palm, pulling the limb back quickly enough to spare my skin of blood. He screeches and jerks his hand off the blade as he pins me with wide, glassy eyes.

“What the fuck? You crazy bitch!” He stumbles back into the wall as I move forward to wipe my blade on his jacket. The irony of his blood soaking into the golden fabric is not lost on me.

I press the blade to his chest until his eyes focus on mine. “You took what you thought you were owed.” I soak the last of the blood over his heart before spinning to stalk from the ballroom. “So did I.”

Chapter Twenty-Two

Caspian

My skin flushes with heat as my body drifts to Bastian where he heaves against the wall, the urge to rip that smug smile off his face is overwhelming. He notices me stalking toward him, a glimmer of amusement entering his eyes; he knew what he was doing when he asked Ariella to accompany him to the ball. He had been here for days, watching me interact with her—he has only ever wanted what I have. And the moment he saw how I reacted to her blade at my throat...

What I hadn't expected was her reaction.

I am not foolish—I know my assassin was attempting to push me away. As if anything less than her gutting me would stop me from following. I chuckle, ignoring the guests that wish to speak with me as I pass.

I break from the thick of the crowd, my cousin's eyes widening—he could certainly feel my rage from Meridian if he were lucky enough to be home. His smile remains, though dulling the closer I become. A blade through his hand was not nearly enough punishment for touching her.

"Something the matter, cous—" His likely imperious retort ends abruptly as my fist connects with his jaw. He grunts, catching himself in time to avoid meeting the floor. Gasps ring behind me. I'm causing a scene. One that will surely get me a lecture from father later and cause gossip within the court...

He touched her.

I grab his collar and shove him roughly against the wall, smirking when he winces at the force. With my arm against his throat, pressure enough to cut off his air and keep him in place, I lean forward until my mouth is at his ear. He will hear every word.

"If you *ever* touch her again," I throw a punch to his abdomen, not relenting in my hold or allowing him to double over. "*I will kill you.*" I force him to see the promise in my eyes before releasing my arm. My blood hums at the pathetic, sputtering breaths he heaves as I jog out of the ballroom in search of my angel.

My shoulders drop at the thankfully empty hallways. I do not have the will to plaster a princely smile on my face right now...there is something much more important to do.

I finally reach the guest wing, my speed increasing the closer I am. My feet swiftly turn the corner that will lead me to Ariella's door as I desperately hope that she didn't choose to go anywhere else. The hairs along my skin rise when I see her walking toward her room, not quite there yet.

"Ariella," I call, my abdomen clenching when she pauses, her body tensing. She doesn't turn at my voice, and I grin.

This woman is impossibly stubborn; she would make the Angel wait for her, if she so wished.

I step around to stand in front of her, and my breath ceases to exist. Her softened features break through every one of the practiced conversations I had with myself on the way here. Those piercing green eyes are missing the hardness they often hold to keep everyone at a distance.

She studies me, a question in her gaze. Her brows furrow when I say nothing, but those soft lips are so enticing that I need to forcibly keep myself still to avoid my imminent foolishness. If I stay near her much longer...

"What?" she whispers into the silence I created, her voice not holding its typical sharp, accusatory lilt. I breathe deeply, heat spreading through my face.

I don't know...why did I chase after her?

I just had the strongest urge to find her—an abysmal need to be near her after Bastian put his slimy mouth on her lips. My eyes widen—I'd intended to replace his taste with my own. To remove the memory of his touch from her skin and brand mine into it instead.

Yes, that's exactly what I need to do.

I do not allow myself to think about the consequences of grabbing the realm's deadliest woman and reach for her face, pressing my lips to hers. She doesn't push me off, though she doesn't kiss me back either. Fuck me...did I misread all the tension between us?

Pulling away just far enough to peer into her discerning eyes, I keep her face in my hands, stroking a thumb over her silky skin. None of the fabric in either realm could compare to the feeling of her. Her pupils dilate, cloaking the disarming green I love so much, and I cannot tell if she's contemplating laughing at me or killing me.

I'll take either, so long as she allows me to stay.

But she surprises me... "Fuck it," she mutters to herself as she grabs my jacket and drags my mouth back against hers. She devours my lips, and my legs nearly give out when she sighs. I slide one hand to the nape of her neck, holding her to me tightly.

I may be just a little afraid she'll pull away.

My other hand grazes down her throat and over the side of her breast—it takes everything in me not to reach my hand in the slit showcasing her abdomen. There's a desperate need inside my chest to grab it and tease the bud until I learn exactly what kind of touch makes her come undone. She seems like she enjoys pain with her pleasure, and I'm eager to give her whatever she demands.

My tingling fingers reach her waist, sliding along her back to press her flush against me. If I didn't know any better, I would say the Angel created our bodies to mold perfectly together.

Every defined curve of her melts into me. It's as if my body is simply just a placeholder for hers to rest on. She gasps when I tighten my hold—I try to loosen it, but that is impossible at this point.

I need her.

I need to witness the look on her face when I bring her the best pleasure she's ever known. I want to examine every inch of her body and memorize each place she likes to be touched. I have to know what kind of pressure drives her wild, and just how she likes to be taken.

I wonder if she prefers to be fucked hard and quick, or more soft and sensual?

It doesn't matter...I'll give her both. I'll give her all of it. I'm desperate to show her exactly how good I can make her feel.

She tugs me forward, twisting a hand to disarm her wards and lead us inside. I use her body to close the door, shoving her against it and swallowing her moans like a starved man. So she does like a little pain...I smile to myself as I kiss my way over her jaw and down her throat, pausing at her pulse point to bask in the speed of her heart.

She may be able to hide her outward reaction to me, but this isn't something she can control. It reveals all I need to know about how she feels.

She begins unbuttoning my shirt, her movements frantic, groaning when she cannot get them undone fast enough.

I chuckle against her jaw. "This doesn't feel like you hate me, angel."

"This changes nothing, prince." My cock twitches at her breathy voice, responding to the sound of her pent up need. I drag my lips back to hers, shivering as she slides her incredibly wicked hands over my abdomen, gripping just above my hips to meld us together.

"We'll see about that." I breathe against her swollen lips and claim them again before she has the chance to speak the denial I know is waiting on her tongue. I suck her words in, groaning at the intoxicating taste of her. I have to have all of her—I need to know if she's as sweet as I've imagined.

Stepping back to release her from the door, my hands make quick work of her dress, undoing the belt and sliding the straps over her shoulders. The fabric falls to the floor, and I don't have one moment to appreciate her incomprehensible body before she's shoving my shirt and jacket off. One would think her no better than a rabid animal as she reaches down to just as swiftly bare my lower half, freeing my painfully hard cock. She grasps my length in one hand, squeezing and stroking as I jerk in her grasp. This beautiful creature has no hesitations in taking what she wants, and I'm unashamedly just a man ready to give her anything she desires. She will have whatever she asks for.

I bend to grab her legs, lifting and never taking my mouth from hers as I lead us to the bed. Her sultriness encases me, a significantly finer scent when it's from the source. Fingers grip onto my hair and neck like I'm their lifeline as I lie her down on her back gently, though I want nothing more than to ruin every inch of her. I want to fuck every hole, bruise all of her skin with my mouth, and bite into her neck until she bleeds.

Maybe these urges of mine are not so crazy, because it feels as if she would like the same thing.

But before I do any of that, I must suck her throbbing core into my mouth. I lift myself from the bed and pause for a moment to admire her. Her skin is soft everywhere—not just her lips. Her breasts showcase hardened, dusty pink nipples that I want to twist and pinch until she comes undone. I run my fingers along her waist, down to her hip and over her toned thighs. I'm in awe that something so beautiful lies before me—that I have the honor of bearing witness to a phenomena very few get to see.

My jaw clenches. No one else should ever see her like this...it will never happen again.

She's mine.

"Have you never seen a woman before, prince?" I jolt like the idiot I am—standing here as sinful thoughts consume me instead of giving her everything she needs. Her bright eyes narrow, obvious amusement dancing along her features.

If I had any artistic capabilities, I would paint the stunning sight before me so that I could hold on to this memory forever. Though I know even the finest painter in the realms would spend a lifetime striving to perfect her beauty and still fail to capture it fully.

I want to stare at her forever, but she's waiting for me. My eyes travel to her glistening pussy and roll. Fuck, every bit of her is perfect.

Why *did* it have to be her?

I bend to sink my tongue through her arousal, but stop when one of her heels connects with my forehead. My brows furrow as I look up at her smirking face.

"Beg." I smile menacingly at the demand, dragging my lips over the straps of her heel.

"I think you underestimate just how badly I want to taste you." The huskiness in my voice surprises even me. My mouth works slowly up her legs, removing her shoes while I continue. "My desire reaches much further than meager *begging*...I would crawl across the lands to you under the judgment of every curious eye in the kingdom. I would forfeit my claim to the throne without question, merely because you asked. I would stand against the Angel itself just for the chance to sit at the foot of your altar.

"Ariella," I breathe, reaching the apex of her inner thigh. My gaze slides to her hooded eyes, swimming with questioning hunger. "Every heartbeat of mine is a promise to you. And if you so wished, I would force both realms to bear witness as I sliced the organ from my aching chest and placed it in your hands—so there would be no question about who I belong to.

"So..." I hover over her heat, barely able to restrain myself. "Will you allow me the pleasure of tasting you?" I refuse to point out the confusion on her face, and how I never thought *the* assassin could ever be so befuddled. My declaration was quite intense, though—even *I* am addled by how strongly I feel.

Her parted lips do not say a word when she gives a barely perceptible nod. Not a moment later I descend, running my tongue along her swollen core. My eyes scrunch closed as I groan, muttering something about how

I'll refuse death's every call—because the only way I will accept my demise is from drowning in her.

My arms slide up her hips, grabbing her waist and tugging her closer. She gasps when I flutter my tongue, my skin flushing even more at her pleasure-filled sounds. I am so consumed by her that everything else in my life pales in comparison.

I should fear these feelings. Push her from my mind because the Angel ordained societal tiers, and royals do not belong with anyone under a noble status. I chuckle when Ariella latches onto my hair.

Fuck the Angel. And my father—he believes himself discreet, though I am aware of his dislike for the woman below me. And after Gavriel informed me of my father's *visit* with Ariella—in the treasury, no less—I've been watching him and Varrick more closely than before.

I suck my angel's clit deeply between my lips, barely containing my smile when her thighs squeeze my head. She mutters curses to herself as her hips gyrate against my tongue. I reach a hand under my chest, struggling with how hard I press into the bed. Once high enough, I circle the heat of her entrance lightly and nearly come when a shuddering moan leaves her.

"Fuck me," she drags on a whine, gripping my hair so hard it borders on too painful. I continue to circle my fingers, pressing further into her slit with each rotation.

I hover just above her pulsating core. "Don't worry, angel, I will." Her inebriating taste floods my tongue once more as I relent to her cries and sheathe two fingers inside her walls, pressing my cock into the bed for any kind of relief.

This woman is unbelievable.

I undulate my hand, becoming possessed when her thighs begin to shake—I need to unravel her. I maintain the same rhythm when her breathing deepens, peering up her tense body, silhouetted only by the moonlight drifting through her window.

To have this deadly, cunning, unforgiving assassin melting at my touch...

Her body tenses a heartbeat before she comes, her coarse moan settling into my abdomen. I slow my movements as her spasms lessen, wringing out every spec of pleasure I can. When her legs release me—much to my disappointment—I lower my head to gather the waves of cum seeping from her.

Fuck, does she taste good.

Her hips jerk when my tongue sinks into her heat. "Fuck, Caspian, I can't—I need you inside me." I pause, sitting back to look where she leans elevated on her elbows.

"Was I not just inside you..." I tease, running the top of a finger over her slit.

She groans, snatching my hand to haul me over her. Her legs wrap around my hips in a manner that tells me they will not let go until I oblige. She pinches my chin, pulling my face down until our lips connect.

"You know that's not what I mean." My cock twitches at her sex-addled voice, and I line myself up to her entrance, swaying my head to massage her swollen mouth.

"You're right," I chuckle as I drive my throbbing cock into her with one thrust.

Chapter Twenty-Three

Ariella

Caspian enters me in one thrust, and I gasp into his mouth as my hands grip his hair tighter. He's thicker than I'd anticipated, lining my walls with a momentary burning sensation before it melts into something exquisite.

He pauses, breathing hard. "Are you okay?" I hum, pulling at his skin to continue, too lost in the bliss to acknowledge when he mutters about how needy I am.

His lips drag over my blazing skin, and my head tilts to provide him more access. My hands slide to below his shoulders, gripping tightly when he pounds into me so hard that I'm certain the crease of my legs will be bruised in the morning. No one has ever fucked me like this before—I fear how easily I could become addicted.

One of his hands skims over my waist before latching under my leg and securing it next to my chest. "*Fuck me*, that feels so good," I moan deeply, completely losing my ability to mask any emotions.

"So she does like it rough, huh?" The prince's voice is teasing, and I have a feeling he's about to take it a step further.

"I swear to the Angel, prince—if you even think about stopping, I will actually gut you this time." He smiles against my neck, kissing an extra sensitive spot that causes me to clench around him. My nails embed into his skin, though instead of protesting, it seems to encourage him. If he feels any pain, he sure as Aether isn't showing it.

He hovers next to my ear and whispers with a seductively deep voice, "Don't worry, Ari...we're not done here until you come on my cock at least twice." He finishes his sentence with an extra hard thrust, and I let out a guttural moan, arching into him. I somehow spread my thighs further apart, allowing him even deeper; the feeling of him so far inside me is the most unbelievable thing I've ever felt.

He drives into me at an astonishing pace, and I wonder more than once why the fuck I haven't allowed him inside of me before. He grinds his pelvis into my clit, and I cannot hold back anymore. My core squeezes as his mouth latches to mine, inhaling my moans like they're the only oxygen left in this realm. After the waves of pleasure recede, I'm coherent enough to kiss him back. I suck on his tongue, savoring everything I won't allow myself to have again.

I press his slick skin further into mine, nausea sweeping through me at the thought of this being over...I can't get enough. Though I remember he did insist on two orgasms, so I must keep going, right?

I chuckle to myself—this is certainly the only time I will listen to anything he orders me to do.

I hook my foot behind his knee, and use the leverage to push him to the side and roll us over so that I'm straddling his hips. I keep us connected the entire time, his arm sliding from my other leg to give me back control. I roll my abdomen to ride him the moment I sit up, my head falling back when his cock thrusts perfectly along my front wall. He lifts to level his face with mine, resting his forehead against my own and sliding his hands around my back to meld our bodies together.

This feels way too intimate—something I would never do with other men. But the minimal light catching his eyes highlights his expression, keeping me from changing our position again.

"How interesting..." I purr, taking my turn to kiss up the side of his neck. "The heir to the ruthless Eldorian throne enjoys being fucked slow." I sink back onto him in a way that matches my words. Brushing my lips over his, I smile against him. "And soft." I follow this with an unhurried roll of my hips, causing him to groan—the sound is pure ecstasy. As much as I'll love to tease him about this, I cannot deny how nice it is. I'm so used to using sex just to get off, but I'm not even thinking about my own pleasure at the moment. I'm enjoying his far too much, and I'd have no problem staying here for hours just to drink in the sounds he's making with every one of my movements.

I will never confess such thoughts aloud, though.

"Fuck you, angel," he retorts with a smile, pressing his lips to mine fully, and I wrap my arms around his neck to hold his head as I shift us to lie back on the bed again.

"Oh, no, Caspian. I'm fucking *you.*" My eyes nearly roll back from this angle, but I manage to keep myself aware enough to hold control. "And you are loving every damned second of it." I feel his cock twitch inside of me—he's close. I angle my hips to push him deeper, leaning forward to touch my lips against the outer skin of his ear.

"Come for me, prince," I whisper demandingly. He does. His length jerks, and the warmth crashing into my inner walls sends me over the edge once more. His eyes seem to glow brighter in the minimal light before mine roll back as I shove my face into the side of his neck.

This is so sensual. So intimate. But, by the Angel is it the best sex I've ever fucking had.

He nods. "I completely agree." Did I just say that out loud? I spring up, biting my cheek; he's likely too dazed to remember that little slip.

But just to be sure...

I grind my hips a few more times, prolonging his pleasure before his hands grab at me to stop the movement. I laugh, running a hand down my sweat-coated abdomen. Heat radiates from him as he breathes heavily. His moonlit eyes meet mine—we study each other for a moment before he grabs my hair to pull me down into another deep kiss, meeting me halfway. He tastes of wine and satiety, my selfish mouth consuming every drop it can before breaking our contact.

I wince as I lift from him and fall to my back, covering my chest with both hands. The bedding rustles as the prince shifts, my skin flushing when I *feel* his stare.

This is the part where I usually dress and leave before the other person forces me into an awkward exchange of words. But as my heart slows and breathing settles, I strangely wish for more...

No—I cannot allow him to dig under my skin any longer. This is already much further than I should have gone with him. My foolish, desire-saturated body blurred my resolve and now I've made my plans significantly more difficult for myself.

My stomach drops.

I would prefer anything to this. I would set foot inside the Aether realm and face every obstacle just to fight the Angel. Because battling things that exist beyond any form of human comprehension? Simple. But this—confronting feelings that Caspian has planted so deeply inside me that I can feel them in my bones? Impossible.

The prince groans, snapping me from my pitiful internal rambling. "You're not going to let me stay, are you?"

The comforting shadows hide my smile. "Absolutely not." He curses, rolling next to me before resting his head on a palm.

"Look me in the eye and tell me you don't feel this connection," he implores, my chest tightening at his soft tone.

I turn my head to find the eyes that peer down at me. "I don't feel this connection, Caspian." The words taste like acid on my tongue, but he chuckles and shakes his head.

"I'll get you to admit it one of these days..."

I jerk up to stand, backing toward the bathroom. "But that's what makes this so fun," I tease, attempting to coax him back to our playful banter. "You thinking there will ever be more to this than what we just did." I pause in the doorway, raising a brow in his direction, though I doubt he can see it.

"Whatever you say, angel," he mocks as he rises to grab his clothes that are strewn over the floor.

A finger taps against my thigh. "Goodbye, prince." I shut the door more forcefully than intended, turning the shower on immediately. I don't hear him leave, but a familiar solitary atmosphere spreads through the room after a few minutes, forcing me to swallow around the object lodged in my throat as I focus on washing him from my skin.

Chapter Twenty-Four

Ariella

I've never been so blurred in my resolve. Knowing what I want, how I need to prepare for it, and executing a routine that will get me there is easy. Kill the king. That was the only goal I've had for two decades. But the moment I arrived at the castle? It shifted into killing the prince. And now? My head feels...off.

I shouldn't have fucked him.

It didn't seem like such a difficult choice in the moment, but I know better than to allow my desires to shadow everything else. I stretch my neck, attempting to forget the many spots along it I had to heal this morning—not my proudest moment.

The hairs along my skin rise when a piercing scream resonates through the halls, so deafening I am certain it will wake the Angel. My feet carry me through the severely empty castle, and I sprint faster when a large crowd of people enters my view. My stomach turns.

Something isn't right.

I am unashamedly frustrated as the horde forces me to push them aside, when normally they run at the sight of me. I curse when dresses tighten around me.

My eyes close as I breathe deeply, calming my fretting heart. "Fucking move or you die," I scream, and the whispers finally cease. Heads turn my way as bodies push back, creating a path. Habit insists I threaten several of them with my eyes, though I do not yield as I no longer see them.

The metallic notes in the humid air strengthen as I step toward the fountain. What is normally a beautiful sight now represents the worst of my nightmares. The griffin's bright stone possesses a red hue as an endless stream of bloodied water pours from its mouth. Below, swirls of deep crimson dance through the pool, darkening by the second.

Whatever is causing the color change must be submerged.

My breathing shallows, saliva thickening to an unbearable point. Something knowing gnaws at my conscious, but I do not acknowledge it. One step further shows me the tips of fingers bobbing in the water. Another step, a skinless arm.

So many thoughts race through my mind, but there is just one pounding its way in, forcing me to see the scene for its truth.

I know what it is. *Who* it is.

And I know why.

The realms collide when my toes press against the stone, and my eyes confirm everything.

The last time I cried was the day my father was taken from me. I watched as the king whipped him endlessly for a crime he never committed. They had him chained in front of the castle gates, because that revolting excuse of a royal could not be bothered to leave the grounds to execute someone he charged with treason.

The crowd wouldn't listen when I screamed my father's innocence and begged for them to investigate the accusation further. Not one single person looked my way, even as my voice broke from the overuse. Instead, they yelled obscenities at him—cackling as he became weaker and his life drained from the wounds.

When I realized the people did not care about my words or that they just witnessed a blameless man be executed, I stared at the stone below his feet. I watched his blood run in rivulets through the cracks as they soaked up the last of his existence like starving beasts.

I didn't blame the stone for taking what did not belong to it.

I envied it.

In that moment, I wanted nothing more than to be it. To be the thing that consumes the warm blood of those who have mistreated and walked all over me for their own convenience.

I stood un-moving for hours, fascinated with how unapologetic the stone was. Even when they carried my father's body away, I did not waver. I watched. Memorized.

I shifted into something new that day. No longer was I the girl who allowed others to think for her, or tell her what to do. Dead was the child who was too weak to fight for herself and those she loved. Forgotten was the daughter who let others carry her heart, as she wouldn't live through ever feeling like that again.

They wanted to be monsters? Then I would be worse. I would become their every fear. The subject of each scary story told in the quiet of the night.

I would become their worst nightmare.

And when Marek found me and insisted I follow him to the guild? I wiped the last stray drop from my cheek and vowed that the only tears ever shed in my presence again would be from those I sunk my blade into.

I've broken that vow today.

Salty liquid cascades down my stoic face, the taste a reminder of what it feels like to be weak. I cannot find the will to care that so many others watch me, questions on their tongues.

Isaiah. My best friend.

The one person I've allowed myself to get close to, even knowing what it would do to me to lose him.

His body sways with the water, flayed skin breaking the surface every few seconds. The only part of him not sliced to pieces is the scar running over his cloudy brown eyes.

I kneel against the ledge, warring with my need to break down and my will to claim the life of every single person here. I am close to doing both when something creamy appears in Isaiah's mouth. My hand reaches for it, trembling slightly when my fingers push past his slimy lips and sharp, jagged teeth.

Something solid presses against me, and I pinch it, blinking when the crinkling of paper breaks through the utter silence of the courtyard.

Three words sear through my every nerve like fire when I un-crumple the small bit of paper.

I warned you.

If that message did not solidify my resolve, the sound of the prince's voice would have.

"What's going on?"

No one speaks as his footsteps get louder. I rise from the ledge, stuffing the confession in my bra before crossing my feet to face the worried eyes of the prince.

"Ariella. What's going on?" he repeats, his leg twitching to take another step but halting when my gaze darkens.

He was a fool to become attached to me.

I am not good or kind. I am not the girl you marry and enjoy a life with. It's unfortunate he will be reminded like this...in front of dozens who wish for nothing more than to capture any gossip they can on the royals.

"This is your fault." My voice is menacing and cold, causing him to wince. "You just couldn't stay away from me, and that was your first mistake. Even after I've told you time after time that you mean *nothing* to me. That you are no more than a moment of entertainment. Even after I agreed to go to the ball with your fucking cousin, you *still* couldn't leave me be."

His nostrils flare, features glazing over before he remembers our eager audience. "I—" His stormy eyes flick to Isaiah, shoulders dropping when he sees just what could make the Silver Wraith cry. His throat bobs, a haunted expression overcoming his face. "I swear to you, I will find who did this and make them pay."

"I *know* who did it! Are you that fucking ignorant, Caspian, that you haven't a clue?" He bristles and rubs at the stubble along his jaw. His gaze searches mine for several moments before he nods, looking away.

Is that all? A nod of acknowledgment for what he and his family have done?

I don't fucking think so.

I unsheathe one of my blades and fling it, ignoring the warmth that blooms in my abdomen when the prince catches it just before it sinks into his heart. Exasperated noises fall from the mouths of the crowd. They retreat as a group, though do not leave the courtyard—always looking for a show.

I'll give them one.

Guards rush me, swords drawn to take what they think will be my life. "Leave her be." The prince raises a hand, gesturing for the men to stand down. They share confused glances before obeying, though they do not return to their original positions. "You want someone to take your anger out on, angel? That's fine—I'll have whatever you wish to give." His arms widen, a clear invitation. This is a dangerous game he's playing, unaware of just how thin a line he treads.

"Take my anger out on you? As if you do not deserve it?" My voice rises as I take purposeful steps toward him. He watches me with sympathy, waiting until I'm just inches away to speak.

"I do. I'm sorr—" My fist strikes his jaw, familiar pain radiating through my knuckles from the contact. He catches himself on hands and knees, heaving as he spits hot blood to the ground.

"Do *not* pity me. You are not sorry," I hiss, grabbing the collar of his thick jacket and dragging him to his feet so that our chests press together. My eyes find his as they demand him to hear my next words as if they were his last. "But you're about to be."

"Ariella—"

"No. There is *nothing* you can say that I will listen to. Isaiah is dead. Your entire family will pay for this." His brows furrow, skin paling as he registers the blade in his abdomen. "Starting with you."

I release his collar, not taking my eyes from his pained ones as I step back. He falls to his knees, hands trembling around the protruding metal.

He laughs, groaning at the movement. Bile rises while my chest constricts every available muscle. I barely notice people screaming and hurriedly running from the scene. The guards advance once again, though

I do not move to protect myself. I refuse to look away and break the connection between Caspian and me.

"You are *forbidden* from touching her!" he roars, coughing at the last word as blood spills from his mouth. He hunches forward, struggling to hide the pain in his features. They pause, unsure of what to do in such a situation, eventually relenting when the prince pins them with a sharp glare.

Has he learned nothing?

I should heal—*no.* He deserves this.

When the courtyard is empty, his heavy eyes find mine, pleading for promises and confessions I will not give. I look one last time to his blood soaking through the stone—a stark reminder.

In my peripheral, guards peek from around the castle doors, clearly arguing with each other, though none come for me. One barks for another to find a healer. I chuckle to myself—it won't matter if they find one or not. Caspian's fate will not change.

The prince's legs give out as he clambers to his side, barely holding his body up with one arm. He struggles for a few moments before exhaustion overcomes him, eyes closing as his back thuds heavily to the ground, hands clutching the blade.

"That was your second mistake, prince."

I return to Isaiah's cooling body, my hands trembling as I step into the bloody water to pick him up. I cannot look at him as we walk through the castle gates, back to our home.

Tears continue to fall, but their meaning shifts. They began shedding for the harrowing murder of the only person I had left...the kindest, most reliable person to have ever graced either realm.

Now they shed because there is simply nowhere else for the rage to go.

I lost focus of my plan, and Isaiah paid the price. He was supposed to win the competition and find a life outside the one we were forced into as children. He may not have admitted it, but I know he only stayed at the guild this long because I refused to leave. He never understood why…and now he never will.

I let Caspian ease his way under my skin when I understood why being with him was impossible. Yet I foolishly convinced my logic otherwise.

I barely comprehend the screams of Valorian's as I stalk through the main streets. I'm used to people fearing and running from me—they're lucky I've a job to do, because I'd have no reservations about using any of them as an outlet.

Why should I? These are the same people who laughed as my father was whipped before their eyes…and now they scream because it's me—and not the king—showcasing a dead body.

I'm certain some are running to report this to the king himself.

Good. He will hear my screams this time.

My limbs threaten to give out as I ascend the steps to Isaiah's and my home. I kick the door in, unfazed by the clink of metal pieces dropping to the tile.

I stop just past the entrance and fix my eyes on the back wall next to the hallway that leads to Isaiah's room. "Marek!" I scream, my lungs burning from the effort. Several of the students to my left jump, spinning to face me.

"Oh, look who it—" Isolde trips over someone on the floor as she rushes over with a few of the others. "By the Angel…is that…" She slaps a hand over her mouth, holding in what someone in the distance cannot.

Why are you at the fucking guild if you're going to vomit over a dead body?

"Marek!" A sharp pain laces my throat as my voice cracks. He rushes up the stairs with Velora and Jaxon directly behind him.

"What is it?" His hurried steps falter when his eyes find me and slide to my best friend. His lips thin as he steps forward, blinking several times.

He searches my face when his feet stop in front of me. "Ari..." he whispers imperceptibly.

"Don't." He knows why I ended up at the guild. How much Isaiah means to me. I look between his down-turned eyes, willing him to understand. "Give him a proper death," I demand hoarsely, holding Isaiah out to him, even though I never wish to let go.

He hesitates, breathing unevenly as he reaches out to gather the unnaturally cool body. My tongue presses roughly to the roof of my mouth—a warning, I realize. I need to leave.

I spin on my heel and walk around the crooked door, pausing when Marek speaks. "And you? What will you do?"

I look over my shoulder, raising a brow in a way that says, *"the king's head is mine."* He nods, and my chest somehow hurts more when he mouths his next words instead of allowing me to interpret them from his expression.

I'm sorry.

My throat burns, but I lift my chin and cherish the last look I will ever have of Isaiah Cheral before turning to descend the steps.

Two fingers tap firmly against my blade. The king just killed the one thing he could hold over my head...now he can watch his kingdom burn.

Chapter Twenty-Five

Ariella

Pain. I ignore the slice across my palm as I continue to twirl my blade, walking mindlessly through Valoria. I've paced this block a dozen times, unable to convince myself to just go in.

The sun disappeared nearly an hour ago, so there isn't much time before I need to be within the castle's walls once more. My fist clenches around the blade and hot blood seeps down my fingers, the droplets splattering lightly at my feet.

"Get it the fuck over with, Ariella—we have a king to kill." I swallow thickly and halt in the dark street, pivoting left to face the one place I'd never wanted to come back to.

Until now.

It's been twenty-years since I've entered my parents' home. Two decades since my father died—even longer for my mother—and yet the house sits here with barely a change to its appearance. As if it's been preserving itself.

The dusty brown exterior touches a familiar place in my mind, but it feels like a stranger to me. Vines and unpicked weeds overrun my mother's garden. I breathe deeply, closing my eyes—I can almost make out the rows of lavender she loved to grow. Her favorite day of the month was exchanging the wilted plants around our home for fresh ones, sitting on the floor at the center of the house while the windows allowed breeze after breeze to grace us with the light scent.

My chest squeezes. She was happy…

Before she killed herself.

I shake my head and walk over the stone path that leads to the portico, which looks less aged than I've become. Interesting considering no one lived here after my family *left*.

People claim its walls are haunted—one parent shoved a blade through her heart, and the other was whipped to death in front of the castle.

They were right about one thing…something haunted *did* live here. But she's been out of these walls for many years.

My fingers wrap around the cool handle and twist.

Musty, stagnant air rushes against me as the door creaks open. I listen for the closing click before tugging on my luminal strand, shaping enough light in my hand to illuminate long-forgotten memories.

Dust motes drift lazily around the familiar space, though my eyes quickly focus on what lies beyond them. The hall in front of me is lined with faded tapestries and yellowed paintings. The wooden floors lead to the large staircase at the back wall, some of the boards slightly upturned. Surprisingly, the chandelier still hangs from the coffered ceiling, though its once bright jewels are covered in layers of dust—as are the high-backed chairs and previously tan curtains.

The colors that seemed so vivid in my memories are now dulled and desolate. I take hesitant steps forward, the house almost seeming to breathe with my movements as the groaning of settled wood and stone fills me with chills. I push open a door to my left, pausing when the faint echoes of laughter are nearly audible—a distant memory of what once was.

This room was where we spent most of our time; the cushioned chairs and couch ideally placed for conversation and activity. What used to be the vibrant red of all the fabric is now a deep, foreboding scarlet. The shapes of my parents laying together near the blackened fireplace flickers in and out of my vision, and I suck in a breath as my feet lead me through the open space into the kitchen.

The back of my throat burns when I survey the area, my heavy eyes pausing at the crusted vase on the windowsill.

This is...more difficult than I'd anticipated.

I clear my throat and spin on my heel, speeding back through the doorway and up the staircase. I do not realize my body's intentions until I'm standing in my bedroom. The white bedding is yellow and threadbare, curtained by the transparent fabric that I was always convinced hid me away completely. It felt like my own private world, where I could just let my thoughts run free.

Pathetic, really.

I circle the room, fascinated with how the last time I was here, the furniture seemed so big compared to my six-year-old body. Now? I tower over the decaying pieces.

My back straightens, heart fluttering as I walk to the closet. My hand lifts to illuminate the carvings in the doorway, where my parents used to mark our growth. Something tugs at my lips at the two highest lines with *Ariella* written on top.

They are a couple inches apart, yet were carved the same day.

On my sixth birthday, my parents brought a blade to my room the moment I woke—it was my favorite time of each year. I was obsessed with growing. In height, mind, strength...I was constantly pushing myself to be better at everything.

Including my parents.

Each year, I insisted I was so close to reaching their carved lines at the top of the doorway. But on this particular day, I was frustrated with how far I had left to grow. My father carved a line at the top of my head and attempted to hold in laughter when I became angry because my hair was tied up, making me taller than he'd carved. After very little convincing from my mother, and a dramatic eye-roll, he carved a second line.

He chuckled as his body straightened and told me how crazy it was that I grew two inches in the matter of minutes.

"That's why you should always be scared of me...I'll be taller than you before my next birthday!"

Dramatic, but true.

Not one year passed before I stood higher than his crumpled, bloodless body.

I sigh, rising to my full height. Something deep tugs at me when my mother's line rests just above my vision.

Valyria.

How similar would we look now?

My shoulder bumps the corner of the doorway as I pivot to stalk from the room. I halt just outside, gulping several measured breaths before turning right to stare at the uncanny hallway that leads to my parents' room. My hand trails the walls while I trudge forward, upturned pieces of wallpaper catching my fingers every few steps.

They began leaving the door to their room open when nightmares plagued my every sleep. I would wake screaming of chaos in the realms and beg them to never leave me like they did in my dreams. I chuckle, tapping a finger against my thigh.

I falter before their room, bile rising to my throat.

I do not wish to remember that piece of my past as a deteriorating, musty space. I just barely can recall its details, and I know seeing it in this state would erase every good memory I still hold on to.

The moment I commit to avoiding that area, my lungs allow me to inhale a full breath as the tightness lessens in my chest.

"Why the fuck did I come here..." I whisper to myself, turning back toward the staircase. I'm muttering to my weak mind when something grabs my arm; I jolt, immediately pulling my blade to shove it in their throat, but freeze when I turn.

There's no one there...

My ears become hypersensitive, listening for the smallest of movements but finding none. I look to the floor, where only my footsteps imprint the layer of grime coating it. Slowly, each of my muscles loosens and I drop my arm while keeping hold of the weapon. I tug on my umbral strand and send a pulse through the quiet house—I'm the only one here.

Unless whoever is here doesn't have essence? I snort and sheathe my blade.

A strand of light catches my eye, my head snapping up to the crack in the door next to me.

My father's office.

I push the creaking wood open, my heart beating faster with each foot of space presented to me. My jaw clenches—his office somehow still smells of stale paper and worn leather. I step into the room and run my fingers over the stacks of paper and folders that are still on the large desk, all of them addressed to *Lord Erendor Mistaire.*

He was a nobleman—always in the castle, meeting with the king, other nobles, and advisors. Somehow that makes what happened to him even worse...Thalion knew my father on a personal level. Anyone that knew him would have seen just how dedicated he was to his work and the kingdom.

So when Thalion executed him on accusations of treason, without investigating or even defining what he did that was treasonous?

Metallic liquid covers my tongue, and I release my cheek, forcing my fist to let go of the paper it has crumpled. I adjust my stance to move when something catches my eye...

Fix the accord.

Three words scribbled over and over in a notebook—journal, I realize as I pick the small book up. I fan through the pages and catch dozens of entries written by my father's hand. My abdomen clenches when I stop on a random page and the words Valyria and death seize my eyes. I slam the journal closed and press a hand to my chest, willing my breathing to slow.

"Fuck this." My hand clutches the journal as I stalk from the room, hurrying down the stairs and through the front door. I pull back my luminal strand before returning to the portico—knowing the king, he most certainly has someone trailing me.

I'd thought being outside would ease the lump in my throat, but it doesn't. Shaking my head, I walk down the steps, faltering slightly when my vision blurs at the edges, creating a tunnel to the street. The moment

I'm off the property, I crouch and scrunch my eyes closed. It takes heartbeats longer than it should to gather myself and will the emotions away once more.

I do not have time to feel things I've already dwelled on.

My mother, father, Isaiah...they are dead. I am not. There is no room for anything other than the sheer truth.

The king and I have matters to settle, starting with his son...whom I just stabbed in front of the entire court. I force my feet to run before the pressure inside my head becomes more than I can handle. Bitter wind cools my skin, my brows furrowing when the exhale of my breaths becomes visible ahead of me.

He's going to hate me...and I deserve it. Even if part of me wishes I didn't.

Chapter Twenty-Six

Caspian

Stitching along my abdomen tugs when I trip over my own foot and tense the muscles to keep myself upright. I wince, breathing deeply until the sharp pain subsides.

Elowen insisted on healing each of my wounds, but I only allowed it for the worst of them. She's intelligent, so I'm certain it wasn't difficult for her to surmise why I refused.

I deserve to heal this on my own and live with the scar that will no doubt replace it.

Ariella was right…she had tried again and again to push me away, and I did not leave. Even now I'm pacing the castle gates as I impatiently wait for her to return. My steps grow faster with each minute that passes—it's nearly midnight.

I know she'd truly kill me if I showed up at the guild to drag her ass back here, but I'm a moment away from taking such a risk. I freeze. She must think my father will have her head regardless of her return. She did shove her blade into me…in the courtyard, of all places, so there was not one chance for me to twist what happened to the king. I should be embarrassed with the amount of begging and arguing I did to halt my father's execution order, but I'm not. If I hadn't managed to convince my father that I fucked up by challenging her, he would have sent a search party through Valoria with orders to kill on site.

When he finally relented, I asked about Isaiah. As much as Ariella attempted to hide her love for him, it was clear just how much he meant to her. And just like everything else I've asked him, my father shrugged and said he didn't know, but he was sure an answer would turn up.

The thing is, they never do. And I never cared enough to look deeper.

But now I have something to care about.

My shoulders drop the moment she appears on the street ahead—thank the fucking Angel. The lights surrounding the castle wall highlight her hair and face, both splotched in deep red. There's likely much more coating her clothes, though it's impossible to see with the black fabric.

My chest squeezes impossibly tight. Seeing her tears earlier...

She's several feet away when her eyes look up, quickly examining my body before shifting to something past me.

I know my suspicions are correct when she pauses momentarily before shutting down everything except the raw hatred seeping from her. I groan when she marches right by me, carefully jogging to catch up.

"Ariella, wait..." She does. I step around her stiff form, forcing my hands to remain still when all they crave to do is hold her. She looks so...empty. Vacant eyes glare at me, while her skin lacks its natural glow.

She's hurting.

"Are you okay?" I scoff—stupid fucking question. "Of course you're not...I just mean, how can I help you get through this?" She rears back, lips parting and closing twice before her eyes search mine.

"You're serious? You wish to know how I am after I attempted to kill you?" A sad smile pulls at my lips.

"If you were truly wanting to kill me, why were you not shocked that I was waiting for you?"

She blinks. "What?"

I laugh, the movement bizarre given our current circumstances. I make a show of looking around the courtyard before speaking, "It's just us two here...there's no need to hide." Her tired eyes narrow as she crosses her arms, covering a small book she holds. "Elowen informed me that your blade missed every organ and vital piece of internal flesh. That you'd merely scraped inside enough that I coughed blood." She shifts, pursing her lips as she avoids meeting my gaze. "Angel. She said the chances of that happening incidentally are nearly zero..."

"Okay, and? What the fuck do you want from me, Caspian? It doesn't matter what I did—I was not lying when I said your entire family will pay."

"I know." She huffs, rubbing a hand over her face. A haunted glimmer passes through her eyes when dried blood flakes into her hands, but she quickly stifles it. "I want to help you."

She chuckles cruelly, stalking past me once more. "I'm serious—I don't know what the fuck is going on, but I wish to figure it out just as much as you do."

I swallow thickly when she spins to look at me as if I've lost my mind. Her eyes flit to my abdomen where spots of blood appear on my cream shirt. "You misunderstand me, prince...I don't fucking care about figuring out whatever it is your father is doing." She's so close—her blazing eyes glaring up at me—that the heat of her breath fogs the space between us. "I'm going to kill him."

I search her eyes for a deeper meaning, or evidence of a lie, but there is neither. This beautiful, deadly woman is threatening to murder my father—the king of Eldoria.

The confession should anger me. It should provide my addled heart with enough evidence that she must be stopped. She's openly threatening my family...

And yet...

My attention catches on the book peeking from under her arm. I stiffen so quickly that I feel my stitches strain. I am certainly the most foolish prince to ever live.

Lord Erendor Mistaire. Written carefully across the leather is the name that has created an unstable wedge between my father and me for years. Just because he is king does not permit him to give orders above the law. My head tilts to the cloudy sky, the murkiness a mirror to every nerve alighting under my skin.

Above the law...says the prince who has fallen for the assassin.

The daughter of the man my father executed just outside the gates behind me. How did I not piece it together before?

"Okay."

"Okay?" I nod weakly, dropping my chin as I attempt to breathe through the uncertainty warring through me.

"I will not help you kill my father, and I will interfere if I catch you. I intend to learn what he's hiding, not take his life. I know what he's done, but he's still my father, Ariella...and as much as it goes against everything I've been raised to be, it's not my place to deny you a chance at revenge." She bursts out laughing, throwing her arms out dramatically.

"Are you fucking kidding me? I just told you that I'm going to kill your father—the king, Caspian—and you still wish to care for me?" She's right...it's crazy for me to stay.

"No," I state darkly, and her head whips to face me again. "I don't *wish* to care about you. I have begged the Angel to remove your presence from my mind after eliminating you from the competition was no longer an option. Fuck, Ariella, we should hate each other! We come from opposing backgrounds—I should want your head for everything that you've done...especially now that you've threatened my entire family *after* shoving your fucking blade into me." I'm nearly shouting, my heart beating up my throat.

I don't think as my hand reaches for her face, wrapping to cup the back of her head and tug her to me. She doesn't resist. I rub away flaking blood as I search her eyes. "I don't want to feel this way about you. I shouldn't—*I can't*. But I do...and maybe my feelings are far too intense to be normal, but I don't fucking care." Her forehead creases before I graze my lips over her trembling ones. "Did you think I was lying when I confessed that I wish to bathe in *every* depraved part of you?"

Her breath hitches before her tongue sweeps across her bottom lip. "You're a fool, prince." I grin as my lips press to hers; she melts into the touch, her panting chest pushing into mine.

The kiss is soft and far more intimate than either of us is used to. Her free hand latches to my arm when I tilt my head to deepen the contact, my stomach churning as she arches into me. The metallic scent of her envelops me, settling into my head like a traumatic memory. Pure sorrow slams through me, serving as a reminder of what happened in this very spot just hours ago. When I watched the last bit of mercy leave her glassy eyes, the weight of both realms crushing me the moment she turned around.

I pull back, my heart dropping as her features immediately harden when her eyes flick behind me. She reaches for my hip, pushing me to the side as she saunters ahead where my father glares.

"Just the king I wanted to see!" His disappointed gaze slides from me to her. I'm torn with what to do...I'd confidently admitted I would stop her if she attempted an attack on my father, but now that it is only us three in this dark, eerie courtyard, I cannot find it in me to get in her way.

She halts a breath away from my father while tapping the blade on her thigh; her other hand holds her father's book at her back, but I've no doubt she could end him with no hands if she truly wanted.

Duty eclipses emotion, and I move to step between them, though my feet remain glued to the ground. My eyes widen as I glance at my father, who thankfully focuses all his angry attention on the assassin. She's fucking warded me in place...heat slides through my limbs as I readjust, crossing my arms as if I'm merely waiting for their conversation to end.

Cunning little wraith.

Like she heard my thoughts, she peers over her shoulder to regard me with an amused look. My father's gaze shifts to me as well, though he is everything but amused. She smiles evilly, saying one last thing to him before she stalks into the castle. The pressure around my feet dissipates, though I remain in place for a few moments more as my father studies me. My father's fists clench and unclench, the expression he wears telling me that he's struggling to keep his word.

"You said you would not harm her," I recount, shuffling around him when he doesn't respond.

The icy wind does nothing for the sweat building along my neck, which worsens when I enter the castle. I'm uncomfortably warm in these clothes—perhaps a cold shower will help. I look down as I speed through the dimly lit hallways that lead to my room; blood continues to spot through my shirt, and I sigh heavily. Elowen will scold me to the Aether for tearing any of my stitches.

Silver hair clouds my mind with ideas I shouldn't entertain. I cannot tonight, anyway. She's going to be pissed when I visit her later.

I nod to Gavriel when he appears next to me, too caught in my thoughts to defend myself when he grabs my neck and shoves me into a room.

"What the fuck, Gavriel?" I whip around to confront him, pausing as he slams the door and closes the distance between us.

"Are you out of your fucking mind?" I put my hands to his chest and force him back. He groans, swiping a hand over his mouth. "I was against you being near her from the beginning—I even told her to stay the fuck away from you! But clearly you're both children who do not know how to follow simple directions!"

My brows scrunch together, something acidic shuffling around my stomach. "Gav...where is this coming from? What do you mean you told her to stay away from me? Why would you do that?" He doesn't need to specify who he's speaking of; I already know how he feels about the wraith.

He curses and paces the room—I look around to the rows of towels, linens, and cleaning supplies. He's shoved me in a storage closet. Fucking bastard couldn't wait one more minute until we reached my room?

"Okay," he announces, raising his hands as if he's just relented on an internal argument. His dark eyes meet mine. "You're going to listen to me, Caspian. She is not good for you...she kills the people you are destined to protect when you take your father's place on the throne. I don't know how else to explain that it's impossible for you to have her, even if I did agree with it. Fucking Aether, prince, she *stabbed* you and the first thing you do upon waking is beg for her life to be spared? That should be evidence enough for you to realize she doesn't fucking care about you!"

He's wrong. "That's not true."

"Not true? She threatens your life each time you're near her—"

"Shut the fuck up, Gavriel. You have no idea who she is or what she's like. You only see what you wish to see, and that's fine, but you *will not* lecture me on my decisions."

He chuckles, though there is no humor in it. "Right...and what about your father?"

I scoff, shaking my head as I lean uncomfortably against a set of shelves. Their wooden edges press into my ribs, and the towels tempt me to use them as a barrier. "What about him?"

"He undeniably also has something against her! He may not have said so much in words, but the attempts on her life are a clear enough sign that you should be running the other way. Why do you *insist* on pursuing her still? I thought you were smarter than this..."

I clear my throat, the day's events quickly catching up to me as my eyes become heavier. "Ouch."

He sighs loudly, dropping his head back. "I just don't want you to get hurt—again—or killed because of a woman you barely know."

I wait until his eyes meet mine. "I know enough," I whisper, my tense muscles relaxing when he nods. I know he'll drop the subject, regardless of how he feels. I cannot fault him for his words; he's like a brother to me and was terrified when he'd found me bleeding and unconscious outside.

"I wandered the halls last night..." he trails off, and I raise my brow expectantly. "I walked past the south entrance that leads under the castle, and there were two sentries stationed in front of the door."

My face scrunches deeply as my mind whirls through a hundred things that could explain why guards were assigned there. "To the tunnels, right?" He nods, leaning a shoulder against the shelves next to me. "Why the fuck would that require protection? Did you check the other entrances?"

"No—and before you ask, I didn't go down there, either. Do I look fucking stupid to you?" He holds up a hand when I grin. "Don't answer that." I laugh, my chest feeling lighter than it has in hours.

"Okay, well I need to sleep before we talk about what to do next. Are we okay?" I gesture between us, narrowing my eyes.

He rolls his, slapping my hand away as he walks to the door. "I'm still angry with you." I burst out laughing when he stalks from the room, muttering about my clear lack of self-control.

Chapter Twenty-Seven

Ariella

Weaving my umbral strand, I string together more wards than I normally would—something I'm becoming annoyingly efficient at. I toss the journal onto my bed and step into the bathroom, my breathing finally slowing. My palms press to the vanity as I study myself in the mirror.

This is the monster I've become.

Stiff hair matted with blood that looks darker than it should, courtesy of the fucking silver strands. The same hair I once loved for the reputation it gave me, but now hate because it's colored with Isaiah's—

A deep breath.

It's difficult to see how much blood soaked into my clothes, but the imperceptibly dark patches are enough of an answer. The cream tile clashes with my hands, making it painfully obvious how grotesque they look. The same hands that just carried Isaiah back home.

There's a light tinge of red covering parts of my face, streaking where the prince grabbed me—I've never been so conflicted about someone. The sincere hope in his eyes when he claimed to know what I did caught me off guard...Elowen seems to know more than I'd like her to, especially because she feels it necessary to inform the prince of every detail. Caspian would have lived with or without her help, so it was not vital that he know the manner in which I chose to impale him.

I am fucking weak.

I should have sliced through his heart, and this would no longer be an issue. That's what I've been planning to do—the only thing I've wanted for years. My blade was a moment away from following through...but when I had the chance to uproot the king's life?

I can fuck with him in other ways—that's what I told myself when I held my trembling blade to the prince's abdomen.

"I bet you believed killing Isaiah would get you what you want?" The king stands unmoving with a smugness only royals could exude. "That's where you fucked up, Thalion." The prince tugs against my wards, but I don't release him immediately. He does not need to be privy to my words.

"I don't think so, Ms. Mistaire. Your reaction confirmed this; though I am still debating on forgetting my son's ridiculous begging for your life and taking it, anyway." He sighs, bored. "No matter, I have a feeling something else will do that for me very soon." I fail to care what he means as I lean in to make sure he hears my next admission clearly.

"You just took away the only *thing in my life that would have made me comply with your demands. Now I've nothing left to lose...so your precious son, Thalion?" I look at the prince over my shoulder before facing the king's cold eyes once more. "He's mine."*

My lip curls at every memory from today rummaging through my head—I will allow myself one minute to feel everything I need to before shutting it all down once more.

My body sags at the concession, and I press my eyes tightly closed as I lean over the vanity. The night with Caspian and every uncomfortable thing that settled inside me when I gave in to what I'd convinced myself was just pure lust. The horrific anticipation I felt walking toward Isaiah's body, already knowing what I would find. Driving my blade into the prince after ignoring the half of my body that pleaded for me to spare him. Looking at my best friend one last time, before impulsively deciding to visit my parents' home because I wasn't ready to face Caspian yet. Or the king.

Any of it.

A strangled breath leaves me, and before I can fully comprehend what I'm doing, my fist connects with the mirror. A comforting pain rushes from my knuckles to the top of my arm as the brittle glass cracks with a sharp, skin-tingling sound. The hairs along my skin rise when I meet the eyes of my fragmented reflection; a desolate image void of any lingering emotion.

I can handle emptiness. I prefer it.

My time in the shower is significantly longer than I'd anticipated. The blood from my clothes stained my skin, especially heavy where the water surrounded me when I stood in the fountain. I scrub my body so hard that I cannot tell where my blood begins and Isaiah's ends. I watch the last of his life slip away, his entire existence folded into a few drops of crimson sinking into the drain.

Something inside me cracks when I turn the water off, drying quickly enough that I'm not tempted to look at my skin before exiting the bathroom. I don't want to see what I just did—how easy it was for me to wipe him from my body. I scrunch my eyes, shoving a shirt roughly over my head, groaning when it gets caught on my nose. Crumpling of the bedding fills the silence; something I would have once found comforting, but cannot stand right now.

I reach for my father's journal, only to pull my hand back. Something frantic tugs inside me, wanting to know everything he wrote, didn't write, crossed out, smudged...all of it. But I do not think it is the right time—there's too much happening in my head to process anything he wrote.

I sigh, sliding under the sheets, my eyes drifting closed before I'm even fully settled.

A blade is in my hand before my eyes snap open at the loud knocking on my door. I scan the dark room twice before I'm confident it's only me in here. I quietly rise from the bed, tensing when another round of pounding sounds ahead of me. I slip on my training clothes and tie my hair up before walking to the door, my heart racing. There's a sliver of light that passes through the bottom, adjusting with the person that is on the other side.

This could be a trap. Whoever it is must have discovered my wards when they weren't able to break in...unfortunately for them, they will not walk away knowing my secret. I tug on my umbral strand and pull apart the essence just as the person frantically knocks again.

"Ariella, please open up!" My head falls back at the prince's whisper-shouting, flutters moving through my abdomen. "I don't have much time before someone else comes to get you." My brows furrow as I yank the door open, being met with Caspian's loose-fitted pants and unbuttoned shirt. I avert my eyes to find his—interesting he appears upset instead of hungry, as if he didn't wander to this side of the castle for one thing.

I cross my arms and rest my chin on the blade, using the sting to ground my reaction. "If you woke me thinking I'd fuck you, I fear you are incredibly mistaken on how well you use your dick." Misleading, but partially true.

"What?" he questions, his eyes looking to the right momentarily. "I'm not—I mean I would. I want to but—wait. Did you just say I'm bad at sex? Because I distinctly remember you admitting the opposite when I made you come a third time." My eyes narrow at the fist he holds against his side.

"Did I?" A smile plays at my lips as I lean against the door frame. "I don't recall making such an inaccurate statement."

He chuckles, his cheeks reddening. He runs a hand over the back of his neck as his eyes drink in my body. "Fuck, I wish I didn't have to do this right now. I'd love nothing more than to stir up those missing memories of yours."

"What *are* you doing here, if it's not to talk your way into my bed?"

Every sense heightens when he looks down the hall again. Maybe this is a trap, after all. "I'm sorry, angel." I straighten at his pained expression, gripping my blade tighter.

"What do—" I falter when his closed hand reaches up to toss something at my face. Powder. "What the fuck, prince? I will..." my words slur off as my entire body grows extraordinarily heavy. "Why?" He lunges forward to grab me when I stumble back. I fight with everything I have to stay awake, but the last thing I hear is the prince apologizing over and over again.

I lurch up, coughing violently at the freezing powder I breathed in. My hands immediately reach to cover my face as it gets belted with what feels like shards of ice. I will my body to stop shivering so badly, though my attempts are useless. The cold bites into my skin, burning each nerve it touches.

The only thing I can hear is the incessant howling that masks even my heavy breathing. I cup my eyes and peek through my hands—snow. When did it start fucking snowing in Valoria?

Something flaps from under my sleeve, and I pull out the paper, struggling to read what it says.

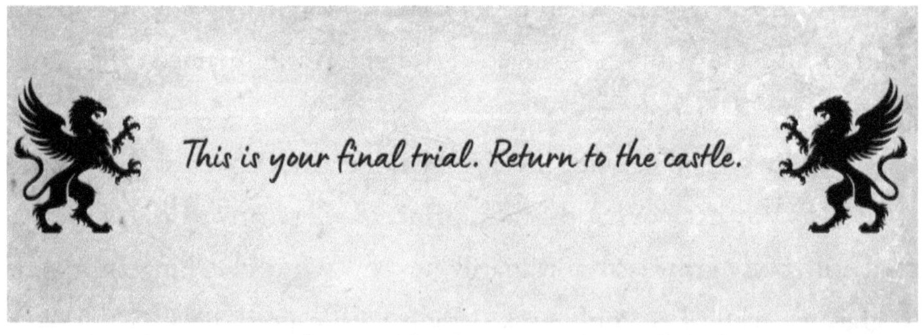

My hands touch my face and body—everything *feels* the same...

"That fucking bastard drugged me!" I scoff, tucking my face into the bend of an arm.

I need to move. Quickly. I've no idea how long I was unconscious for, and I can already feel my limbs weakening as their resources are directed to the center of my body. I carefully push up, barely managing to stand without the frenzied blizzard forcing me back down. My lungs burn as I sigh deeply when my fingers touch the blade at my thigh—Caspian must have sheathed it before he brought me here.

How *did* I get here?

I wince as a strong gust of wind attacks me, my fingers dotted with blood when I pull them back.

Heat, then move.

The only things I can think about right now, lest the king get his wish after all. My eyes scrunch closed as I attempt to concentrate on calling to my pyro strand; it takes several tugs before the familiar essence comes forward. I coax it over my skin, only enough to prevent the worst effects of the storm. Even just that small amount of warmth feels like it was gifted by the Angel itself.

Covering my eyes once more, I scour my surroundings, clearing my throat when the dryness tickles it. It is impossible to see more than a few feet in any direction, though the slope under my feet and the amount of snow already on the ground tell me everything I need to know—for now.

Unstable memories threaten to thwart my focus, but I shove them down and begin wading down the mountain. At least, I think this is the direction I need.

I chuckle, the movement feeling how I imagine sands in the Cindara Desert do. My legs move too slowly through the snow, and after only minutes I am panting and sweating. This is not good—I've no food, water, or reliable clothing. My sweat is quickly depleting my body's heat, though I can weave more. For a while. The most pressing issues are how damp my clothes will get from the sweating and how quickly I will become dehydrated.

"I could melt some snow..." I scan the area once more, decently confident that no one would witness my use of undocumented essence. It would be a big risk, but so would not having water.

I straighten and continue inching forward, shoving each hand under an arm to conserve essence. I've never determined just how much I can use before my body gives out from exhaustion—and I'd rather not discover that at this moment.

I've no idea how much time passes before I'm cursing the Angel for not creating any useful essence. It would be a dream to fly down the fucking mountain, but instead I'm anticipating another several hours before I reach the castle. My sweat has coated the collar still imprisoning me, allowing the blizzard to quickly dry the hard material to my skin. I'm certain that moving it will only tear my skin with it; it burns, but it's not yet important enough for me to weave my pyro strand until it lets go.

The blizzard seems to have lessened—possibly. It is a challenge to know for certain, as everything is still just as white and blinding as before. My brow attempts to furrow, barely moving from how stiff my skin has become. I've yet to see another competitor...the Elysaran mountains reach north for hundreds of miles, but I wouldn't expect that we were all placed so far apart. They must be close. Or dead.

Hopefully the latter.

Images of lying down and being lost in the snow forever flood my mind. It would be so easy to succumb to the call of the mountain—give my body to it in exchange for ridding me of all my ridiculous problems.

I wheeze in another burning breath and drive myself forward. Isaiah's death would mean nothing if I let go. My father's death. Even my mother's. The king is responsible for each of their murders.

It may have been my mother that shoved the blade through her heart, but instinct tells me that Thalion was the reason for her decision. I'm unsure of how, but I'll never figure it out if I die here. I must keep going.

I struggle for hours, carefully weaving heat into my limbs when I've no other option. I have never known such exhaustion—tugging my pyro strand becomes harder with each attempt. It slips through my calling, forcing my body to become colder while I continue to sweat more water than I can physically consume. The amount of heat I can weave is minimal at this point; it's as if the cold is overpowering that strand. It could be affecting all of my affinities, though I will not test that theory in these conditions.

Nor will I allow myself to fear what will happen if I do not reach the base—or at least make it through this fucking blizzard. The shards of ice no longer strike me hard enough to bleed, though I can feel the rashes they're creating along my exposed skin.

My surroundings have brightened slightly, and I'm certain I can see a bit further, though it does not feel like enough compared to how long I've been walking—stumbling, mostly. However I imagined I could keep Isaiah alive long enough to win...I'm not sure. My body is barely listening enough to save myself, so to ensure the safe descent of two?

My best friend's unimpressed eyes flash just ahead, as if he's telling me just how pathetic that sounds. He's right—the reminder sinks into my skin, providing energy I couldn't detect before. I'm the fucking Silver Wraith...I will not yield to a bout of snow.

I look up, nearly groaning at the hint of shapes coming into view. I squint when the shapes appear to move—no, shape. Just one.

My stiff fingers find the icy blade on my thigh and unsheathe it. The distinct features of another person fill out the closer I get. They must hear my shuffling as they spin, screeching before they stumble to their back, indenting the snow with their flailing body.

I take a step. "Please don't!" the person croaks. A woman. "I don't want to die on the mountain! Please just let me get down so that my family can have my body!" I recognize that voice.

I march forward and rip trembling arms away from their face to be met with—"Ally?"

Chapter Twenty-Eight

Ariella

"Fuck's sake, you couldn't have died already?" I blow out a long, grating breath. I shouldn't hesitate—she will be killed by something else, if not me—but her presence reminds me too much of Isaiah. Memories flicker through my resistant mind, but I quickly shove away the thoughts and focus on Ally.

She frowns at whatever she finds upsetting about my words and pushes weakly to her feet. "That was rude...so glad to see you, too!"

"You shouldn't be." She smacks her cracking lips, coughing dryly. The tips of her eyelashes and brows are frosted over, creating an eerie aura around her eyes.

She scoffs, hunching into herself until she looks no more than a child. It would be so easy to leave her and allow the mountain to handle her death. Isaiah is no longer here to reprimand such considerations. Perhaps the Angel allows him to watch from the Aether realm, but why should I care? What is he going to do—resurrect himself just to tell me that I must be nicer to a woman he had a crush on?

That's exactly what he'd do if the Angel permitted...just to annoy me.

"Listen," Ally croaks, rubbing a hand over her throat. "I know I'm not going to live through this, but I truly just want off the mountain before I die. My family deserves to have my body."

My forehead creases—this is the second time she's said that. I may have let it go once, but twice is no coincidence. "Your family?" A slow nod. "How exactly did you come from the guild if you have a family?" Her eyes look to my left as she searches for an answer.

Her impassive laugh is a little too forced. "I forgot you wouldn't even consider anyone at your guild a friend...but they're my family." I hum and tap on my blade, her eyes catching the movement.

"Is that why they sent *you*—the weakest member—to a deadly competition? Because they're your *family*? I remember you admitting similar thoughts only weeks ago..."

She shivers as her arms somehow slide around her torso further. Her voice shakes as she mumbles, "Whatever, Ariella. Can you just please wait to kill me until we're down? It's what Isaiah would want you to do..."

I flex every muscle I can, if only to keep from sending the full force of my shadows over her to drain all the pathetic bits of essence resting under her skin.

If I found *her*, there are likely others nearby. Watching.

"Do not *ever* speak his name again, or you'll be begging me for death long before we're off this fucking mountain." If it was possible for her skin to pale further, it would have. Quiet rage flashes in her eyes before she looks away. I nod behind her and change my grip on the blade. "Go—before I change my mind."

There is no delay to her movements as she spins and stalks through the snow. The blizzard has calmed, the wind less biting, though I still cannot see too far ahead. I keep a good distance behind Ally, and the crunch of her footfalls identifies the amount of warning I would have before an attacker reaches me.

I fixate on the back of her head for the next hour, debating on whether saying fuck it and sinking my blade into her skull would be the right decision. I don't—the prominent awareness of what happened the last time I said that sticks obnoxiously to every thought.

I'm unsure at what point every breath that entered my lungs turned from burning to only slight discomfort, though the possibility of being close to the bottom energizes my nerves. I twirl my blade through a hand, surveying the dull landscape around me.

My feet move before my mind registers the scream up ahead—I'd have to thank the Angel if another competitor killed Ally before I had to. But it's not another person...I slide to a stop just behind her, rearing back to avoid stumbling over the cliff edge like it appears Ally did. She lies flat on the ground with her legs dangling over the edge as she clutches to a blade I was not aware she could use.

She tilts her head into the snow, eyes immediately finding mine. "Thanks for the help!" I truly was unaware that such mindless fools existed in this realm.

"Why in the Aether would I have helped?" She gapes at me as if I'm the ridiculous one.

I straighten as a prickling sensation skims down my neck. I flip my blade to hold the tip before stepping one foot back and flinging it at a barely perceptible shadow. Another blade zips past my head—where I'd just stood—before succumbing to the endless drop over the mountain. Forever lost.

My eyes narrow when the shadow grunts, muttering curses under its breath before marching closer. A figure with red hair and an arrogant swagger comes into view.

Jeth.

Fuck me, I do not wish to deal with this.

His dark eyes lock onto mine, a wicked smirk cresting his face. "Ah, my favorite cock-blocker!" He yanks my blade from his shoulder and tosses it to the side. "Well, only for a day...Sivara was more than willing to take your place."

I raise a brow, keeping my voice as low as the storm will allow. "And where is my place, exactly?"

A toothy grin. "On your knees, of course," he taunts, searching my face for any reaction.

He'll find none.

"If I recall...it was you who got on your knees for me. Actually, I have been curious..." I saunter leisurely in his direction. "Was the healer able to repair every part of your cock? Or are you even more of a disappointment now?" His lip curls, a manic expression coating his eyes and features.

"You stupid bit—"

"Ah, ah," I lilt, holding up a mocking finger. "You'd do well to remember the consequences of such words." I'm sure his thighs press together, though I am too focused on his snarling face to check.

He lunges for me, swinging his arms like a crazed beast. Under normal circumstances, it would be easy to block him—but these are not normal circumstances, and my feet slip on a sheet of ice just as he reaches me. I fall back into the snow, grunting when Jeth's weight drops onto me. He snickers, and I expect him to pull out a weapon or hit me, but he does neither. Instead, he reaches for the buttons on my pants, yanking at them frantically as he mutters about the things he's going to do to my dying body. I drive my knee into his ass hard enough that he screams and use his distraction to slam my fist in the center of his throat. He chokes, scrambling to the side as jump up and run to grab my blade.

"I do not have time for your stupid games—it is too fucking cold," I bark, grabbing his hair and dragging him to his feet. "Give the Angel my worst wishes." He makes to grab for me, but I drop my hold on him to kick his chest hard enough that he falls off the side of the mountain. His piercing scream is the best thing I've heard in the last day.

"Oh shit," Ally whispers as she steps next to me and peers over the edge. "Please don't do that to me." I almost laugh.

Strands of my hair whip around my face as a strong updraft curves over the mountain's mouth, as if to thank us for the sacrifice.

Perhaps it will allow us to descend now.

The sun rises, the snow finally ceasing—my breath catches. I knew the Elysaran Mountains swept across days worth of travel, but I think it is impossible to imagine the kind of beauty in front of me. Ranges of summits that stretch significantly further than even the Angel could see, creating a valley where part of the river runs through. The barely peeking sun highlights opposite sides of the mountains that surround the river, their ridges blinding. I spin—each direction but one filled with the same vastness. Above, not a single cloud threatens to cover the orange morning light.

I wonder if my mother ever saw this....she always loved being outside. She'd tell me stories of grand adventures in the lands and homes resting in the clouds themselves—they were never but fables to me, but now I'm not so sure.

I clear my throat when another gust of wind stings my tired eyes, and I turn left to continue walking.

"Thank the fucking Angel," I announce. Ally startles at the coarse sound in place of peaceful silence. I snort—as if anything about this is peaceful. I wave Ally along when she pauses to look at me, eager to finish the last bit of our journey off this merciless mountain. The rows of buildings that make up Valoria are much closer than I'd expected, so there is maybe an hour left before we reach the base.

The snow melts to jagged terrain, the muscles in my legs trembling by the last step before I drop onto the path that connects Grenport to Valoria and Meridian. I rest my hands just above my hips, greedily breathing in the significantly warmer air. I squint at the mocking sky—it's barely morning, yet now so hot that beads of sweat slide down my neck. I sigh at the crunch of footsteps next to me. What to do with her...

"Okay, how do you—" my question ends on a gasp as sharp pain radiates through my upper arm. My blade is in my hand before I spin to block Ally's advance, slicing deeply down her forearm. She screams and pulls back, clutching the wound to her chest.

"Really? You actually thought to try something so foolish?" I reach over my chest to pull her blade from where it impaled me, wincing at the sting.

She laughs as her teeth pull a piece of torn fabric tightly around her arm. "You truly think so highly of yourself... *Valoria's Silver Wraith is someone to be feared*, they told me. *She's the deadliest, most skilled killer this realm has ever known*, they said." She cackles, sliding a handful of star blades from her pockets. "You know what I see? Someone who makes everyone else think she is this strong, fearsome assassin, but is only just a weak whore of a woman who throws herself on every royal cock she can find." My brows raise as a giddy smile tugs at my lips—she has my attention.

"Is that so? Well, certainly feel free to kill me now, as I am too *weak* to defend myself."

Someone else settles in Ally's light eyes...no, this is the real her. The person she's been hiding behind some feeble, idiotic mask as she feigned ignorance in everything.

She smirks. "When the king came to me with his offer, I would have agreed without the promise of a throne. Your reputation is a topic of everyday conversation in the rest of the Kingdom—the people, they're scared of you, but they love to talk about you. It's disgusting...so many lies spoken of your *talents*.

"Anyway," she sighs, stretching her neck from side to side. "When the king asked me to get close to you before finally killing you...it was one of my happiest days. *I* would be the one to show the kingdom just how pathetic you actually are. Show them that your name truly means nothing; just scary stories woven by fools with nothing better to do."

I am still stuck on one thing she mentioned. "He promised a throne?"

Her eyes brighten as if she's been waiting to tell me her next words for so long and is giddy to finally do so. "Oh, yes...I know how much you love your pretty prince, but the king promised me his hand—and bed—for your secrets and death. And now I'm going to bring him your head." I refuse to acknowledge the nauseating rage that simmers in my gut from the image of her in Caspian's bed.

Fuck if I would *ever* allow her near him.

But... "And you believed him? You didn't take one moment to consider why he asked you, of all the people in the kingdom, to do his bidding? You're from a distant guild, brought to a city where no one knows you...any way you die could easily be blamed on the competition, Ally.

He was never going to allow you Caspian's hand...you were just easy to convince and even easier to rid of when he's done with you."

I step closer as she shifts, her forehead creasing deeply. "No," she whispers, shaking her head. "He said I'd be the prince's wife if I did this!"

"Did he?" A resolved nod—she's getting angry. People make mistakes when they're angry. "Where is the contract he had you sign? Or the witnesses to the conversation he had with you?" Another step, and she notices my slow advance this time, holding a star up threateningly.

"None of that matters! I'll just tell—" she pauses, realization drooping her features.

"Now you get it," I say sweetly. "Even if you were to live through this, who the fuck would believe you over the king? And even if the king admitted to saying that...who is going to force him to follow through? The Angel?

"Honestly, Ally, I thought you were dense before; but this—" I gesture to the space between us with my blade. "This is pathetic. Embarrassing."

"Shut up! You're just bitter that he'll be mine, and I'll give him enough heirs to carry our family's reign for centuries."

I burst out laughing, the events of the last few days quickly catching up to me. "If you truly believe I'd be upset about not being the prince's breeding tool..." I chuckle again, ducking when a star blade whizzes through the air. "You'll have to do better than that—" My words cut off when she tosses several more in succession, wincing when one scrapes the top of my leg.

She runs for me when her hands are empty, jumping to catch her legs around my waist and flip us over. We roll through the dirt, both grappling for the upper-hand—she's a significantly better fighter than she ever let on. I'm almost impressed.

My elbow flies into her jaw, my other arm growing too weak to continue much longer. I may have trained myself to heal in moments like this, but actually living it is utterly different. My focus wavers when I attempt to reach for my vital strand, allowing her several hits that she shouldn't have gotten. It's useless to attempt healing my arm right now.

She must have trained hard for this, being a more worthy opponent than anyone I've ever fought. Part of me wishes to prolong our sparring, but my faltering muscles and limbs protest such a foolish idea. I crouch as she stalks toward me again, twisting up to hurl a fist full of dirt in her eyes. I do not stop to catch my wheezing breath before I grip the hilt of my blade and slice it across her throat. She sputters, all but forgetting the pain in her eyes in favor of the mass amount of blood draining from the wound. She trips as she backs away, landing with a thud on her back and attempting to find purchase along her throat—the sweet blood too slick to be anything but helpful.

I grimace, wiping my blade along her tattered shirt. I cannot keep back a yawn and sit heavily on a rock a couple of feet away—I am so fucking tired. I should hurry back to the castle, lest my collar blows my head off for taking too long, or something else just as ridiculous.

My eyes snap to the gurgling woman at my feet, rolling when she continues to struggle for breath. I lean back on a hand and silently beg for clouds to appear.

"Would you like to know something, Ally?" I wait for a hiss of air to wheeze from her lungs and nod. "I knew you weren't nearly good enough for Isaiah...and I am quite disappointed in myself because I would have let him have you. That man has been through so much shit that even the Angel would balk, but he deserved to be happy." I groan when she doesn't answer, instead twitching as her body makes one last attempt for air.

I lean forward to rest my elbows atop my knees and smirk as her eyes become unfocused. The blood leaking from her throat slows to trickles, small droplets causing ripples in the pooling beneath her neck.

"As you leave this realm, I want you to remember one thing." I push from the rock to crouch, grabbing her chin to force her eyes on me—she likely cannot see or hear me, but that's not my problem. "If I have even an inkling of you attempting to taint Isaiah's spirit, I won't even bother calling to my spectral strand. I will march right into the Aether realm, find your soul, and tear it from the Aether's grasp. Then I'll feed it to the first creature I cross paths with, because you are worth nothing more than a beast's disappointing snack. Stay. Away. From. Him." I shove her face away, feeling lighter than I have in days.

Chapter Twenty-Nine

Ariella

Hairs along my arms rise the closer I get to the castle. Every home I pass, every shop and tavern, all empty. The city is quiet. Desolate. Abhorrent heat beats down on my exhausted body—the irony of me all but begging the cold to disappear just a few hours ago is not lost on me.

My tongue weakly attempts to provide any moisture to my mouth and lips, even knowing the only solution at this point is water. My head pounds harder than the sun as every muscle in my body aches, as if they've been pushed past their limits for days.

I'm so caught in the throes of my discomfort that I breeze through the castle gates before noticing the lack of red and gold attire that normally surround the entrance. I pause, wincing at the strain looking over my shoulder causes in my neck.

There is not a single royal guard in sight. I scan the courtyard, purposefully skipping the fountain—no one. No movement or chatter. No wary stares in my direction. Nothing. Until a booming cheer sounds from the left, my feet moving toward the arena before my mind catches up.

The noise gets louder as I step closer to the large structure behind the castle. What the fuck could they be cheering for? And while the rest of us are dying on a mountain? Pathetic.

Two royal guards donning those unbecoming red masks straighten when they spot me. One nods his head before pivoting to enter a tunnel several feet away from the door they're stationed in front of. A finger taps on my blade as I follow the guard, smirking each time he looks back as if I'm about to attack.

Maybe I will just because of how fucking annoying he is.

Stale, dry air thickens; the man ahead nothing more than a barely perceptible silhouette. It takes longer than I remember before light grows in the distance, and I can feel my heart's racing tempo in my throat.

The noise becomes near-deafening as the guard gestures ahead, and I step through the entrance. I stop my restless finger to unsheathe my blade.

This does not feel like a crowd that is ready to congratulate a winner. They're hungry, basically drooling around their pleas of a *final round*. It is not difficult to discern their meaning when my eyes lock with Sivara's, who stands idly at the center of the arena. I swallow down every bit of pain and tiredness as I saunter to the only other person in the grounds with me.

At least I am not alone in having struggled my way back. Her normally pristine hair falls around her in hardened chunks, a hint of red glistening when the light hits it right. Her leathers are torn in several places, faring better than the flayed pieces of skin hanging from her arm.

I avert my eyes—too fresh of a reminder. Images of Isaiah's body will only render me at a disadvantage.

My knees almost give out when I stop a dozen feet from my opponent, turning right to face Eldoria's illustrious royal family. My eyes pull to the side where the prince sits already watching me—always watching me. He winces, mouthing *I'm sorry.* I memorize his lips as they wrap around the simple words; the same ones I wish I had the chance to tell my best friend.

Caspian offers a sad smile, as if he knows where my thoughts went. But now they veer in another direction...tension, heat, those lips devouring mine. Feeling wanted and cherished when it is the last thing I'd ever deserve. His contorted features when my blade met his flesh. Blood seeping from the same lips that gave me so much the night before.

What he did last night.

When I'd gone from wanting to kill him to needing to protect him, I'm not sure. Truthfully, I'm too exhausted—physically and mentally—to be sure of anything at the moment.

I meet his warm, gentle eyes and return his smile, if only to silence my head so that I may focus on whatever the king is about to say.

The bastard himself stands, gesturing to the audience with his arms. "My great people of Eldoria, welcome to the final trial!" Cheers. It's baffling just how invested these people are in trials they've barely seen—that is until I'm reminded of how these same people laughed as my father was whipped in the same streets they walk each day. "Before you are the two remaining competitors—the others have been confirmed deceased." So they *have* been watching us somehow.

The king leans against the railing in front of him, gesturing to my left. "Sivara Dhuri, here from the cliffs of Invalle," he booms, grinning widely before narrowing his beady eyes at me. Uncoordinated stomping rings from behind me, likely those who know Sivara personally. "And Ariella Mistaire, the legendary Silver Wraith, and a member of Valoria's very own guild!" I don't want their admiration or applause. I have half a mind to test just how widely my essence can spread, so that I may kill every fool from here to the Aether.

If for no other reason than silencing their vexatious cries.

"There may only be one crowned victor..." His attention sweeps between my opponent and me. "Sivara. Ariella. Do whatever you must to wi—" The entire arena silences as Sivara's body drops to the ground, my blade protruding from just above her ear.

He wanted a show? He will not get one from me.

I'm fucking sick of being paraded in front of the good citizens of Eldoria who want nothing more than to watch me bleed. Suffer. I'm done wearing this collar and taking part in this sham of a competition.

The next blade I throw will meet the creased space between his eyes. I glare through him and ensure he hears my message clearly.

He's next.

My eyes scan the audience, most of them tense with shocked expressions. Some laugh. Others carry their children out of the arena. When my attention flits back to the royals, a ghost of a smile settles on the queen's face. She's fitted in a silken, gold dress with straps that reach around to hug her neck. Gold chains fitted with jewels I cannot make out wrap around both wrists. Her long hair falls in waves over a shoulder, a lighter piece framing her severe face.

Next to her, Vespera stares at Sivara's body with her jaw hanging as far as I'm sure it will go. I pass over the king to focus on Caspian, who covers his mouth with a hand, eyes glimmering playfully as if he's struggling to hold in a laugh. He straightens and bites his cheek when the king pins him with a disapproving look before addressing the utterly silent arena.

"I suppose we have our champion! Ariella Mistaire, you have proven yourself worthy of such a title. The awarding ceremony will occur in two days time. For now...*rest.*" The manner in which he spits the word churns my stomach, guaranteeing I will indeed *not* be resting.

But no longer will I remain here, either.

I cross my feet to turn back toward the tunnel, stalking from the arena without acknowledging any of the cheers or questions aimed my way. The moment I enter the castle, I pause to breathe. It's over—and I'm still alive. Isaiah will not be crowned the winner. I did not murder the prince or his father. Not a single one of my plans succeeded, and I am now left with dozens of questions that I did not have before.

I sway, pressing a hand to a cream wall and opening the eyes I didn't realize I'd closed. I need to return to my room before I fall unconscious right here and render myself vulnerable. Then I will sleep before thinking further about any of this.

No—water first, then sleep.

I attempt to swallow, a phantom of the motion gliding down my throat.

I wander through several halls, filled with paintings and decor that scream *royal.* Something touches my shoulder, my hand snapping up to grab the wrist of the prince, who immediately covers it with his other in a placating manner. He says something.

"What?" His brows furrow as he examines my body, focusing longer on the bloody spots. "Not all of it is mine." I'm not sure why I felt the urge to calm his nerves.

"Are you okay? I was calling for you, but clearly you did not hear me coming," he whispers, his thumb rubbing heavily over my finger that taps against him. I pull my hand back and continue walking.

"I'm fine." He says nothing, walking next to me as if we're equals. His steps are sure—confident in a way that only the gait of someone who is familiar with their route would be.

"Ariella, I'm so sorry for last night..."

I stop abruptly, reaching to pinch his chin and force his eyes to mine. "I'm not angry with you." Why do I care what he thinks? The heaviness in my body turns into an intense ache as adrenaline wears off. "I just can't talk about it right now, okay?" He peers down at my hand, a question flitting through his curious eyes. I say nothing, allowing him to grasp it with both of his. His lips brush over my fingers as his gaze locks with mine, a flickering sensation running down my arm.

"Okay." He squeezes my hand before dropping it lightly, grinning wickedly. "Though I will walk you to your room...you look a heartbeat away from death." I scoff, my eyes widening before I shove at his chest. He snorts, catching up when I stalk away from him.

"You really know how to make a woman feel good," I attempt to say coldly, though it comes out much softer.

"Would you like me to make you feel good, angel? My mouth is *excellen*t at so much more than just producing charming words." I can't help the laugh, though I don't hide it, either.

I struggle to weave my umbral strand enough to undo the wards at my door...only to groan when I remember there couldn't be any because I was drugged the last time I was here.

I feel eyes boring into me.

"What?"

I roll my head to Caspian as I lean against the door. He shrugs, sliding his hands into the pockets of his pants. "Nothing—I just love hearing you laugh." I suck in a breath as his hand reaches to push a loose strand of hair behind my ear. I shift, holding his stare. After a moment, he drops his hand and smiles, though it doesn't reach his eyes.

"I know—too much." He sounds almost sad. I shouldn't care...so why does my chest squeeze tightly from his defeated voice? "Get some sleep, Ariella," he breathes, nodding to my room before backing away. Should I ask him to stay... "Actually, shower first, will you?" He scrunches his nose playfully before disappearing down another hall.

I barely make it to my bed before my eyes close—huffing because I know he'll tease me for sleeping in such a filthy state.

Chapter Thirty

Ariella

I sit cross-legged on my bed—one I still need to change the sheets on. My nose scrunches at the memory of waking up surrounded by crumbled dirt, blood, sweat, and whatever the fuck else managed to latch onto my skin.

My chin rests heavily on closed fists, the pain from my knuckles the only thing keeping me here. In front of my father's journal.

Do I truly want to crack open this part of my past? To discover who my father actually was, and blur the too little memories I have of him?

"Stop being fucking pathetic—it's just some old writing." My voice is strange in the stillness of the room.

The leather creaks as I pry it open, breathing in deeply through my nose and out through my mouth. My shoulders ease with every page I turn, a hint of a smile on my lips. My father talked about my mother as if she were the only light in his life...he loved her just as much as I remember.

So many entries pass through my eyes—how beautiful my mother looked when she was pregnant with me. The day I was born, and how my father had dropped to his knees and bawled on my mother's legs after holding me for the first time. He said I was the single most beautiful thing he's ever seen...I clear my throat, blinking the burn away before turning the page.

I freeze as a deep pressure in my chest drops through my stomach. This one is a mere month before my mother took her life. I wasn't expecting the entries to go this far…

June 3

Can't sleep again, not that I've been sleeping much at all lately. The house is too damn quiet, like it's waiting for something bad to happen. Valyria told me her decision today. She's set on it. She wouldn't hear anything I had to say…it hurts. Sacrificing herself for the Accord? For Ariella? My head's spinning. How am I supposed to just stand by and watch? She says it's the only way. That the seer saw what would happen if she didn't. Ariella's so young, too young to lose her mom. And me? I can't even begin to imagine life without Val. This feels like a nightmare that I can't wake up from. How do you prepare to say goodbye to the person who means the most to you?

Something clogs my throat. I turn the page.

June 28

The world doesn't feel right anymore. The skies are darker when they should be clear, the air feels like it's pressing down on me, suffocating. Val sees it too, and every sign of the Accord's weakening pushes her closer to that final decision. I pleaded with her tonight...I dropped to my knees, begging her to reconsider. Begging her to speak with Elara, to try and find another way. But she shut it down. She won't risk going back to the Aether, won't risk what might happen to Ariella. It's like watching her walk straight into a storm, knowing I can't pull her back. I feel so powerless, so furious. So fucking scared. It's like there's this constant pressure on my chest, and I can't breathe, can't think. What are Ari and I going to do without her? How do I explain to a child that her mom died to give her time?

"What the fuck..." I barely breathe, hastily turning the page only for my breathing to increase rapidly.

The nearly empty page trembles as I flip it.

August 22

I haven't been myself. I've been trying so hard for Ariella, but I just feel like I'm so close to an answer and Valyria took her life prematurely. She said that whatever I found wouldn't change her fate. Then she actually did it...left us.

The house feels empty, hollow without her. I've been tearing through every old text and scroll we have, desperate for something, anything that could change this. I can't stop thinking that her sacrifice was for nothing. And I can't let that be the end of her story. I won't. For Ariella, I have to keep digging, have to find the truth. Even if it means standing against the king himself. I just know he's to blame for the balance shift. He's the reason the Accord weakens. I will figure it out. I promised I'd look after our little girl, and I'll fight for her until my last breath.

I begin frantically flipping through the pages, catching pieces of what life looked like for my father after his wife killed herself.

September 12

It's the middle of the night and I'm here, talking to this old journal like it can answer me. Sometimes I think I hear Valyria's voice, telling me it'll be okay. But it's just the wind, isn't it?

September 17

Last night, the horizon looked like it was on fire, the edges of the sky burning. Is that what Valyria saw? Is that why she couldn't stay? The weight of what's coming feels too heavy to bear alone.

November 1

Ariella was holding onto her mother's locket so tightly today, whispering to it, asking it why mommy had to go. My heart shattered right there. I held her, told her stories of her mom, the queen, the hero. But after I put her to bed, the silence was unbearable.

"What does that mean?" I choke, the tightening in my throat almost unbearable.

She killed herself...for me...for an Accord? What balance has shifted? What the fuck was I supposed to learn that I didn't because that bastard of a king—

I slap the journal shut and toss it across the bed.

I cannot think about any of this right now...it's too much.

I push from the bed, stumbling over my boots as I yank them over my feet and release the wards at my door. I don't have the mind to re-ward them before stalking toward the opposite side of the castle.

I swear to the Angel, if he isn't in his room...

I turn down a wide hallway and heat floods my veins as my eyes find a woman hanging from Caspian's arm, looking up at him with stars in her eyes. She's the complete opposite of me, and exactly who Caspian should want in his life. She has long, luscious, brunette hair—every strand curled to perfection. Her round, soft face compliments her lithe body, and the admittedly pretty lavender gown she's wearing hugs her small frame. She is the image of a perfect future queen.

Something I will never be—wouldn't *want* to be.

I do not wear dresses or curl my hair. I'm not sweet or innocent...I murder people for a living, and I love it. I have a dark past, and clearly an even darker future with whatever the fuck is coming.

I know Caspian and I could not work long-term, but I have zero qualms about fucking with any woman who thinks she does have a future with him.

My gaze hardens as I stop directly in front of the pair. The woman's eyes meet mine, hers widening as her neck flushes.

"Ariella...is there something I can help you with?" Caspian questions hesitantly, but I ignore him and continue studying the beauty in front of me.

It's possible she doesn't deserve my wrath...but she's touching what isn't hers.

"And who might you be?" I ask her sweetly, tilting my head.

"This is Je—" Caspian starts, but promptly shuts his mouth when I pin him with a heavy glare before my eyes slide back to the woman.

She peeks at the prince, obviously unsure of what to do in this situation. "Don't look at him." Her flustered stare snaps back to me, redness creeping up her pretty neck. "Look at me."

"I—I'm Jessenia," she stammers, her voice quivering slightly. Angel, she would not live a day outside of these castle walls. I pointedly glance at her arm wrapping around Caspian's. She takes the hint, pushing from him quickly as if he's some parasite—good girl.

"I assume you know my name already?" She nods, her nostrils flaring; she's trying hard to hide her fear.

I step forward, causing her to back away. Two more steps have her pressed against a table, her chest rising and falling quickly. There's a light sheen of sweat beginning to coat her appealing skin. I continue my advance until the front of my body lightly presses against hers and lift my hand to brush it along her cheek. She shivers, and I smirk—that did not feel like a tremble caused by anxiety.

I meet her wary eyes, curiosity and a glimmer of want flick through her sapphire irises. Interesting. "Well, Jessenia..." My hands spread to grab the edge of the table, leaning forward until I cage her in. A prisoner of my own. Our lips are a heartbeat away, though she does not pull back. "How would you like to be...*friends*?" She hesitates for a moment but nods; her breath coats my skin, the sweet and fruity scent tantalizing my nerves—I want to know what she tastes like.

"I would like that, too." I move my lips to press a kiss just under her jaw, testing how far she's willing to take this. She stiffens, but tilts her head slightly. Whether she realizes her body is arching into mine remains a mystery, though I have a feeling she's never experienced what it's like to have the focus on her.

Men have a way of ignoring all of a woman's needs, especially when they're given everything they want either way.

"You see, Jessenia—" Another kiss, to her neck this time. "I treat my friends well. But the thing is," her pulse flutters wildly against her throat, and I smile at her reaction to such simple touches, "you do not wish to know what it's like to not be my friend." I sweep my lips over her ear and whisper, "And if I ever see you near him again, you'll find out."

I lean back to hover her lips again. My stomach flutters as I cup her cheek, dread sweeping over her features before she nods. Her eyes flit to my lips before looking back up to me. She's definitely wondering if I could make her feel better than any fool she's ever been with.

I can.

My thumb swipes over her soft skin, and I smirk—I'd be caught dead by the Angel before admitting that I quite like her.

I press our mouths together, allowing her the freedom to pull away if she wishes. She doesn't. Her hand snaps to my elbow as her heart races against my breast. She's cautious—but curious—so I deepen the kiss and take all of her into me. She tastes of berries and warm days, and I nearly groan into her. My free hand traces her hip before grabbing her waist and pulling her closer. She's so eager to take everything I'm giving, holding onto me as if she never wants to let go. She's sighing into my mouth and arching in a way that molds her entire body to mine—and I am drinking in every moment of it.

Fuck Caspian, I want her.

No, I can't. I grip her hair, tugging her back just enough that the slick of our lips just barely touches. "Do we understand each other?" I murmur over her puffy skin. She nods again, and I chuckle at her inability to speak.

My features darken as I free her and step back—a simple reminder of who I am, and what will happen if she doesn't listen. "Now leave." She presses a hand to her chest, breathing deeply before scurrying away. She weaves around the prince as if he were a curse, not even bothering to look him in the eye as she goes.

I face Caspian fully, who leans against the wall with an eyebrow raised, smirking at me. "I never took you for the jealous type, angel." His amusement floods the space between us.

"Jealous?" I close the distance to him. "No...Jessenia and I just came to an understanding, is all."

"Is that so?" The smile he's attempting to hide tells me he doesn't believe a word I'm saying. He shouldn't.

"Yes. You and I have plans—she was in the way." I'm directly in front of him now, and I know he sees the heat in my gaze because his eyes narrow as his teeth graze their bottom lip. I snatch his hand and lead him down the hall toward his room.

"I must admit...what you did back there?" He laughs, taking a dramatic breath before sighing deeply. "That was hot as fuck." It's a struggle to hold in my smile, not answering him as I continue leading us through the castle.

Once we reach his room, I open the door and pull him inside, spinning to glare at the guard who is always there. As sweetly as I can manage... "Oh, Gavriel?" He narrows his eyes at me, knowing that whatever I'm about to say is going to piss him off. "If you don't want to hear your prince being thoroughly fucked, I'd cover your ears." I tap one of mine in point and wink before slamming the door shut.

Turning around, Caspian is watching me with bright, wide eyes. "You are inconceivable on the worst of days...but today? Fuck, I'm about to slit my own throat for daring to be in your presence."

He somehow never ceases to surprise me with the things he says. But I'm nearly bursting with too many emotions, my stomach churning wildly. I do not wish to deal with them right now. "I was being serious to

Gavriel. If you don't want this, tell me right now so I can go find someone else to fuck. I've no time for games." All lies.

He must see the desperation in my eyes, because his gaze darkens as he steps forward.

"You're *delusional* if you think I'll let another man touch you," he spits, grabbing my neck tightly and holding me in place. "Unless you wanted to go play with Jessenia? I may be convinced to allow that, as long as I can join." The humor in his voice shoots heat through my body. I snarl and grab his throat, shoving him roughly into the wall.

"You. Will. Not." He bites his lip, smiling.

Fuck, I fell right into his trap.

"I knew you were jealous." He presses into my grip to kiss me, my body immediately relaxing. When he pulls back, his features harden, serious once more as his astute eyes search mine. "What do you need, Ariella?"

All of my walls drop, and it's no longer the assassin and the prince in this room—it's just me and him. Two souls with opposite lives and the same goal.

Every instinct in my mind tugs me away from him, afraid to show anything that isn't the cruel, emotionless mask I'm so comfortable in.

"I need to forget," I whisper, wincing at my admittance of weakness.

But...the prince has never used those things against me, though he has every reason to. He's in the perfect position to fight me at every step, but he doesn't. He's always chosen to protect me—so I choose him now. My control is breaking, and the only person I had left in my life that wouldn't judge me is now dead.

Because of exactly what I'm about to do again.

The prince doesn't ask for any explanation, nodding as his hands seek the hem of my shirt, lifting it from my body. His lips find mine in a fervent kiss, not separating for one moment as we continue to undress each other. I stumble over my boot for the second time today, laughing when Caspian follows me, barely stopping us from falling to the rug.

"Fuck, I love that laugh," he murmurs, walking me backward.

My hands greedily flatten against his abdomen before sliding around his waist. He groans into my mouth when I grip the lines of muscles running along his spine, snapping whatever semblance of control I'd thought to maintain. As my ass meets the cold back of a wooden chair, I reach behind me to shove it aside before blindly swiping my hand across the prince's desk.

Stacks of paper, gilded pens, and Angel knows what else clank to the floor. He smiles, running his tongue down my jaw as his hands lift the backs of my thighs to place me on the desk.

"You're going to make Gavriel run in here thinking you've murdered me," he chuckles, my back bowing when he bites into the side of my neck. His fingers cup my breast, pinching hard, and my hand shoots out to catch myself from falling back at the onslaught of sensations. My forehead creases when I grab something sharp, looking over to see my pants somehow landed up here.

"Are you worried, prince? I'll invite him in myself, if it would make you feel better...though he couldn't do a fucking thing to stop me if I did wish to kill you."

He rises fully, kissing my needy skin until he reaches my ear. "I don't know," he grinds out, thrusting his cock through my center, leaving me writhing under his full attention. "How many times—" Thrust. "I have to fucking tell you—" Another, then one more. My fingers grip his shoulders tightly, as if they are the only things holding me together. "I am not scared of you, Ariella." In one movement, he tugs my head back by my hair, pushing the tip of his length just inside my entrance.

My legs shake when he pauses, grabbing my free hand to drag it down his chest until we reach a rough line of skin—his scar. He places his forehead on mine, and I have half a mind to shove my pelvis forward for any kind of relief as he remains still.

"Do you know why I refused Elowen when she attempted to heal this?" I feel utterly pathetic when a whine escapes me as he pushes in just a fraction more. I shake my head, if only to distract my trembling limbs from the overwhelming throbbing at my core. "Because as much as you refuse to admit it, this is a reminder that you *are* affected by whatever the fuck this is between us, just as I am. That you try so hard to convince yourself to hate me, and yet cannot find it in your deliciously murderous heart to truly hurt me...and I will wear this scar proudly for the rest of my life."

I pant against his lips, scrunching my eyes closed. Too much.

My hands pull us into a comfortable familiarity, my tongue searching for his until they caress each other in a demanding dance. He grips my wrists, ripping his own skin as my nails scrape over him when he pulls them off—I barely notice his chuckle from the way he undulates his hips, giving me not nearly enough of him. I can no longer draw him into me as he plants my hands on the table, encouraging them to hold me up as his cup my back and force me to arch forward.

"Caspian, please," I cry when he continues to deny me.

He pauses, peering up from where he was just about to suck my breast into his mouth. "I get the feeling you've never begged for anything in your life..." A mischievous glint enters those silver eyes. "I quite like the sound of it—I should tease you more often." My retort gets lost to his mouth—Angel, the things this man can do with his tongue. I shudder when he swirls my nipple gently before dragging his teeth over the bud.

My head falls back, only to snap up as he slides lower. A heartbeat later, he halts when a dagger meets his throat. "No. You're going to fuck me—right now."

He lifts to bring us at the same level, smirking before roughly thrusting forward until he's fully seated inside me. My mouth drops on an airless moan as my hand slackens, lowering the blade from his heated skin. Before I can drop it back to the desk, the prince grabs my wrist and brings the cool metal back to his throat. He leans forward, our bodies still connected, until his nose rests against mine. The only sound in the tense space is the heaviness of our breaths.

Instinct demands I pull away and not let him hold me in such a vulnerable position.

I ignore it.

Instead, I watch him. I do not blink as I absorb the silver irises staring deeply through me. This is too much.

My breaths quicken, heat sliding up my neck. As I'm a moment away from breaking the trance, his eyes darken and he presses further into the blade. One drop of crimson slides down his neck, spreading over the lines of his chest.

"Should I fail to fulfill your needs, I want you to use it." His hardened tone caresses my senses, causing the hair along my arms to rise. He drops his head slightly, his lips brushing a light kiss over the tingling skin of my own. "Because I wouldn't dare live in a world in which I cannot satisfy your every desire."

A dense shadow pushes against the inner walls of my chest, and I part my lips to compensate for the tightness. He doesn't give me a chance to process the meaning behind his words before his mouth devours me, their urgency speaking of a desperate need to claim. He pounds into me furiously, his groans burrowing into my bones.

I am thoroughly lost in his taste, his smell. Can barely form a thought beyond the pleasure of each part of my body he worships.

This man that I hate, that I planned to kill to get revenge for his father's actions. This man that I sunk my blade into before I left him bleeding in front of the castle he is to one day rule. I have told him time and time again just how little he means to me, regardless of what I actually feel.

Because I don't fucking know.

I roll my hips in time with his, my arms securing around his shoulders. I shove my face into the crease of his neck, sobbing through every merciless thrust as he gives me exactly what I need. He presses his thumb into my spine and pushes as he slides his nail down to my tailbone, gripping my ass to shove himself harder into me.

"Oh fuck, Caspian, I can't—" I clench around every inch of him as heat builds quickly at the base of my abdomen.

The hand holding my head to him tugs until my neck is exposed for whatever he wishes. "I got you, angel...let go," he breathes over my skin before sucking just below my ear.

Release finds me the moment his cock swells, and the glide of his mouth feels desperate as it searches for mine. He bites down on my lip, drawing another wave of pleasure from me. His thrusts slow as we fall into a companionable silence, both of us trying to regulate our breathing. My eyes flit open to find his, the silver irises seeming to dim as he calms.

The intimacy of this moment is not lost on me, but the memory of why I'm here hits me hard—a distraction. But if this was merely a distraction, then why does admitting it hurt so badly? Why can I never just be honest with myself?

I sigh a long breath...because everyone I care for ends up murdered. And suddenly the thought of the prince dying is more frightening than what might happen if he lives.

Chapter Thirty-One

Ariella

"What?" Caspian shakes his head idly, scrutinizing a strand of my hair. He shifts inside me as he leans forward to look at it more closely, my overly-sensitized intake of breath snapping him from concentration.

"I just thought...it's nothing." He smiles brightly, dropping my hair. He smirks in an utterly satisfied male way when my features contort as he slowly pulls out before pointing a finger at me. "Stay right there, or I won't let you use your blades on me any longer." My stomach dips. I do not need to tell him that he doesn't *let* me do anything—he knows. The look on his face begs me to fall for his attempt at annoying me.

He disappears into the bathroom before walking back toward me with a wet cloth. When his feet stop mere inches away, I avert my eyes from his still partially hard cock. He chuckles.

"Like what you see, angel?" A playful smile pulls at my lips as my eyes unhurriedly drink him in. I scrunch my nose and shrug before leaning back, bored.

I hum, "It's all right." He bellows a laugh, throwing his head back. I fight the unsettling heaviness in my chest and push to drop from the desk, blocked by his *all right* body when he steps closer.

"I swear the Angel sent you to this realm just to humble me." He reaches the cloth toward my thighs, my hand snapping to grip his wrist.

"What do you think you're doing?" His confused expression does not match the hardness of mine.

"Cleaning you?" That...is not what I'd expected him to say. I search his face, though he only watches me with growing understanding. "Do not tell me your other...*partners*," he spits, "have never made sure you were cared for?" I think I shake my head—I've no idea why this seems so important to him.

"I don't know who you think I am, but I'm certainly capable of cleaning myself, prince." My head tilts. "Though, if it's pregnancy you worry about, I can assure you I consume the cilla leaf each month."

He waves a hand. "As do I, but that's not what I'm referring to." Still distractingly naked, he shuffles between my legs once more. "I was going to tease you—how I finally know something the Silver Wraith does not..." His hands slide over my hips, cupping my backside before pulling me forward. The chill of the cloth causes my skin to pebble under his touch. "But my amusement is not worth the expense of how you've never been cared for or protected properly."

Why I feel the need to defend myself is lost as I open my mouth to keep pushing him away. "I've learned to do both for myself just fine; I do not need you to coddle me." His sad, pitying smile grates my nerves—a cold reminder of the different lives we come from.

"Sure...you were forced to learn how to wield a blade to protect your skin. How to clean this beautiful hair. How to live on your own, because there was no one left to live with you—"

"I don't need a fucking history lesson. I know what I went through." I swallow around the burning words.

"*But*," he enunciates, pressing a light kiss to each corner of my mouth. "You've never had the chance to be human. You learned to shut off your emotions and desires. You build a wall the moment someone is kind to you because you don't know how to handle it, just like you're doing right now." Am I?

I scoff—of course I do that...if I don't let anyone close to me, no one gets hurt. It's simple.

"And this, Ariella." He brings the cloth to my center, cleaning our cum from me more gently than I thought could be possible. "This is me caring for you. I know you can do it yourself...but I *want* to do this. You shouldn't feel like I've only used your body to fuck, just to toss you aside afterward. You should feel cherished," he breathes, kissing my cheek. "Appreciated." Another kiss. "I want your body *and* mind to feel safe and valued with me. I will not hurt you, angel." It's like he's seen my every fear—how he knows this much is alarming, causing my heart to beat fast in my chest.

But there's one thing he forgot to consider.

"That may be, prince...but I *will* hurt *you.*"

His eyes lighten as he shrugs. "You're worth anything you wish to do to me." He squeezes my thigh before returning to the bathroom. I hop from the desk and hurriedly slide on my pants, pulling my shirt down just as he walks back into the room.

I suddenly feel uncharacteristically nervous, blurting the first thing that comes to my head. "I read my father's journal." I wince—fucking fool. He slips from his closet as loose pants settle on his hips.

Of course, he forgot to don a shirt, and his knowing smile confirms just how intentional that was. I roll my eyes, holding his gaze as he saunters over to me and leans a hip against the desk.

"What did you find?"

For a moment I consider leaving without answering, but something tugs in my head. "A lot, though the most interesting information was written just before your father killed mine." He winces at the reality I haven't directly addressed with him. The horrible truth that intertwines us—the thing that I've wanted his life for while he pitied mine.

I open my mouth to tell him of my findings, but pause when my eyes catch the royal crest glaring at me from the wall. This is the son of the man I've hated my entire life. His father ripped my family from me; forced me into a life that I never wanted.

And Isaiah.

His family took everything from me, and yet I'm standing in his room after fucking him, about to spill all the secrets that had gotten my father murdered in the first place. I cannot trust him...I shouldn't.

But not only do I need to, I want to. He has proven himself worthy time after time, not just with his bewildering words, but his actions. I can surely give him this small piece of me, if only to garner his help in discovering what my father almost had about the king.

"I didn't thank you for the other night...I'd likely be dead if anyone else had come to my door." He smiles, something heavy flitting through his eyes that causes me to tell him of what I found. His forehead becomes increasingly scrunched the more I say, wary tension seeping from my muscles as I watch his confusion grow.

If I'd had a single hint that he knew anything I speak of, his body would already be growing cold on the floor.

He's silent for minutes, and I study his face as he processes my words. "Wait, an accord between whom? I know of no such agreement amongst the cities or the kingdom..." I stop pacing to sit on his bed, falling back and pressing my palms over my eyes.

"I'd gotten the impression that this is not a normal accord. He said it's *weakening*, as if it is not a document but a living thing."

"How is that possible...that does not make sense." He sighs, running a hand over his mouth.

I bite my tongue hard enough that a familiar metallic taste floods my mouth—I left one thing out. "He mentioned begging my mother to find another solution...in the Aether, but she didn't wish to go back." His head snaps toward me, seemingly unaware that his feet drag him to the bed.

"Go back? As in she'd been there before?"

I groan. "I don't fucking know, Caspian! I'm just as lost as you are. How she died to give me time for something I know nothing of...how my father was convinced his search would be able to save her, and how he was certain the answers would lead to your father. He'd spoken as if the realm would perish any day—" Fuck, my head is throbbing. I sit up and cross my legs, facing the prince. "I do not fucking care why my parents did what they chose to do. I want to figure out whatever is going on with your father, and complete whatever the fuck my mother died to give me time for."

His eyes search mine, tired. "Gavriel thinks he may have...stumbled across something." I raise a brow, waiting for him to continue. He hesitates before seeming to decide on the right words. "You remember where the first trial was?" I nod once. "He saw one of the entrances to those tunnels being guarded."

That's his big secret?

"If you have yet to notice, there are sentries posted at every fucking corner of this castle." He chuckles, shaking his head.

"Yes, but never at the tunnels. There's nothing to protect down there, so why were they posted at one of the entrances? Not to mention everything my father has done with this competition and his attempts to kill you...

"I don't know, Ariella—I'm fucking confused." He falls back to the bed, cupping his hands behind his head. "I can't see my father doing anything substantial enough to fit with what you're saying, and yet I also didn't think he could outright murder people for sport. The death of every other assassin was not meant to happen, and yet it did. So whether it's him, or Varrick, that is making these decisions, I am not sure. But something in my gut is telling me there is much more to this than we think."

I should leave. Gather my winnings at the ceremony tomorrow and travel far from Valoria—I'd never have to deal with any of this again. I could go on the adventures my mother spoke fondly of, or visit the cities outside of the kingdom.

That would be necessary, regardless; the king will send others after me the moment I am out of the spotlight.

It would be the smart thing to do, and I've never been someone to make impulsively foolish decisions. And yet I find myself saying...

"So, how do we figure this out?" If it wasn't for my father's journal, I likely would have left. But there's something between his written words that calls to me—begs me to stay. "If I don't remove myself from the castle after tomorrow, he will insist on having my head."

We sit in silence, both lost in our own warring thoughts.

Getting into the castle undetected is the easy part, but remaining unseen long enough to obtain answers?

The door to Caspian's room bursts open, slamming into the wall as Gavriel stumbles in with his sword drawn. He scrutinizes the prince and me with wide eyes, clearly confused that his charge is alive and unscathed—mostly.

"I—" His shoulders slack. "It was so quiet, I thought..." I burst out laughing, hopping from the bed and sauntering to the sputtering guard.

"Did you think I fucked your prince to his death?" I drawl, walking my fingers over the worn leather covering his chest. "I'm honored, Gavriel, that you would bestow me with such a compliment." He smacks my hand away, and I smile brightly when his hatred for me overpowers his worry for the prince.

"You're lucky I even allow you in here, wraith. If that fucking idiot wasn't so obsessed with you..."

"Allow?" Heat builds in my chest, my eyes narrowing. He crosses his arms, smirking. "Well then *allow* me to sink this blade into your heart since you seem convinced that you've the power to order me around." He tenses when the tip of my blade presses below his ribs, angled up toward the rapidly beating organ.

We glare at each other for a moment before Caspian groans loudly. "You two are ridiculous," he mutters, sliding an arm around my waist to pull me back. I shiver when his lips meet my ear. "Why don't we save such threats for me, hm? I seem to get jealous whenever you hold that beautiful weapon to anyone else, especially my guard—" He halts, straightening. "That's it!" My brows furrow as I look between a disgusted Gavriel and a grinning prince.

I twirl the blade through my fingers, pinning Caspian with a hard look. "What's it, exactly?" I swear to the Angel, if either of these foolish men claims any sort of ownership over me again...

"Ariella, you'll be my personal guard—that's exactly how to give you the access you need without my father making an attempt for your life."

Gavriel and I share a look, agreed for once. "First, I would never be something so lowly as your personal guard." I wink at the unimpressed bastard next to me. "Second, perhaps you've forgotten that your father lives in the castle. If I were to live here as well, that would certainly give him far easier access to me."

He huffs, waving a hand. "No, of course I wouldn't have you actually protect me—unless you wished to do so from my bed," he lilts as his eyes roam my prickling body. Gavriel makes a strange noise, and I'm sure his skin is turning green. "But if I announce it during the ceremony tomorrow, there is nothing he could do to refute it. You'd be expected to be seen around the castle frequently, so he wouldn't outwardly attack you, nor would your presence in the halls alarm anyone."

The guard scoffs. "I guarantee everyone that sees her will be alarmed."

I reach to pat him on the chest, forcing him to back away further. "Thanks for the support, Gav." I bite my cheek, watching the prince attempt to hold in a laugh.

"Do. Not. Call. Me. That," he spits each word, his grip on the pommel tightening.

"Oh, you'll get used to it, Gav—especially when we begin working together." I smile sweetly at him, relishing in the way his nostrils flare as he grinds his teeth.

"Gavriel, calm down or get out. You're being dramatic," Caspian laughs, his expectant eyes finding mine. "So you'll do it?"

I do not seem to have another choice...or so I tell myself.

Chapter Thirty-Two

Ariella

Maybe killing the king and forgetting about my father's search is the better option—at least, it truly feels like that at the moment.

"After the harrowing losses of seventeen other competitors, I am pleased to announce Valoria's very own Silver Wraith as the victor!" The king's booming voice bleeds through my ears as I stand in front of his throne. His crimson, floor-length jacket sways with the dramatic movements of his arms as he speaks to the crowded audience behind me. "Today we celebrate Ariella Mistaire's skill, adaptability, and cunning. She has proven herself worthy of the title and will be awarded fifty gold coins!"

The audience cheers as raging heat floods my veins. I want to scream and unleash the monster he created all those years ago. Isaiah's life was worth a mere fifty gold coins? It would be so easy to kill him—and to lose my chance at the answers my father spent the last part of his life searching for.

The impression of Caspian's pleading gaze prickles along my skin, as if he knows what I'm thinking. Feeling. I press my tongue to the roof of my mouth as a finger taps against my blade.

I have waited twenty years to take what Thalion owes me. I can wait a little longer.

I need a distraction. One good enough to keep the part of me that wants to explode subdued. My eyes flick to the queen and her daughter, who both sit straight and still in their seats.

Vespera wears a deep red gown, fitted with golden lace around the bodice. Her light hair is braided down her back, hanging stiffly over a shoulder. Her blue irises scan the audience over and over, though she doesn't seem to be looking at them, but *above* them.

My attention drags to Seraphina when she moves a hand; I watch as her fingers drag lightly over her silky, golden dress; their movement is nearly imperceptible, though understandable. I would hate being tied to that bastard of a king as well. She must feel my stare as her severe gaze slides to mine, her hand halting its writhing. I raise a brow at her scrutiny, a hint of a smile on my lips when hers curl. She shakes her head, tossing her hair back over a shoulder as she tucks a lighter piece behind her ear and focuses ahead once more.

"Ariella," Thalion basically shouts, walking down the stairs to stand directly in front of me. His arrogance must be shining through his eyes as they look irritatingly brighter when he reaches to touch my collar, the wretched material snapping apart before falling into his hands. "Congratulations—do tell us what you hope to do with this new freedom!" A slight breeze of essence touches my lips as the staff member off to the side weaves to amplify my voice along with the king's.

"Actually, father, Ariella will be staying here in the castle!" Caspian yells, nodding to the sweating man to weave his words out through the crowd. The king's eyes narrow on me, hand twitching as if he means to strangle me right here.

I smile, speaking low enough that only he can hear. "I warned you, Thalion. Your son is *mine*." He stiffens, about to reach for me when Caspian's hand comes down on his shoulder.

"It is my great honor to proclaim that Ariella has formally agreed to join the royal sentries as my personal guard. Her skills are...exceptional, and I was pleased with her acceptance of my offer. Please join me in congratulating our victor!" He bows his head to me, stepping forward to fuss with my shirt. I watch as he places a pin of the royal crest over my breast, the sound of my heavy breathing drowned by the audience.

"Let's go," the prince whispers, nodding to a side door. I begin to follow, only making it a few steps when a heavy amount of essence washes over me. I pause, peering over my shoulder at the king. His expression is amused, though he hasn't moved from his place on the floor.

What was that?

I survey the area, pushing out the suffocating noise of everyone else in this damned room. Blinking away a bout of dizziness, I look between Thalion and Seraphina, both of whom watch me with calculating eyes. A finger taps against my thigh. Whatever the fuck that was, I'll find out—the king sees the truth of that in my gaze, spinning to dismiss me.

I hurry from the throne room, sucking in a deep breath; the musty heat of a thousand people cramped in once space will never be appealing. In fact, I may insist the prince no longer attend events so that I am not forced to suffer through such pathetic things.

Familiar hands cup my face before Caspian's lips slam down on mine. I immediately arch into him—an embarrassment for how easily I succumb to my desires.

I pull away, missing the sweet taste of his tongue. "Are you not worried about someone finding us?"

He bites his cheek as his fingers slide to massage the back of my head. "I do not fucking care who sees—in fact, I have half a mind to drag you back in there so the entire kingdom can watch just how good I'm about to make you feel." He leans to kiss me, stopped by a single finger as I press his lips until he backs away.

"As much as I'm intrigued by the idea of making your father hate me even more, you are not to touch me in public." His jaw drops, somehow offended by the idea.

"Yeah, keep that shit to yourselves. It's bad enough she has to be around at all—" Gavriel screeches like a child when my blade sinks into the wall he leans on. He heaves, likely thankful that the blade didn't sink into his cock, but just below it. "You missed, wraith."

I smile wickedly. "Hm, I don't believe I did." His forehead scrunches as he looks down, yanking the blade from the wall, only to expose the gaping hole I created in his pants. He tosses it and cups every small bit of manhood that drops through the opening, cutting his gaze to me. "You were saying?" I chuckle, ignoring the curses he shouts my way as I push a still gaping prince toward our rooms. Which are now across from each other—whether that's convenient or annoying, I've yet to decide.

"You know, one of these days he's going to retaliate," Caspian mutters as we navigate dimly lit hallways. I tug on my umbral strand and undo the wards at my door, pushing it open. I don't look back as I enter the large space—far more than I'll ever need—and frown.

"I'm counting on it," I say, knowing the prince followed me in here.

I rest my hands on my hips and sigh. Everything in here is far too opulent for my taste...I suppose I normally do not have a taste, but the excessive amounts of red and gold are sickening. If I wanted crimson bedding, I'd have a little fun with my blade as I rode the prince.

The bed frame, desk, all the knobs and hinges—gold. Shiny, revolting gold. Every fabric is coated in the deep, royal red that I cannot seem to escape from. It's as if the king himself vomited on every surface in here.

I will change every bit of it.

Caspian drops the pouch of gold coins on the desk and saunters to me, blocking my view from everything except the expanse of his chest. I look up at him, ignoring the rippling over my skin when I find him smiling warmly at me. He snatches my hands, and I allow him to pull me forward until his legs touch the bed.

He drops ungracefully, sliding the tips of his fingers over my abdomen, tracing the curve of my waist. His tongue wets those curved lips when my abdomen clenches under his touch. "So sensitive," he breathes so low I doubt he meant for me to hear.

"If you invited yourself in here thinking I'm going to fuck you, I'm afraid you still think too highly of yourself."

A shrug. "How could I not when you look at me the way you do?" He peers up at me, a clear challenge in his gaze.

"Like I wish to slit your throat? Because that's how I feel when I see you." He hums, yanking my thighs so I'm forced to straddle him.

I leave my arms at my sides, biting my cheek as he leans to press a whisper of a kiss to my throat. "Exactly like that." Instinct pleads for me to retreat—that his words, this position, they're far too intimate.

I don't want to feel the sinking in my gut whenever he's near, nor do I wish for my skin to pebble when he touches me. The warmth that's always present inside my face when he's in the same room, because there isn't one moment that I do not feel his eyes on me. I don't want to desire him and his ridiculous fucking words...and yet I'm addicted. To all of it.

I grasp his hair and tug his head back, running my tongue along his lips—he opens for me immediately. I groan and devour his taste, basking in the hint of lavender that clings to his skin. I grind into his hard length, desperately searching for any sort of friction.

I lose all will when he moans into my mouth, pushing him back to the bed. The hand that catches me lands on a cool, supple object; I blindly toss it away, arching my neck to give Caspian more access. My eyes flit open and land on what I had thrown—my father's journal.

But there's something sticking out from the back...

"Hold on," I murmur, stretching over the prince's head to pinch the jutting paper between two fingers. I sit back, noting his questioning look before twisting the paper, breathing out every spec of air when I find the words *To Ariella* written on one side.

"What is it?" Caspian sits up on his elbows, his voice laced with concern.

After so many years, I still recognize the handwriting. I unfold the paper as I attempt to hide the shaking in my fingers—the effort useless when the inside confirms my fear.

"It's a letter," I breathe, searching Caspian's curious eyes. "From my mother."

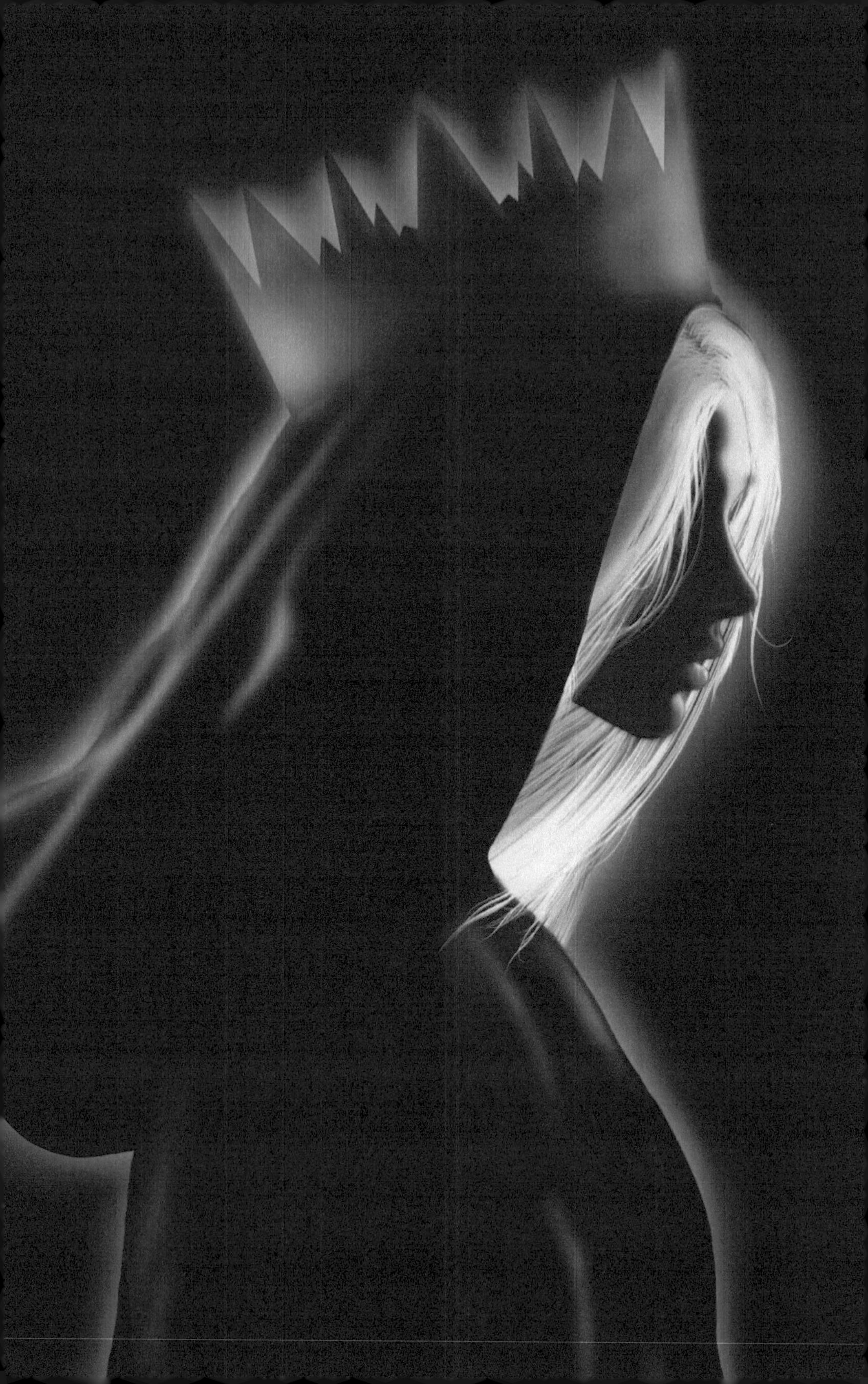

Epilogue

Valyria

"You're certain it's her?" I grip Elara's clammy hands tightly, my voice wavering.

Her pale blue eyes slide to mine as her bottom lip quivers. "I'm sorry, Val. It's her." A broken sob escapes from me, my kind friend wrapping her arms around my torso, not seeming to care as I soak her robe with endless tears.

"I just do not understand how he did this...she doesn't deserve such a fate..." Elara holds me for hours, listening. Comforting. How am I to tell Erendor? I can't do this—

My eyes snap open, greeted by the darkness of the night.

I shove the blankets off, slip from the room, and walk hastily down the hall until I reach Ariella's door. I crack it open and my eyes immediately find my sleeping girl. I muffle a laugh—she always falls asleep in the strangest positions. She lies on her back with one arm splayed to her side while the other falls over her head as if she means to grab the wall; she snores softly, oblivious to everything that's to come.

I wish I could give her more than the knowledge that her fate is tied to things beyond even my control. I clench my jaw, and move to step into Erendor's office, grabbing paper to write all the words I want to say to her. Words that will never be enough.

My sweet Ariella,

If you are reading this, it means the time has come for you to know the truth, both about who I am and the choices I've made. You have every right to be angry with me. I must leave you sooner than I wish, but it is a choice I make willingly, for you and for the balance we are all bound to.

You must grow strong, my love, for your path ahead will be very hard, and I cannot tell you how sorry I am for the burdens that will be placed on you. Being a guardian of the Accord is a difficult life to live, but I know that with your father's help, you will do so well.

Please know that every decision I've made, I've made with you in my heart. I love you more than the stars love the night sky, and it is my love for you that allows me to prepare for what must be done.

Be brave, my beautiful girl. Learn all you can, question everything, and trust in the kindness of your heart. Lean on your father, Ariella – he will explain everything you must know, and he will help you through this.

Remember that I am always, always with you. From here to the Aether, you will find me anywhere I am needed.

I love you so much my special, beautiful girl.

Tears track silently down my face, slapping too loudly against the desk. I know I must sacrifice my essence...I understand it will tip the balance to give her time...but those things do not make this any easier.

To never watch her grow into the beautiful woman she will be—I cover my mouth with a hand to muffle a sob.

Watching her and Erendor spend time together practicing her essence, or picking the prettiest lavender from the garden...even laughing as they argue over the silliest things about who's correct. I chuckle through the tears—too often is neither of them right, but I never have the heart to tell them. Their bond fills me with so much joy, and I know he will take the best care of her after I'm gone.

I sigh deeply, folding the paper and setting it on my nightstand. Erendor will not be pleased, but I know he will give Ariella the letter when the time is right.

That comfort is enough to settle my racing heart and dry my skin as I slip back into bed and wrap myself over my husband. I hope it is also enough to keep the nightmares at bay—I've no desire to watch Elara's visions of chaos and collapse any longer.

Author Note

Thank you for reading Shadows of the Crown! I cannot tell you how honored I am that you've taken the time to give this series debut a chance. If you enjoyed the beginning to Ariella and Caspian's stories, please consider leaving a rating/review. They are so important to authors!

The first installment to the Shadows of the Crown series focuses more on the characters and getting to know them. We dive further into their world and essence in the next books as we learn more about the Accord and exactly what it means to be weakened! However, I know some enjoy reading about inner workings of a book—so if you are interested in learning more about the magic system before book two is released, please visit dakotamonroe.com/shadowsofthecrown!

Starting this series has been one of the longest, most rewarding projects of my life. I have dreamed of being an author since I was a child, and I still have so many written pieces saved that I've never shown anyone. Years and years of writings that haven't seen anything other than my face. But then—over a year ago—Ariella came to me and she had a story to tell. One that needed to be shared with the world...so I got to work. And it is an incredible feeling to know that others who also grew up loving fantasy books are now reading mine. You truly honor me—thank you.

I would love to especially thank the many people who have supported me throughout this journey, and are giving me the motivation to keep going. To my husband, sister, friends, and huskies...you are my everything.

To my PA, Beta Team, ARC Team, and Street Team...there are no words to express how thankful I am for each of you. So many of you have been supporting me ever since Of Bonds and Daggers was released, without having a clue that Shadows of the Crown existed yet, and that means so much to me. I am so appreciative.

PA: Ambria Meyers

Beta readers: Ambria Meyers, Courtney Riley, Nichelle Kistemaker, Payton, and Shannon Young

Street team members:

Aixa Arellano (ig:ax.arell30), Alexis Riveron, Alysha Wilson (tt:Alyshadwilson), Amber Bueno (ig:Smutlover25), Amber Kirsten (ig:amberkirsten95), Ambria Myers (ig:my.chemical.romantasy), Angel Woods (ig:readwith.angel), Ashley Mead (tt:ashyysbooktokk), Aulbanie Olson (ig:aulbz_b), Auriane Hallez (ig:starsxdust), Bailey Scheil (ig:lulu_reads98), Caitlyn Wright (ig:caitlynmariewright), Charlene Bertrand (ig:Fantasmutty.fiction), Courtney Riley (ig:courtney shea.reads), Cynthia Sanchez (ig:cynthiareads__), Darby (ig:darbys. reads), Denisha Williamson-Walker (ig:denishaslibrary), Enola Henderson (ig:whatnolareads), Hannah Fuller, Hannah Grogan (ig:hannahtheawkward), Isabella Cha (ig:bellsreadss), Janelle Fox (ig:smutcartel), Jess Michalski (ig:midwest.kindleworm), Julles Smith (ig:jullessmith), Kaisey Rainey (ig:rainey.day.reads), Karlee Daniels (ig:bookluver2024), Kata Voutilanien (ig:katvou_books), Katelyn Snell (ig:katalyn0823), Katie Tenbroek (ig:bookishk92), Kaye Zellers (ig:kaye_missy_), Kaylin

McIntosh (ig:_justımorechapt_), Kristyn Fairchild (ig:kristyns_lux_library), Kelly Layton (ig:bookscoffeeandrocknroll), Kiara Camper (ig:kiaras_booknook), Kristen Holt (ig:bratzrus_booknook), Kristina (ig:kristinahollidaz_), Kyra Miller (ig:wiccanbookworm), Lily OBrien (tt:lilymarie0619), Magen Odom (ig:magens.book.nook), Melinda Vang (ig:Melluvbooks), Mikayla Laymon (ig:mikaycakesbooks), Nichelle Kistemaker (ig:basicbitchandspicybooks), Payton, Robyn Foster (ig :read.with.robyn), Robin Padilla (tt:squeakydino), Rosalinda Sorola (ig:linda_bookstagram), Rowan Ulrich (ig:rowansdarklibrary), Ruth Hawkins (ig:r_anngel_mua_bookishangel), Sally Cox (ig:whychoose.salsy), Samantha Grimm (ig:Millennial_Sam_Reads), Shanna Layton (ig:bookdirtytome), Shannon Mannion (ig:Notsolittleirishbookworm), Shannon Young (ig:xxkalypsoxx), Sydney Olivarez (ig:syds.bookiish.revi ews), Tanna (ig:bookedbytanna), Tricia Walro (ig:whitefoxreads), Valeria Reyes (tt:_vals.library)

Pronunciations

Characters:

Aether — a-thur

Ally — al-ee

Amada — uh-mah-duh

Ariella — are-ee-el-uh

Bastian — bash-tin

Bessan — bess-on

Caspian — cass-p-in

Corine — core-in

Elara — ee-larr-uh

Elowen — ell-oh-when

Erendor — air-en-door

Gavriel — gae-vree-ell

Isaiah — i-zay-uh

Isolde — uh-zowl-duh

Jaspar — jass-par

Jaxon — jacks-un

Jessenia — jess-en-ee-uh

Jeth

Julia —jule-ee-uh

Lila

Marek — mare-eck

Marion — mare-ee-un

Myst — mist

Noah

Obren — oh-bren

Raine

Saben — sah-been

Seraphina — sare-uh-fee-nuh

Sivara — see-varr-uh

Stella — stell-uh

Thalia — thall-ee-uh

Thalion — thail-ee-un

Valyria — vuh-lee-ree-uh

Varrick — vare-ick

Velora — vell-or-uh

Vespera — vess-pair-uh

Vincent — vin-sent

Cities within Eldorian Kingdom:

Eldoria — ell-door-ee-uh

Frostwell

Grenport

Invalle — in-veil

Lumarna — loom-are-nuh

Meridian — merr-idd-ee-un

Valoria — vale-or-ee-uh

Cities outside Eldorian Kingdom:

Auroria — uh-roar-ee-uh

Ebonwood — eb-un-wood

Skydence — sky-deh-nce

Thalasire — thal-uh-sire

Vexail — vex-ale

Whisterra — whi-stare-uh

Other places:

Angel's Passage

Cindara Desert — seen-darr-uh

Ebelan Sea — eh-bell-an

Elysaran Mountains — ell-ee-sar-an

Meneau Sea — men-owe

Verdantia Forest — vare-dan-she-uh

Weaver's Torrent

Also By Dakota Monroe

The Curse of Gods series

Book One — Of Bonds and Daggers

Book Two — Of Gods and Pain

Book Three — Of War and Realms

*

Shadows of the Crown series

Book One — Shadows of the Crown

Book Two — Releases 2025

*

Standalones

Her Lovely Curse — Release tbd

About the Author

Dakota Monroe lives in a dark world and dreams of even darker fantasies. She has been a fantasy-obsessed reader since she was a child and now brings hers to life through her writing. As a neurodivergent woman, Dakota has always felt out of place with her thoughts and ideas; but books have been her savior, and a nonjudgmental place for her to escape the colorless world we call reality. She hopes her characters, and stories, provide an outlet for others, even if just for a little while.

www.ingramcontent.com/pod-product-compliance
Lightning Source LLC
Chambersburg PA
CBHW020306030826
48979CB00029B/2261/J
* 9 7 9 8 9 8 9 4 7 5 6 8 1 *